I0749884

Devil's Claw

DEVIL'S CLAW

Dark Woods Series

Kasey Hill

Dark Moon Rising Publications | Virginia

Dark Moon Rising Publications

70 Foxwood Drive
Rocky Mount, Virginia 24151
Tel: (540) 257-2861

ISBN: 978-1-945987-89-2

10 9 8 7 6 5 4 3 2 1

Printed in the United States of America

In Memory of Michael Wayne Pugh
June 30, 1970 – September 10, 2012

Other Works

The Guardians of Light Series (YA):
Firefly of Immortality
The Shining Ones
Firefly: The Half-Blood Angel
The Valley of the Shadow of Death:
Nephilim Rising

The Whispering Spirits Series (YA):
The Haunting at Foxwood Village
Dark Coven

Short Story Collections
Tales from the Crib: Collection of Short
Stories and Limericks

Poetry
Tiptoe through the Tulips
Bittersweet Symphony
Angels on the Moon
Careless Whispers (under KH)

Tattered Wings Poetic Series (under KH):

Soul on Fire

Unr3ndered

Paper Heats

Black Balloon

The Sun is Rising

Unbeautiful

Coming Soon

The Guardians of Light Series:

Firefly of Immortality II

Ashes of Immortality: Black Wings of Death

Ashes of Immortality: Crowned by Ash and Flame

Ashes of Immortality: Crowned by Infernal Flame

Ashes of Immortality: The Shadowed Verse

The Guardians of Light: Revelations of Raziel Series

Bloodlines: Into the Shadows

Dark Woods Series

The Haunting at Foxwood Manor

Stand Alones

Camp Redcap

Gaebler's Asylum of the Damned

Tattered Wings Poetic Series:

Razor Blades and Roses

Perfume, Powder, and Lead

Devil's Claw

Part 1: The Diary of Patrick Ingram

WHAT DOES IT MEAN to be alive? Does the humdrum of a beating heart constitute the sacredness of life? Is it conscious awareness that differentiates between ethereal and corporeal? Is it strictly opinionated as to what constitutes a person to be alive or dead? Life is held in such high regard and considered to be an infallible state of being with right or wrong answers, when the very essence of existence cannot be explained outside the structures of religious contempt or theorization of how the world came to be. It leaves little room for the macabre and sinister insinuations that exist within the structure of nature that has spent millenniums eating away at the rot and decay of flesh and bones as if it were a cancer eating away at a living and breathing being.

The expansion of lungs and other autonomic bodily functions that sustain a human's meat suit became scientific reasoning of elaboration as an attempt to answer the deepest question that has burned within the hearts and minds of those consciously aware of their petulant and mere existence within the fabric of space and time on this planet. Within this infrastructure of debate and theological connotation, humans have leant the idea that life is covetable while death is inconvenient to the human psyche. Attempts at immortality have been made by varying cultures to sustain life into the afterlife, and for what? To gain some concept of everlasting life as religion perpetuates?

Did our ancestors achieve this grandeur notion of everlasting life after trying and failing for so long? As the echoes of the past whisper on the wind, bouncing from walls that talk, I can't help but think they did achieve something. The silent screams of those long dead reverberate from the floors of nature as the earth calls out in hungry vibrations, pulling energy in and releasing what it consumes in powerful ebbing waves that only those attuned to a certain frequency can pick up as the rest of the world goes about their day as if the past doesn't lay buried, dead beneath the earth they walk upon.

Most parapsychology books barely delve into the bones of the earth. It never speaks of the constant cycle of life, death, and afterlife that exists within the very ground we tread upon. They don't explain that the very smell of petrichor is the perfume of death, intoxicating your senses on rainy or moist days where groundwater mixes with the rain cycle and brings forth the decay that's buried within mounds of bodies, both plant and animal, even human, alike. Everyone skates around death as if the very mention of it would bring down his scythe upon the necks of the living and drag their souls to the pit in which he rests his head. Death was a familiarity to me, for the landscape of Foxwood Hills sang a siren's lullaby to those who would listen.

No matter how beautiful the vast fields were or how serene the rolling hills seemed to emanate, there was a placid, sinister grip that grabbed you by your feet the moment you stepped foot onto the land. The mirage of serenity that most felt while visiting that had no perception or sixth sense to prickle the hairs on their neck, long passed down by our ancestors to avoid danger, disappeared once you entered the door of Ingram Manor. Within those walls that smelled like stale alcohol and a permeating rot that couldn't be mopped away, those souls whose bodies feed the earthen grounds of Foxwood Hills called out in unrest and disdain. Not only do they call out, but they also lash out and grab onto those alive, feeding from their energies like an IV bag full of pure adrenaline to sustain the hunger the land has left them in.

Within the halls of Ingram Manor was where I spent much of my youth, barricaded inside alone and without much else to do but wander and wait while an evil man, my father no less, treated me in heinous ways, whilst my mother indulged me in ways that would enrage my father in spouts of jealousy. I often heard them arguing, where he told her that it was time to pop her titty out of my mouth so I could be a real man and not a whining pussy of a son he was saddled with. He hadn't always been an evil person. I have memories, very few, of a time when I was little, prior to his father's passing, that I could remember him laughing and being merry. I could remember how affectionate he and my mother were. It all suddenly changed one day.

Oftentimes, my mother would send me to my room not out of punishment but for my own safety to thwart the flares of my father's temper. His drunken stupor, more often than not, landed me on the receiving end of a switch made from the sturdiest tree branch that could be found for the slightest of infractions I may have caused. I was the one sent to hunt the switch down, and if it wasn't to his liking, I had to go find one even thicker. This, by far, was no extraordinary event, and it happened nearly every single day, and the more that my mother intruded upon his actions, the more violent they became.

The manor was situated in the middle of the woods with no other children around for miles. The manor itself was old and styled in a similar fashion to the plantation buildings of Louisiana, hand forged and built over quite some time by my ancestor Benjamin Ingram. Spanish moss, as well as wild grape, often overtook the natural wood harvested from the trees in the area, and our gardeners spent weeks at a time plucking the greenery away so it didn't look like an abandoned estate. The roof looked as if there were church steeples built in place of a normal roof of the century, with its gables and the arched windows lent a subtle yet haunting feel to the place. The antebellum pillars spaced evenly across the front of the house, spanning the entire manor, providing a balcony porch for the second floor.

The inside of the manor was just as luxurious. There were only the three of us, but we had more rooms in the house than a hotel, it seemed. Each room had ornate trim moldings and hand-carved wooden features above the mantles. There were numerous bathrooms and shower rooms throughout the structure. When you first walked into the manor, the sitting area past the foyer looked as if it were handpicked from the British palace, as it led into the library with stacks of books on shelves that required a ladder to reach the top. An old globe of the world sat in the middle of the room, and even though it was never used, it never had a trace of dust. The cleaning staff hired worked around the clock, day in and day out, to keep the house spotless. There were at least fifteen maids staffed that worked in shifts of five.

The fireplace in the middle of the sitting room was hardly ever used except for when the harsh winters of Virginia would strike and blizzards would take out the power. It was a magnificent build that seemed to take up an entire wall of its own. Lions were carved into the wood, much like all the mantle pieces throughout the house. But even as beautiful as it was, it held this sinister feel to it as if it were to eat your soul the moment you sprang it to life with a blazing fire.

The walls of Ingram Manor seemed to climb higher and higher in each room you entered, peaking into the elaborate ceiling that housed lavish chandeliers. I believe Mother had imported a few from both France and Italy to replace the old-style candle-lit ones that used to grace the gloomy airspace. Just as in the rest of the manor, the walls were decorated with hand-carved wood, and each of the windows was curtained with a lace valance and long dark drapery that was only pulled back for a few hours a day to allow the natural lighting to burn away any sins that had transpired. It was unexplainable for a child to put into words how the scenery of the house set the atmosphere. It was dark with a dank feel, as if death waited in the corner of every room.

Both my parents came from money. Money has always been the root of power, bringing with it greed and bitterness. There were many times in my youth that I could remember them throwing extravagant parties and inviting other wealthy families in the area to partake in the evening's festivities. When these parties were held, I was sent to bed early with one of the maids to watch me to make sure I didn't slip down to the party and inconvenience their fun. At times, my imagination ran wild with elaborate stories and reasons as to why my parents never allowed me to walk amongst our guests. In some of the imaginings, I believed them all to be part of some wicked cult that sacrificed children under the full moon to drink their blood and stay young forever. Some of the parties were so well known that actors and singers who happened to be in the area would be invited.

Alcohol and the rich and famous are not a well-combined thought-out plan. It was the era for drugs, alcohol, and rock-n-roll, and from what I read in the paper, all of that was involved the night that the actress slash singer Nelly Roderick went missing on the estate. The last that was seen of her was her stepping outside for a cigarette and a stroll. Father said she must have wandered through the woods and gotten lost, falling into the waters of Devil's Claw. No one's body has ever been recovered from that lake when it swallows you alive. However, I heard the voices that night leading her astray from the house. The very voices that plagued me day in and day out to come outside and play.

I was an only child. Knowing my parents as I grew with age, it was hard not to think my existence was even meant to happen. Those very few memories of my early childhood felt like a fantasy tale I had told myself to cope with my abusive father. My mother most likely fought tooth and nail for my existence. I didn't make things easier for her either after being born. Many would blame a mental imbalance that caused me to have violent and psychotic episodes, such as night terrors and waking hallucinations. The doctors explained it as if I were asleep, even though I was actually awake. I was the family secret and stain. My father absolutely hated that I wasn't a normal child, and alcohol fueled that hatred with every tip of his bourbon glass to his lips. He initially didn't want an heir to succeed him, so having one with mental instability enraged his ego further. However, they wouldn't listen to my strange ramblings and stories about how the dead walked the halls at night and purely believed the doctors and their scientific reasonings as to why I behaved the way I did.

It was quite hard to explain out loud when I tried to tell my mother about my experiences. What the doctors said that I experienced wasn't what I experienced at all. I didn't feel like I was in a dream state or heightened paranoic mood. What I felt, saw, heard, and witnessed was not of this world but rather what was trapped in between this world and the next after death. The only explanation I could fathom was that it was paranormal encounters, and more specifically, ghosts.

I could feel them and see them. I heard them whisper my name and quite often felt their oppressive energy permeate my body as they tried to take over it. I tried to fight them off as best as I could with not only my defiant will but also my hands. Once, a maid ran into my room as I was fighting off an apparition that I could only see, and I accidentally struck her in the face, blackening her eye.

The first time I spent any time in a sanitarium was for a month of observation. During this time, I was subjected to countless tests that went as far as sleep deprivation, sensory deprivation, and pumping me full of barbiturates and varying other pills that they forced down my throat to entice my psychotic behavior forth. When that failed, they subjected me to insulin coma therapy, where they strapped me down and forced me into an insulin coma. Through all the torture, they couldn't elicit a single response from my supposed mental illness, but they took into account everything my parents had told them about what happened at home. The diagnosis they gave my parents was Schizoaffective Disorder bordering on Schizophrenia.

I admit that during that month there, I started to believe that maybe I had been crazy, like everyone believed me to be. The ghosts were hallucinations that were quelled by the medications they had given me and the therapies they had subjected me to. I felt calmer and more myself in that institution and was able to get an objective third point of view about myself in the haze of medicine. My episodes were, in fact, de-realization. However, when they sent me back home with my prescription in hand, the prescription no longer thwarted the hallucinations I had within the manor's walls. I knuckled down with my belief and experience that what was happening was paranormal as opposed to a mental health crisis.

The tickle of a migraine was the first thing I felt upon my return to the manor. This tickle was etched into my brain because it had been a precursor for the voices and visions consuming my everyday life. It would get to the point where it was monotonous yelling, laughing, screaming, and crying without a moment's reprieve from the sounds. The visions were of a time long ago, filled with murderous and malignant people sweeping a black cloud of death across the valley and children dying at their hands. Then, the malevolent beings would laugh from the corner of my darkened room, spewing their spit and blood across the floor in heaves. The number of times I ran a razor across my wrist in an altered stupor of emptiness was more than you could count on your fingers and toes.

My father no longer hauled me to the emergency room but kept a doctor on staff through the night to bandage me up whenever I would walk through the halls in a dazed ambiance, scaring the maids as blood dripped from my wrists and pooled in misshaped rivulets on the exquisitely cleaned floors. I heard the whispers throughout the house that, on occasion, they could see the blood absorbed into the flooring without a trace, as if my very essence was feeding the house and sustaining its malice. The house always felt alive, as if it were eating me from the inside out and carving myself up was the only way I could escape the doom-enclosed mouth of the beast that wished to devour my soul.

Those around me failed to understand the frustration I felt in regard to these attacks. The visions weren't just flashes of pictures or glimpses of faces. Entire storylines would play out as if a movie camera had been turned on in my head with full audio enabled. The voices would whisper to me in between the films that played, pleading with me to help them.

The voices were the determining factor to me that I was not batshit crazy. I had listened to so many psychologists and psychiatrists that I understood that malicious voices that told you to do harm to yourself or others meant you were schizophrenic. However, what I experienced was like a little child from the past wanting or needing me to help her.

The "episodes" would come in glimpses. There would be times I could go for months without any, and then out of nowhere, they would hit me like a bag of bricks, quite literally, without warning. That was how bad the migraines would get. Actually, I would prefer to be knocked out by the bag of bricks from reality as opposed to the suffering I was rendered in my delusional state.

My parents, well, more so my father, wanted to keep the matter hush-hush and began to have me cared for at home, even by the doctors and psychologists, paying large amounts of money to both medical staff and the home staff, so it wouldn't be leaked to the papers that the Ingrams' son was off his rocker. Good things never lasted long with these episodes, and eventually, after one really bad episode, I was possessed by one of the ghosts. It felt almost like the dream state the doctors had warned about with their diagnosis. I was awake, but I was asleep as well while something else controlled my body. Several of the maids tried to stop me as I walked to the fireplace to grab a log of burning wood, the one night we actually used the damned thing. It was as if I had powers of my own, and without even laying a finger on them, I sent them sprawling across the room before they ever had a chance to get near me.

By the time I was able to reclaim possession of my actions, I had already set the sitting room ablaze while the spirit that had overtaken me sat laughing in a chair against the bookcase in the adjoined library. According to the psychiatrist and therapist, I did what all schizophrenics do and listened to the voices in my head. No one would listen to me when I would tell them there weren't any voices, and I could not control my actions. I needed a priest instead of a doctor.

When the doctors believed my adolescent-riddled mind could no longer differentiate right from wrong, my parents locked me down even more tightly than they had initially. I was no longer offered services by the servants. I was locked in my room, and a tray of food slid beneath my door. I was isolated, without anyone to talk to or really call a friend. My parents didn't come to my room to see me. Most times, the doctors there would strap me down to my bed so I couldn't act out any more aggression through the night while loading me with barbiturates that gave me terrifying nightmares I couldn't wake from.

The few servants that had been thrown across the room were paid large amounts to continue working even though they agreed with me and said the place was a haint spot. Some of them had families that had lived in the area nearly just as long as my family had. Gabriella was one in particular. She didn't come out right and say it, but I knew her family came from old magic. Being locked up for so long, I had read about so many varying mythologies as well as looked through grimoires of magic left by my ancestors throughout the years to understand who had the gift. I had watched Gabriella add special oils and herbs into the mop buckets she washed the floors in, as well as the unusual wind chimes she made for my parents and stuck on their porch. I quite honestly believe my parents fully understood, as well, that her family came from old magic. However, not a single one of the maids, especially Gabriella, dared to speak against my father with such ramblings of the deep-seated land rot they whispered about in hushed tones.

Oftentimes, they would read to me in soft, light voices so no one would hear them from the other side of my door as I sat on the floor listening to the maddening words of Edgar Allen Poe's tales of misery and woe. My only solace, my only escape from both my torturous mistreatment and the malign assault of the supernatural, was those stories the maids read to me. They often apologized for having to leave sooner than we had hoped they could stay, as bells rang throughout the house, calling them for service. I always told them thank you before they pandered off. I will never forget their generosity to me.

After the final consultation with the doctors they had hired, my parents had me committed for a time at Gaebler's Sanitarium. My parents told me how grand and luxurious this place was and that it would be a resort-style facility, a retreat center. I would be cared for properly and be able to unwind and relax without the worry of the "ghosts" messing with my head. This would all help reverse my schizophrenia, along with medications and treatments. However, it was all a bullshit lie. Do you know how many people have died in this sanitarium? Before it was even a sanitarium, it had been a place where they treated those afflicted with tuberculosis and, prior to that, the Spanish Flu. It was like stepping into the Twilight Zone when I entered the establishment. Spirits reached out to me, grabbed me, and latched onto me as I screamed, shackled in my bed, for someone to help me. I couldn't escape them, and when a spirit knew you could see them, they never left you alone.

Gaebler's Sanitarium was a government-funded asylum that was cleared for medical practices that were still being treated as clinical trials. It was the initial treatment center for those clinical trials for cutting-edge psych medicine, and the patients were unethically made the guinea pigs. The medical director who ran the sanitarium believed in extreme methods of persuasive medical treatments, such as forced lobotomies, involuntary sterilization, both accidental and incidental, and electroshock therapy paired with enough tranquilizing barbiturates to kill a horse. Afterward, you were strapped into your bed for weeks at a time to writhe in your own shit and piss because the medical staff was a sorry lot that shouldn't have been in the medical field, to begin with. I was starved beyond starvation and usually hooked up to an IV bag of fluids to stave off dehydration as I bounced to and fro into consciousness and unconsciousness.

For a person my age, all I wanted to be was normal. I didn't want to have some extraordinary gift, especially not one that had me locked away from family, friends, and the general public. I just wanted to be normal. So, I prayed. I prayed, and I pleaded every night to God to help me. I don't know if it was the praying, electroshock therapy, or my near-death from starvation, but something worked. Whatever it was, whatever happened, it was like a curtain closed on the realm of the unseen for me. The voices in my head ceased, the apparitions faded away, and the medication they had me on was dosed just right that altogether, the paranormal activity I had experienced faded from my memory. I couldn't remember the visions I had experienced over and over any longer.

After a couple more weeks of being poked, prodded, and shocked some more, the quacks at the sanitarium contacted my parents and told them I was cured of my schizophrenia, and I was ready to reenter society. When my parents arrived, I sat idly in the sunroom, waiting for them for weekend visitation. Timidly, they approached me, and when they were given the proof they needed of my rehabilitation and cured of the malady that had stricken me, my father did something he had never done before. He wrapped his arms around me and hugged me while my mother sobbed happily into her palms pressed into her mouth. They didn't waste any time getting me home. I had been committed for four years, and purgatory couldn't even compare to what I had experienced.

The impact of that place on my psyche affected me more than what the paranormal experiences had, and not a day goes by that I still don't suffer from tremors, night sweats, and flat-out fucking terror from my memories of that place and what they did to me every single waking moment I could remember. Many years have come and gone since those alienated days of my childhood. My parents were young when I found myself burying them in the family cemetery. My father went first, followed shortly by my mother. Even though they were young in terms of age, their bodies had grown feeble throughout the years. It was as if the house itself had sucked the life right out of them when I was locked away. I was utterly alone after their passing and locked myself away in the manor they bequeathed in their stead. They left me the kingdom of my childhood that was just a rotted parcel of land in what is called Franklin County, Virginia.

The property was located right beside the old Thompson Estate along Doe Run and Ballpark, a few miles from the Highway 220 exit to Rocky Mount. It had since been broken up and parceled out upon their death. The only living heir they had was a young girl who was placed into the care of the state when found by social workers, when a friend of the family insisted there was something wrong. I had purchased every single piece of the land once parceled, so now owned both the Ingram's lot and the Thompson's lots. Before they took her away, I told her that whenever she was ready to move back into the manor, it would be waiting for her. The emptiness in her eyes as she left that day with the social worker told me I needed to tear it down just as much as I needed to tear down the manor I lived in. Even though the Thompsons had owned the land, it was still considered part of Foxwood Hills, and thusly, the manor had been named Foxwood Manor.

As I have attested, my parents came from money. More, in particular, my father was rooted in old money. When my family first immigrated here from Ireland, we were not destitute immigrants looking to escape into a new world in hopes of striking gold or none of the sort. My ancestor Moira had been accused of witchcraft, so the church was hunting my family to wipe the blight from the hills of Ireland. Moira was what those in Ireland called a banfháidh, a seeress. She also worked her own type of conjure magic, making witch bottles for the locals being played by evil magic. Just as Gabriella's family had been root workers, my ancestors were as well.

Moira's husband, Benjamin, came from a wealthy line of men. From the family journals I had found in the library, I understood they had struck gold and had a sizeable lot of land in Ireland that they paid workers to work for them, growing their crops and tending to their livestock. The McGradys were one of those families that had their own small estate on the property and were treated just as if they were part of the Ingram legacy. When the church began to point their finger at Moira for baneful sorcery, the McGradys were the only family that stayed while the others fled to escape persecution themselves by partaking in the witchcraft. Their loyalty proved to Benjamin that they indeed deserved a better life than what they all were having in Ireland. So when Benjamin packed his family up to come to America, he extended the invitation to the McGradys as well, who, in turn, accepted without hesitation.

The Ingrams' escape from Ireland meant they couldn't travel the conventional ways that most would by going to Staten Island and being logged into the book of immigrants. With the Church of England now in charge of Ireland, it made an escape from religious persecution harder to come by. Benjamin paid a supply ship a great deal of money to smuggle them into the colonies of America. This was not long after the fight for Independence in the Revolutionary War, so England still had left their mark on the colonies as well, and still kept impeccable records of those who arrived by boat to the immigration harbor.

Benjamin packed up everything from his estate, leaving behind centuries' worth of legacy land, and headed for the colonies for a fresh start, even changing their identities. Ingram is the name they chose at the port, switching from the legacy name of McElwee. They landed on the beaches of Virginia, and before they could be spotted, they quickly made their way deep into the mountains of unsettled territory. It was a treacherous journey because the natives were not kin to the pale faces that had taken over their land with such brute and violent force. It was safer to stay on the coasts of Virginia, and those who traveled deeper into the territory of the "savages" were found murdered and scalped.

However, Moira had this special gift of her own that would compel empathy from people, much like the owner of the ship that granted them refuge on board to escape the Church of England's grasp. Even though there was a language barrier between her and the natives they happened across, there was an understanding of souls. The natives granted them safe passage as well as helped them navigate the untouched woods until they came to what was known as Franklin County. Moira wrote in her journal that once they touched the red clay mud of the county, the natives immediately stopped traveling with them as if the dirt itself was impassable. Fearful that other tribes of natives would mean them harm, Moira told Benjamin this would be their spot.

Moira wrote quite often about her time spent with the natives and their teaching her the secrets of their people. There was one in particular that she took a shine to and taught to speak English while he taught her the Iroquoian language. Her journal entries soon became scribbles of hysteria as she wrote about the history of the land and how the natives had abandoned it because of its impure energies. Her native friend warned her of the dangers of cultivating the fertile soil and feeding the beast that lay beneath the foundation they lived upon. It was safe for the most part to eat the food given by the land, but it was imperative that they didn't dig deeper into the grounds, or else they would unleash the spirits of what they called the Kâ'lanû Ahkyeli'skï.

Benjamin didn't care about the fairy tales of the natives. He was born and bred in Ireland, where many stories revolved around malevolent and benevolent spirits of another world. Instead of heeding their warning, he broke ground building their plantation. Once the land had been torn, what few natives that had remained departed quickly, including the one that Moira had taught English. The land was claimed in the Ingram name, and Benjamin was given a writ stating he was the owner. Throughout the years, the heirs of Benjamin bartered using the land as leverage and slowly eroded the legacy land that Benjamin had bequeathed to them.

For over a century, we've had costly disputes with one of our neighbors, the Willards. What started as a simple disagreement about ownership over land grew into a scene much akin to the Hatfields and McCoys. I never understood why they wanted the land as badly as they did. They had the same acreage as we did. They had the same fertile ground as we did. They were always growing gardens that produced mighty fine pickings. However, they have wanted to battle it out for years in court. It is always the same verdict with different judges, and the only ones gaining anything from the proceedings are the court officials and the blasted lawyers.

You would think after losing so much money and not gaining anything but headaches and gray hair, they would leave well enough alone, but we can't even mow the lawn or use any type of machinery near the property line, or else they call the police. I then have to explain to the cops while they are running my license that it's a land dispute, and they have no jurisdiction over the matter. That is when they drag their lawyers in as well. If it weren't for the fact that the state wouldn't allow any impediment to our shared driveway, I would cut off communication with them entirely by blocking off the roadway and putting up a security fence around the entire property.

They also like to stir up trouble for anyone who takes the wrong way down the driveway coming to Foxwood Hills Resort and using their end of the drive. It's always an elaborate show of guns and threats to scare away customers, but people have grown used to it, and when they stop and ask for directions, the folks around here tell them not to enter through the Doe Run gate and to come to Ballpark instead to avoid conflict.

Chapter One

IT HAD BEEN NOTHING but scenic hills, trees, and mountains as Carter drove his family of four through Virginia from Maryland. It was such a change of perspective driving through the rural and urban areas compared to the city life he and his wife, Candace, were used to. He glanced at his watch and then glanced at the signs they passed on the roadside.

"How in the hell did we end up in Martinsville instead of Roanoke?" Carter asked, running his hand through his hair before grabbing his cheap cup of coffee, which they had gotten at a gas station.

"I don't know, dear," Candace flippantly replied as she thumbed through a magazine she had grabbed off a stand at the convenience store. "Maybe you should ask Alexa since her directions are the only ones you have been following."

Carter grumbled under his breath as Candace continued to ignore his irritation.

"What happened to us staying at some top-notch resort closer to the lake?" Carter asked his wife, Candace, as sweet sarcasm fondled the air between them, his forced smile plastered on. "This hillbilly hell is halfway between bum fucked Egypt, and *you have a purty mouth.*"

"I double-booked us just in case something happened to either of the spots that I put a reservation in. Apparently, some sort of accident happened to where they had to shut the resort down for a week, and they couldn't hold our spot. Something about a staff member catching a room on fire with a joint, I don't know," she huffed, tossing her magazine onto the floorboard and pulling her phone out to use Google Maps.

"So, where are we going then?" Carter asked impatiently, the bitter irritation flaring in his rising temper. "I don't know about you, but I need to get out of this car and take a piss."

Candace rolled her eyes. "We are about ten minutes out from it," Candace replied, pulling up the directions from her GPS. "Merge onto the exit and then take the next road up there on the right. It's called Doe Run Road. The resort is about three or 4 miles from there. Looks like there are two ways to get there. Which one do you want to take?"

"The one with the least turns would be nice," Carter muttered.

"Fine. Just drive straight, and then we will be turning down Foxwood Drive on the left," Candace replied heatedly, shutting her phone to sleep mode and tossing it in her purse at her feet.

Carter's old college roommate, whom he still kept in touch with, cordially invited Candace and Carter to attend the boating Regatta and the annual Virginian Smith Mountain Lake fishing tournament. He also just happened to be the mayor of Franklin County. Smith Mountain Lake was 580 miles of aquamarine blue waters, emerald shores, and sapphire blue skies. It was comfortably nestled in between the Blue Ridge mountains and was the largest lake in the area, next to Kerr Lake, which bordered Virginia and North Carolina.

Carter was finally able to take his mandated vacation from work. He couldn't have chosen a better time, either. He had been swamped through his residency at the hospital and now that he was no longer a resident and hired medical staff, he had some breathing room. Their children, eight-year-old Joshua and six-year-old Isobel, were homeschooled, so taking a couple of days off from school wouldn't count against them attendance-wise. Plus, they hadn't been on a family vacation in a while, and the family really needed a break from reality.

The kids were so excited about this trip that they had packed their clothes a month ago and bugged Carter and Candace every single day to see when they would be leaving. When the morning came for them to load up the car and leave, the kids had already put their suitcases in the back of the van and sat waiting in the backseat patiently for their parents to finish loading up their things. Things had been running smoothly so far this trip, and they hadn't had any hiccups other than their first-choice resort being burned down by a pothead.

"Here's the exit," Candace stated, pointing through the windshield at a small turn.

Carter didn't even have time to slow down and veered sharply to the right. "Next time, a little bit of a warning so I don't get pulled over, please," he asked, gritting his teeth.

Lights flashed in his rearview mirror, and he quickly glanced at his wife with pursed lips while she silently mouthed, "*Sorry.*" He pulled his vehicle over to the side of the road, looked for his license and registration, and then rolled down his window as the officer walked up to the car.

"Long ways away from home," the officer stated as he leaned down in the window, scanning over everyone's face from front to back. "It's nice to see kids properly strapped into booster seats for once," he muttered.

"Yes, officer. We are on our way to Foxwood Hills Resort. We were invited down by the mayor for the tournament," Carter explained, handing over his papers and ID card.

"Ah, Foxwood Hills, of course," the officer replied. "Do you know how to get there?"

Before Carter could even ask directions, Candace jumped in to answer, "We sure do!"

Carter rolled his eyes and lolled his head back to the officer with yet another forced smile. "The wife knows the way," he smirked.

The officer stifled a grin. "Try and take the exits a bit slower around here. There isn't 90-mile-an-hour traffic, so merging onto and off exists is a bit easier," he said as he tapped the roof of the van and handed Carter back his paperwork and card.

"Thank you, Officer..." Carter began.

"Tatum," the officer replied.

"Thank you, Officer Tatum," Carter said with a nod.

Carter rolled his window back up and looked over at Candace as she sat in the passenger seat with a huge grin on her face.

"Shut up," Carter replied without even letting her speak. "Is this the road I need to take? You said Doe Run?" he asked, pointing at the road about twenty feet away from where they had pulled over.

"Yes, that would be it," Candace replied.

Carter put the vehicle in drive as the sheriff passed by him with a wave. He waved back and pulled out behind him, slipping his blinker on to take the next right. He hated not knowing the directions himself. Back in his day, they would print out MapQuest directions and read them as they drove down the road, as if they were land pirates searching for buried treasure. Candace, however, didn't approve of him gracing the white line while reading the paper, so she took over the mapping and barked out directions right at their turns.

If she tells me one more time right as I am passing a turn that I need to turn, I will run the car off the road into something on her side, Carter mused.

They passed by a cemetery and a church whose sign read Henry Fork Church- The Brethren, then right beside it, another church that read Living Waters Assembly of God.

"They sure do like their churches here," Carter mumbled as he began to pass by an array of houses that looked like what could only be described as a rural ghetto. The people who congregated in their yards or on their porches wore ratty, dirty clothes. Most of them that they passed by had a cigarette held between their lips while they fussed with kids or dogs, while others lifted pipes from their pockets to hit. Within minutes, they passed by another convenience store on the left that had gas pumps, U-Haul rentals, and a sign that said apartment below available for rent.

Carter snorted as they drove by and said, "If you can't make money with the store, rent to the crackheads down the road," Carter chattered, amused.

A sign loomed over the gas pumps, naming it as One Stop Truck Shop.

"You know what they say about them lot lizards. Do you need some extra money?"

Carter laughed as Candace popped him on the back of the head.

"Hey, at least there is gas close by. The last time we took a vacation, I ended up having to walk over ten miles to the next gas station to get gas when our car ran out," Carter said, looking over at Candace. "Remind me again why we ran out?"

"Oh, my God! It happened one time, and you will never let me forget that I didn't remind the *driver* to stop for gas," Candace huffed, crossing her arms in irritation.

Joshua and Isobel were like church mice in the backseat as their parents bickered back and forth playfully. They stared out of the window and watched the rural countryside pass by as they drove past small, trashy neighborhoods, mobile homes, and trailer parks. Their proximity in age allowed them to remain close while growing up. There were times that Candace could swear they were meant to be twins instead of being born apart because of the silent conversations they had with one another. Candace glanced in the visor mirror to see what they were up to in the back since they had been so quiet during the trip. They had hardly spoken during the entire drive down from Maryland. Both Carter and Candace exchanged glances with one another as Carter stole a glance into the backseat himself through the rearview mirror. Normally, Joshua would be talking a mile a minute and trying his best to irritate Isobel while they drove down the road. For them to be on their best behavior was both suspicious and yet serene, considering that at least once a week, Candace would jive to the TikTok video singing "Fuck them kids" because they were such little "assholes," as she would put it. Carter would always follow with, "I bet you wish you had taken more anal now, huh?" to which she would slug him in his shoulder. Carter glanced once more in the rearview mirror, acknowledging the quiet children.

"Are you two alive back there? We haven't heard a peep from you the entire ride. For two little ones that bugged us for an entire month over this trip, you sure are quiet. Are you two still excited?" Carter asked, grinning at the two of them like a circus clown in the mirror.

They both glanced at Carter in the mirror with solemn stares, then silently returned their gazes back out the window and shrugged their shoulders.

"Really? Nothing?" Carter asked.

They seemed almost callous about the question, which pushed Carter's button just a bit. He breathed in deeply and held it for a moment before releasing the inhale and whispering "woosah" under his breath. He looked over at Candace with his eyebrows furrowed and mumbled under his breath through gritted teeth, "You better get your kids before I do."

Since they had Isobel, times had gotten a little tough, and Carter had found himself buried in work to stay afloat with bills, not to mention how taxing and draining a hospital residency is already. The mortgage, the car payment, and then the new baby expense were working him to the bone. So, the yearly vacations they had come to enjoy became too much of an expense to partake in. Truth be told, this was the first time in several years they had the spare time or money to be able to do anything aside from travel to the local county fairs. They were able to scrounge up enough money and set it back to be able to travel.

Candace rolled her eyes and shook her head, irritated at his short temper with the kids. "Enjoy the fucking peace, Carter," she groaned. "It won't be long until they are driving us insane wanting us to take them here and to take them to go hiking or whatever else they want us to do, and you replying 'after my nap.'"

"Bitch," Carter muttered.

"Forget to smoke your weed this morning, love?" she smirked as he flipped his middle finger up at her. "Make a left up here," Candace declared as they came to a slow stop.

"Are you sure this is the right road?" Carter asked.

"According to their website, this is the back entrance to the resort," Candace assured as she minimized the browser on her phone that had Foxwood Hills pulled up with the directions from Martinsville in the map section of the site.

Carter pivoted the steering wheel and pulled onto the road, which, in reality, was a small gravel road that led them through nothing but trees or a small forest area.

"Are you sure those directions are right? I mean, I don't want to argue with the owner of this place, but this looks like a scene out of Deliverance or Wrong Turn where everyone will die if they don't turn around and leave before the local inbreds kill them," he asked, putting the car in park and pulling out his own phone to verify where they were.

Candace pulled her phone back out of her purse once more, looked at the directions, and nodded her head. "It says that the resort is right up this road, about three or four-tenths of a mile."

"This isn't a road! It's an end-of-state maintenance beginning of hillbilly hell driveway that farmers make to lead cattle to their deaths!" Carter exclaimed.

"Would you just drive the damn car!" Candace yelled. "Geeze, enough with the sarcasm and hick jokes."

Carter mumbled, pulling the gear shift out of park. He put the van into drive and began a slow ascent toward their possible doom. As they crept up the drive, they came to a clearing on their left where a large, white, two-story house loomed with a garden behind the house. He slowed down to a crawl as they began to pass it so they wouldn't disturb the occupants of the house when a menacing gray-haired gentleman jumped out from the woods to their right, holding an AK-7 and spitting a wad of chewing tobacco on the ground. Carter rolled Candace's window down so they wouldn't come off as rude or snobby.

"Afternoon," Carter stated.

"You have any idear where yer at, boy?" the man asked, pointing the gun at the car. "Yer trespassing on my god dern land."

"I'm sorry," Carter replied, looking uneasily from the gun back to the man holding it. "The directions on our phone led us this way."

The man took a swig from the mason jar he held full of some clear liquid with fruit in the bottom as Carter swallowed the lump forming in the back of his throat. Candace glanced at him nervously as they waited for the man to either lower his gun or fire at them.

"We are looking for Foxwood Hills Resort. Have you heard of the place? We don't mean any harm, sir. If we took the wrong turn, we surely apologize for it. The directions on their website said we could take this road to get to the grounds," he replied as politely as he could.

The man spat another wad of tobacco juice from his lip as he lowered his gun. "God dern commies. How many times do I have to message that God forsaken *Resort* and tell them to remove this entrance from the directions? Once, I let the drive grow up, but they took me to court. The damn owners at that place claimed since I was tearing up their driveway with my semi when they know good and god damn well I don't drive it anymore," he muttered. "I paid for that driveway with my taxes, whether they say it ain't state-maintained or not. Those money-grabbin' bastards live o'er there," he said, pointing through a valley that had trees covering every inch of the property.

"So, we are in the right location?" Candace asked nervously.

"Ye' yer in the right place," the man replied, shaking his head. "Get on outta he'a," he huffed and flapped his hand at Carter.

"Once again, I apologize for the inconvenience of trespassing on your land due to poor directions," Carter replied.

"Just make sure to leave through the actual gate when you're done prancing around with them holler folk," he huffed and staggered back over to his porch, lifting a joint from the front pocket of his overalls. His eyes were already glazing over from the few swigs of grain alcohol he was drinking from his jar.

I bet he has a still somewhere around here, and that's why he is so jumpy, Carter thought as he watched him blaze a joint. *On second thought…*

Carter jumped as the sound of the storm door flapped shut on the two-story house while an elderly woman stood on the porch. She looked from their vehicle to the old man blazing his green and began to ask him questions.

"Ah, marriage," Carter said as he looked over to Candace, who returned a scowl back at him.

Carter smiled with a slight nod and a wave of his hand as the old woman continued her assault of questions on the old coot about who they were and why they were trespassing on their land.

Just by her appearance and mannerisms, she didn't look like the kind of person who took kindly to strangers. Carter rolled up Candace's window and once again began the long haul up the drive to the resort. A pylon sign stood at the end of the drive with Foxwood Hills Resort painted across the wood, announcing their arrival to the resort alongside the no trespassing sign pointing in the direction they had just come from.

"That was... frightening," Candace gasped, breaking the silence.

"Yeah, no kidding," Carter replied.

He heard a sneeze from the backseat and glanced in the rearview mirror, startled for a moment. He had forgotten they were even back there, as quiet as they had been the entire ride.

"You two," he said, holding their attention, "I don't want you straying too far from your mother's sight, you hear? Wherever we are settled into a cabin, you are to stay within looking distance of us. Understood?" he asked.

The children nodded in unison.

"Lord knows the hillbillies from Deliverance are walking the woods," Carter mumbled under his breath as he leaned over to Candace.

Carter looked around as they drove through the resort and half expected more hillbillies to come running out of the woods with torches and pitchforks. He watched the kids in the rear-view mirror as they drove through the resort, and they didn't even bat an eyelash. They were acting stranger than their usual "Omen" selves, but Carter brushed it off. *They're probably just tired or something,* he thought. *It **was** a six-hour drive.*

They took the road that led into the park and stopped at the main office, which was a lavish white cabin. There was a stop sign and a plaque with information about pricing and main office hours. **See Main Office Clerk for Check-in** was embossed on the plaque.

Carter pulled into one of the parking spots, switched off the ignition switch, and then turned to Candace and said, "Alright, you sit here while I go in and pay for our cabin."

"Ok," Candace replied as she glanced through her magazine again.

"Lock the doors, and don't roll your window down for anyone or anything," Carter urged.

"Ok..."

"Anything!" Carter reiterated. "The president, the Pope, no one. If they look crazy, don't roll it down. If they look like that insane gun-toting hillbilly from down the drive, don't roll it down. Blood-sucking zombies, nope. Or even," sucks in a breath gasping, "Elvis invites you to his new, back-from-the-dead concert; Don't do it! You never know who will pop out of the woods next around here... with a gun... looking to eat us for dinner or use us as their sex slave."

Candace nodded, agreeing sarcastically with her mouth twisted in a mocking mimic, and pushed the automatic door lock button as he closed the driver's door behind himself. He gave all those instructions on when not to roll the window down, when they could just pick up a large rock, or use the butt of their gun to break in her window if they really wanted.

She glanced in the backseat and smiled at Joshua and Isobel. They only replied with blank stares. "Come on, kids, where's your enthusiasm from yesterday? I mean, you ran around for weeks yelling and hollering about this trip, and when we take it, you are quiet as church mice without any enthusiasm," she asked, a bit downtrodden by their attitude and response to the trip.

Joshua and Isobel sighed while plastering the fakest smile they could muster on their faces, then returned their attention to staring out the window. Candace huffed and looked out her window as well. The resort was walled in by a forest, with the office being the only other thing visible in the area. The way the trees bent and swayed as the gentle wind blew across the resort caused an uneasy feeling to settle in, causing Candace's heart rate to climb in an anxious, rapid-fire rhythm as storm clouds gathered in the sky, casting silhouettes that appeared alive against the ground.

Candace had always been an outdoorsy type of child. She grew up riding birch trees to the ground, climbing the huge oak trees to swing from their branches, and tapping the maple trees for fresh syrup. However, there was something different about the way these trees loomed over their car, almost as if their presence alone caused the trees to peer closer and listen to their conversations as if they were animate.

The pines were at least forty feet tall, if not larger, looking all the world like giants emerging over the area from a fantasy world that had been tucked away quietly in the backwoods of Virginia. Oaks, maples. Poplar, locust, and other trees from the distance danced within the pines with their emerald green leaves flittering in the wind on the branches. Goosebumps prickled her skin, and in turn, she ran her hand down her neck to make the hair standing up lie back down flat as her nerves fired off warning sirens. Joshua and Isobel acting as strange as they were only intensified the knot of dread in the pit of her stomach. Maybe if she walked in, she could talk Carter into finding somewhere else to camp.

A loud pop against her window brought her back from her deep thoughts quickly, as her heart fluttered, causing her to catch her breath. She jumped slightly in her seat and let out a small squelch. She peered out the window to see what or who it was that thumped the glass with a loud thwack. On the other side of the glass stood a man around forty years old, with dark, black hair that had begun to gray, and was dressed in a white t-shirt and blue jeans with a short sleeve button-up shirt that had his name embroidered on the pocket. He motioned for her to roll her window down, but her husband's warning floated around in her head. Once he realized she wasn't going to roll her window down, he spoke to her loudly so she could hear him through the glass.

"My name is Mikey. I am the resident handyman or, what do the city slickers call them... oh, maintenance man," he stated with a grin.

She cracked her window an inch. "Nice to meet you, Mikey," she replied cautiously.

"Your husband is inside filling out the paperwork and parking permits," he replied. "After that is all wrapped up, I will take you down the trail and show you the cabin we have picked out for your stay this week."

"Wait, how did you know he was my husband? I mean, he could have been a friend for all you knew," she asked, narrowing her eyes, about to roll the cracked window back up.

He smiled and gave a small chuckle as he lifted a walkie-talkie from his utility belt. "The front office called me so I could show the new arrivals to their cabin. Told me a wife, husband, and two children," he replied, glancing into the backseat and giving a wave to Joshua and Isobel.

Candace smiled and let out a sigh of relief. "I'm sorry," she chuckled. "My anxiety is ramped up a bit, as well as everyone else's. We followed the directions on the website, and they brought us in a back way? Anywho, we were met with a shotgun-toting," she watched as

Mikey's eyebrows raised before changing the tone of her sentence, "older gentleman, that wasn't thrilled we had come in that way," she said, pointing in the direction they had driven.

"Yeah, that's Nathaniel," Mikey said, grimacing. "He's a bit of a prick, and that's putting it mildly. He causes all kinds of problems for my boss every chance he gets because he can't stand the fact that my boss's family never comes off this land, so that he could buy it all for himself. Wanted to turn it into a dairy farm or somethin' other."

"Oh, now that makes sense," Candace replied, but eyed the trees suspiciously.

"Yeah, don't let those trees fool you. This is all agriculturally zoned here. Hell, most of this was clear-cut just to put the campground in."

He turned his attention to the kids in the backseat. "Hey, guys! What do y'all like to do for fun?" he asked. They sat silently and unanswering. "I have all kinds of fun activities for the youngsters around here. We do walk-throughs of trails while I teach about the indigenous plants of the area. I show you what's good or bad for you. I teach some survival hacks if you ever get lost in these woods, or any woods for that matter. What berries to eat, what plant leaves are fine to wipe your butt with. You think y'all'd like that?" he asked.

Joshua and Isobel sat there solemnly and quietly, staring at Mikey. Mikey's grin began to twitch, and he glanced at Candace for reassurance that he hadn't scared them or anything.

"Do they talk?" he whispered.

"After the fiasco earlier with... Nathaniel, was it? I don't believe my husband is going to let them go far out of our sight," Candace replied apologetically. "He's a clinger," she joked.

Mikey laughed. "That's alright. I make the offer to all the kids. Sometimes, parents need a break from their kids, and even kids need a break from their parents. This is a perfect buffer for the two. They get to have time alone with other kids and learn about nature. Other than what few games the attendants provide, there really isn't much for them to do in the resort, so I always leave an option on the table to go on a little nature hike," he replied. "The resort is more so geared for the adults activity-wise. Not many kids like to sit and watch the adults play poker or fish."

"There are fishing spots here?" she asked, surprised.

"Yeah, there's a huge lake off in the back of these woods. Devil's Claw Lake. I don't like taking the kids over there in large numbers in case one slips off and gets too close to the water. I am not certified in CPR or anything," Mikey replied. "But we allow fishing and even hunting on the campgrounds. Swimming is allowed as well, but as I said, we don't have lifeguards on duty or anything, so it's at your own risk and liability-free. That's some of the paperwork your husband is signing right now."

Carter made his way out the door of the front office, carrying keys, papers, and a placard to hang on their rearview mirror.

Mikey waved at him. "Ready to get to your spot, Mister...?" Mikey asked.

Carter squinted in the sun as he stared at Mikey, taking in his appearance. Like the people in the office, Mikey was dressed for the backwoods life. He gave a nod and replied, "Carter is fine."

"Just follow me in the buggy then, Carter," Mikey said, smiling and nodding.

Mikey walked over to an old beater, late 80's model Jeep Wrangler, and got in. It appeared to have been a white Jeep at one point in time; however, rust now overtook every piece of metal on the cab, and there were just bits and pieces of white left behind from the original paint job. Dents and dings littered the surfaces, as well as scratches. The roofing must have been damaged because what would normally be a removable soft or hard top was now a tarp that replaced the entire top of the vehicle, presumably to prevent rain from damaging the inside if the interior isn't already ragged out.

Carter hopped in the driver's seat, muttering about the piece of shit Jeep the maintenance man owned, and looked annoyed at Candace.

"What?" she asked defensively.

"What part of anyone or anything did you just not get?" he asked.

"It's not like I dropped my panties for the first midlife crisis to walk up on the door," she retorted. "Besides, he explained who he was and showed me his badge and all before I spoke to him. Plus, it isn't like he couldn't have just broken the window if he wanted to carry me off like Tarzan."

Carter huffed and replied, "He would have brought you back," as he started the SUV and slid it into drive.

Candace sat in her seat quietly, miming the words her husband had said since they arrived, and rolled her eyes. She glanced over at him and sweetly smiled as he stared back at her, unamused by her antics. They followed Mikey in the Jeep for a few minutes as they took a gravel road deeper into the trees that had panicked Candace earlier. Right before Carter figured he needed to switch his headlights on because of the tree coverage darkening the path, the vehicles emerged on the other side of the drive, where they arrived at the cabins.

Cabins lined the sides of the drive, nearly stacked on one another. Carter had sprung for a cabin that was by itself, as opposed to the efficiency condo cabins the campground offered. It gave them a little extra privacy apart from the other resortgoers. As they drove slowly through the lane, they noticed that there were already people scattered throughout the park playing games and being entertained by resort employees.

The rust bucket came to a stop in front of them, and Mikey hopped out of the truck so he could motion to Carter that the cabin to the right was where they needed to park. Carter pulled into the parking space for the lone cabin and then shut the motor off, taking the keys from the ignition.

Everyone clamored from inside the vehicle and stretched their legs out after the long journey. Carter stared at the cabin, impressed by its structure. It was more of a miniature mansion than a cabin. It looked as if the Addams family had built it compared to the other cabins they had passed by coming in.

Mikey whistled. "The Penthouse Presidential Cabin. You folks should have an excellent stay with this bad boy."

"Is it nice?" Candace asked. "I didn't even know there were different types of cabins available."

"This one is the top dog of all the cabins. It is secluded away from the efficiency ones, as you can see, so there aren't people walking through your yard to bother you at night. It has blackout curtains, a jacuzzi in the back, and your own minibar. Let's see, what else? Oh, you get your own internet router box with a TV and Xbox hookup. You get on the house satellite TV, and it comes with a stove and fridge," Mikey replied proudly.

"Oh, how nice, dear!" Candace said through gritted teeth. "How much did that cost us?"

"For the week, it usually goes for a grand," Mikey replied without missing a beat.

"Thank you, Mikey, for all the helpful information," Carter smiled sarcastically.

"What else makes it the best?" Candace asked. "And can you tell us more about the land here and all?"

Candace and Carter walked over to Mikey as he began explaining the history of the area. Joshua sighed and walked over to where Isobel stood, staring into the trees. They stood side by side, gazing at the dancing light of the sun beaming through the tops of the tall trees.

"I don't think it is safe in there," Isobel whispered to Joshua. "It's scary and looks like bears live in there."

Her eyes glistened in the sun as she stared into the dark of the woods that surrounded the back of the cabin.

"All the more reason to explore the first chance we get," Joshua replied quietly. "That dude Mikey will keep us safe from bears on his hikes."

Shrieks and giggles interrupted the darkness that was creeping its way into their thoughts. They quickly turned to find the origin of the laughter. A small group of kids played kickball in a small section of a field off to the side of some of the cabins across the way from them, while others tossed a football back and forth, and a select few painted on easels.

Carter and Candace had also become distracted by the noise of the kids in the campground. Joshua and Isobel glanced over to their parents, asking with their eyes to join them.

"Get out of here," Carter said while shooing them away with his hand.

Joshua began to sprint over to the group of children, but stopped quickly when he realized Isobel wasn't following him like usual. Isobel had instead returned her attention back to the woods and continued to stand there peering into the quaint dark of the forest. Shadows continued to dance throughout the thicket as the wind rustled the treetops, allowing them to cast glints of light onto the forest floor through the parted gray skies above.

"Come on, Lizzy," Joshua called.

The wind began to pick up in intensity, and little dust devils began to form at the tree line, kicking up the recently fallen autumn leaves and twisting them along the ground, tossing them into the air every now and then. Isobel didn't flinch and remained in the same spot, just standing there as the small whirlwind circled her, catching her hair and tossing it around as it breezed by. Leaves caught in her thin, blond hair and her modest blue, print dress kicked up a bit in the mild winds, but it still didn't faze her. She didn't bat an eyelash. Instead, she peered harder and deeper into the shadows that danced like ballet performers before her. The ups and downs of the trees were as if dancers were being lifted into the air and gently sat back down on the blankets of moss growing on the forest floor. Her eyes were fixated in almost a near squint as a vacant gaze crept across her face as if something had caught her full attention.

Joshua was quite the opposite. He shuddered as the zephyr reached him, and its cold tendrils of death and decay wrapped him in an embrace. It had started off as a rather warm day for fall weather, but a wall of frigid air that followed the wind hit him and chilled him to the bone. Goose bumps prickled his body, and the tiny hairs on the back of his neck stood at the root.

Anxiety washed over Joshua with a nagging sixth-sense sensation that someone was watching them from within the woods. Once more, his nerves were set on edge as the hairs pricked up on his arms. He grabbed his arms quickly and rubbed them, shaking the feeling off. He didn't want Isobel to see him acting like this or think that he was scared. He was the big brother. His job was to make her feel safe and to let her know that he could and would protect her at all costs. She didn't need to see him being all paranoid or something. However, his anxiety sank in deeper because no matter how much he rubbed his arms, he couldn't shake the feeling of utter dread that was starting to settle in the pit of his stomach. Nausea swept over him, and he felt suddenly like retching up the lunch they had eaten.

"Lizzy," Joshua called again,

Once again, she didn't respond to his calls. He walked over to her, grabbed her by the shoulders, and gave her a gentle shake.

Her eyes looked like they were glazed over before she gave them a blink and looked over at Joshua. "We need to go," Joshua whispered to her.

However, no matter how much he willed it, they both continued to stand there in the deafening quiet, where the only audible sounds now were the rustling of the leaves in the wind as it whispered in the woods.

As the sunlight continued to cast shadows and shapes, the darkness seemed to mutate and transform before them. A picturesque scene of doom and terror spread out before them. Faint voices, as if whispers of children in the woods floated on the now gentle breeze. Joshua and

Isobel both heard the child-like voices calling out to them. Joshua glanced around, and none of the others in the campground seemed to notice the voices. These voices weren't anything like the sound of the children playing rambunctiously in the field. The voices even knew their names as the whispers grew louder but softer in their ears. It was mesmerizing, haunting even. It had a lilting timber, almost ephemeral even, that vibrated and buzzed within their very cores. It pulled at them, begging, almost pleading with them to come. To come to the shadows and play. It pulled them, drew them toward the woods, toward the darkness, a tainted beauty of death and peril.

Quiet settled around them as the wind died down and then disappeared altogether, along with the voices. It was moments before either of the children even spoke. Joshua was the one who said it first...

"There's something in there... Something not right... something… dark and evil…"

Chapter Two

NATHANIEL PROPPED his foot up and leaned into a tree stump with red-rimmed eyes as he took another swig of moonshine from his corn liquor jug. He glanced over at his wife as she pursed her lips and frowned at him, her resting bitch face tugging at every wrinkle visible. He watched the SUV disappear as it continued up the gravel driveway, another vehicle passing through their side of the land. He had half a mind just to let the trees and brush grow up so no one else could use the driveway, but then he would have to chip in on maintenance of the main entrance, and he didn't want to deal with that hassle.

"You feelin' ok, Nate?" Ozell asked as she eyed him closely.

Nathaniel muttered incoherently.

"Nate!" she demanded.

"Confounded woman, what?!" he hissed in response.

"Don't you take that tone with me, you ol' bastard. I will slip rat poison into your stew meat and dance on your damn grave," Ozell barked.

"What do you want, you old biddy," Nate rasped as he drew another slug of corn liquor from his jug.

"You've been acting funny, and I was worried, you scoundrel. I don't know if it's the heat or the shine getting' to ya, but you let them there people off without even firing off a shot from your gun. It don't make no damn sense. Why you being so nice all of a sudden? I ain't ever seen you let people keep on getting it without threatening them within an inch of their life and the law showing up to tell you you can't do that. Besides, they'll tell their friends, and before you know it, our driveway will become a confounded highway," Ozell spat.

Nathaniel stood there, half listening to Ozell and half thinking about the kids in the back of the vehicle that the Yanks drove in. He had no idea why or how, but they had mesmerized him like a snake charmer. They felt oddly familiar, and he absolutely hated children, so he was never around any for those young ones to remind him of anyone. Yet here he stood, strangely enamored with the vision of their faces in his mind like a newspaper clipping filed away in his brain. The hairs on his body pricked up, and goosebumps prickled his skin. He gave a shake from the heebie-jeebies and took another long swig from his jug before tuning back into Ozell, still rambling behind him. His paranoia was getting to him, and it was most likely either the liquor or the bud he smoked doing it. Either way, he needed to shake the feeling for good.

"Woman, why do you insist on graying every hair on my head with that mouth of yers? Ye'd think that after all 'em belt lashings you got over the years, you'd mind that tongue of yers. But here ye' are wagging it like a dog's tail looking for a bone to pick. Make yerself scarce. Go do some'in' for once instead of hanging over my shoulder with that useless attitude ye' like to wear." Nathaniel stared Ozell down, daring her to backtalk him.

Ozell muttered under her breath, and Nathaniel's eyes widened in anger.

"Speak up! I can't hear yer sass!" Nathaniel bellowed.

"What would you like me to do, *massah*? Milk the chickens?" she asked sarcastically. "I got my shit done for the day. The housework is finished, and the garden has been weeded and the vegetables that were ripened have been picked. Want me to start doing your chores, too? Show you how useful you are? I bet I can swing an ax and bust that pile of wood that's been *seasoning,* as you so call it, and get it all done before nightfall, unlike your lazy, no good for nothing codger loving son of a beehive—"

Nathaniel clapped his hand across Ozell's face, and she quickly grasped the reddening handprint with the palm of her hand, wide-eyed. "I warned ye' about yer sass, and I have had just about 'nuff of it. Get yer ass in the god damned house now. I expect my dinner on the table within the hour."

"Don't you *dare* take the lord's name in vain in front of me, you two-timing, low-down piece of horseshit. I have put up with you being a bastard lately, hell, a fucking dick even, but you ain't going to treat me like cattle *and* do it while sinning," she fired like Yosemite Sam.

Nathaniel brought out his big boy voice while raising his hand and bellowed, "Listen here, ye' little wench. I am the man of this house, and you will watch your tongue, or it will sit on the mantle in a mason jar of shine. Now get!" he slurred as the liquor started to impair his ability to speak.

Ozell flinched away from his hand. Nathaniel became a downright dick whenever he drank shine. There were times in the past when both of them had been alcoholics. Fighting was always the main component of both of them getting sloshed. Ozell could never handle Nathaniel's mouth.

During her drinking days, she never flinched away from his pops and instead would lay her own punches in. They would fist fight, and hell, sometimes they even pulled out guns and spent an hour sloppily trying to shoot one another. Calling the cops on domestic violence wasn't a thing in the past. Most neighbors kept their noses in their own houses, so there wasn't ever any police involvement, and they would taper off once a family member intervened. But as Ozell got older, her age caught up with her, and the blows were more painful. Even on the night of their wedding, they got into a slap-down fistfight that escalated into a gun display.

Ozell had caught Nathaniel slipping around with one of her bridesmaids. Luckily, her sister, Margaret, stepped in to stop the feud before the church did, in fact, call the law.

"What in Sam's hell are you two doing!" she yelled at them as she ripped the shotguns from their hands.

"It's only birdshot," Ozell defended.

"You are in the house of the lord using profanities and guns, and I will not let drunken Bonnie and Clyde tarnish our family name. Sober yer asses up and get out to the reception. It's time to cut the damned cake."

They did as ordered, and the reception continued on as planned. There wasn't much of a honeymoon, to Ozell's disappointment. She had planned for Hawaii, but Nathaniel blew all their money on poker, so they had to rent a camping spot at Philpot Lake for the weekend in its place. She never forgave him for it, either. She had an advertisement picture of Hawaii hung on her kitchen wall that she looked at every so often, wishing he would surprise her with the trip. The years went by, and the only thing he surprised her with was a flaccid dick.

"One of these days, Nathaniel, you're going to wake up dead, poisoned, and then buried under my endangered roans, and ain't a damn soul going to miss yer scrawny ass but me," Ozell threatened.

Nathaniel waved away her nonsense with a flick of his wrist as he picked up his watering jug to wet his flower bed. As he passed the jug over the tops of the flowers, he noticed whole apple cores, potato peels, and other bits of food that were supposed to have gone into the compost pit out back.

"Dammit, Ozell, how many Go- how many damn times do I have to tell ya that the food goes into the pit, not directly into mah flo'ers," Nathaniel yelled, tossing his watering jug aside.

The jug bounced and rolled some down the yard before coming to a rest. He spun around to strike her, but all he saw and heard was the screen door slamming shut to the house. She had already walked inside.

"Daggone wench, she will be the death of me, and it won't be her poisoning me either. Ima stroke out because of her ass," he said, picking his straw hat from his head and wiping his sweaty brow.

His white, greasy hair was matted to his scalp as the humidity caused every pore to rain down over his eyes. He could hear the old turntable begin to roll out Elvis Presley's notes, and he couldn't help but smile for a moment, thinking of Ozell shaking her hips as she walked around the kitchen preparing dinner.

Nathaniel mopped the sweat from his face and put his straw hat back on his head. He walked up the steps to the screen door and popped it open, grabbing his .30-06 hunting rifle from the mount on the wall.

"Honey, I'm going to go do my patrol and get some hunting in," he called sweetly as a truce.

He started down the steps when he heard the music turned down low.

"What was that?" Ozell called to him.

"Going out to hunt and patrol!" he yelled, then picked up his pace to the shed.

Ozell had barely opened the screen door before he had torn through the field on his hunting side-by-side ATV.

"Just stay away from them damn ruins," Ozell commented to herself.

Nathaniel floored the gas pedal to the max as he took the trails he had carved out through the woods. He didn't even know why he patrolled the area every evening, but he felt compelled to do it like he had to protect what was his at all costs. He thought back to his childhood and remembered how his father had gotten obsessed with the Ingrams. Every single day, his father would take him along on a walk and tell him about the history of the Ingrams and McGradys and how they had always been bad news since the moment they bought the property adjacent to theirs. Even the caretaker was a no-good piece of dirt that needed to be watched.

Once the ruins were discovered by the land surveyor while marking the property lines, Nathaniel had become mindless over the area. He felt like a salvage yard dog chomping at the bit to protect his junk and couldn't control the anger that came with it. His gut told him that Patrick was going to snake his claim away on that gold mine.

He hadn't always felt this way toward his neighbors. There was a time, even when his father ranted his crazy ramblings, that Nathaniel had his own thoughts. When he was a young boy, he would often run into Patrick out in the woods playing. It was long before they ever sent him off to that insane asylum. He was quirky, but Nathaniel knew Patrick wasn't crazy. There were strange happenings in the woods when they were kids that he wrote off or blocked out.

Now, all he felt was a deep-seated rage that bubbled beneath the surface. He couldn't help but be angry at the thought of them. Nathaniel dropped the side-by-side's speed down and slowly crept around the bend that ended where the old plantation's homestead had stood. It was your typical foundation from the early settlers' days, where boulders and logs were stacked for a base. Age and weather had whittled the remains of the house down to just that. The petrified logs that remained looked as if they had been burned, whether from the original damage to the house or from lightning strikes throughout the years.

Nathaniel climbed from his side-by-side and walked to the right side of the rubble. The only thing left besides the actual laid foundation for the bottom of the dwelling was the chimney that had seen better days. Weathering had worked its toll on the hearth, and it was crumbling, barely staying together through the wind, rain, and lightning storms that had torn through the land since its erection. Apart from these few markers, one would never have guessed that any type of estate sat on the land here.

Now, Nathaniel had the wreckage marked as his and had set a hunting blind smack dab in the middle of the decaying bricks. He hunted deer, squirrels, and pretty much everything else that could be thrown into a stew kettle. Nathaniel's 30-06 was strapped to his shoulder as he climbed into his hunting blind. He had two other weapons cases that he kept in the blind at all times. One was his crossbow, and the other was a .22 rifle to shoot small game such as squirrels and rabbits. He could destroy most of the meat using his .30-06 rifle.

In his old age, a crossbow was easier to use than a drawstring bow since the best hunting ones were 75-pound draw. His rheumatoid arthritis had riddled his bones with calcium deposits, and his shoulder had undergone rotator cuff surgery years prior. With a crossbow, all he had to do was load arrows, pull the drawstring back, and hook it into its locked position. Its accuracy was also more efficient than a drawstring bow. He had no complaints.

Nathaniel zipped down the door of the blind and eased his old bones down into the camping chair he had purchased from the Walmart in town. It was collapsible and easy to carry around, just in case he needed to carry it in for cleaning. It was perfect for his blind setup as well. He used pallets to keep him up off the ground so it wouldn't get anything muddy that he kept in there. The blind was waterproof, so when he zipped it up tight, no moisture could get in.

He set up his rifle on a small desk he had in the hunting blind, using a tripod for the gun. Along with the rheumatoid arthritis pain came shaking as well. The tripod helped steady his shot instead of wasting ammo and losing dinner for the next week. He scanned the area and also looked through the scope of his rifle for any signs of animals wandering through the area.

A breeze began to rustle the leaves around his hunting blind, and he took a whiff of the air. He could smell the damp ground and dying leaves succumbing to mildew, creating a perfectly scented petrichor perfume in the air. He could smell the pine tree sap that seeped to the surface during the hot and humid days of summer that had trailed over into the fall. Nathaniel pulled slightly on one of the boards of the pallet, and it popped loose, revealing a mason jar he had hidden beneath. He pulled it out and loosened the lid, taking in a good whiff of corn liquor made with damsons. He tipped it back and took a long pull from the jar before putting the lid back on the jar and setting it on the floor of the blind.

He sat quietly, listening to the sounds of the forest as the wind blew, the trees moved, and the animals scurried. He wanted a good-sized deer today, so Ozell could make him some tenderloin steaks. The tenderloin was the best part of the deer, and he'd argue that point until he was blue in the face.

The sounds of nature soon blended with one another, sounding almost as if they were whispering secrets in his ear. He smirked to himself and then quickly jerked his head. The whisper sounded more audible, more like the voice of a person. He picked up his binoculars that he kept in his rifle case and scoured the area to see if there were any of them campers from the resort who had wandered off and got lost in the woods. It wasn't uncommon for them to find themselves down here. It was easy getting turned around in those woods. Up is down, and down is up, and the light seems to go in a circle instead of a steady line.

The voice he heard didn't repeat itself, and he didn't see anyone in the woods, so he shrugged it off with a chuckle and took another drink of the damson shine. He held the jar up to his face while grinning like an opossum. *This shit must be stronger than what I thought. I need to give a tip next time when I load up on it.* Nathaniel nearly dropped his jar when the voice once again popped into his ear like a whisper.

Nathaniel...

He jumped to his feet, looking around frantically.

"Whoever is out there, show yerselves." He waited silently for any type of sound or voice to float on the breeze again. "I am hunting and can easily shoot you by accident. Once again, make yerself known." The air went quiet, almost as if the wind had died permanently.

"I hate having to talk," Nathaniel muttered. "Scares away the damned deer."

No sooner had he spoken the words than a doe and her fawn walked from the brush and into the clearing. Nathaniel quietly positioned his gun's scope on the two of them and sat watching them as they grazed on the bait he had scattered around the area. Deer couldn't resist sweet feed, cracked corn, and persimmons mixed with apple chunks. It was a concoction he came up with on his own, and it surely worked, too.

He clicked his sights on his gun and watched the doe munch on her food. At one point, she had stopped eating and stared directly in his direction as if she knew he was there. Her ears twitched as well as her nose as she sniffed the air, most likely smelling the alcohol he had lavished in greedily. But she didn't seem frightened of his presence at all.

He was about to let the deer go, and so he could find a nice buck, when something eerie settled into his bones. He felt like he wasn't in control of himself anymore. He pointed the gun at the mother and pulled his trigger. He hit her directly in the heart. She moved a few steps and lay down one leg at a time, panting before falling over to her side dead.

Nathaniel excitedly congratulated himself on his perfect shot. The strangest thing, though, was the fawn didn't run from the sound of the gun. It stood beside its mother, sniffing at her as her heart finished beating and the blood trickled from the wound that the bullet had made. Empathy tugged at Nathaniel's heartstrings, and he felt terrible for what he had done. He never hunts the doe when she has a fawn at her side. *Why did I do that?*

Nathaniel started to walk over to the carcass of the mother deer, and the baby fawn still didn't budge from its spot beside her. It, too, now lay down beside its mother and made bleating pleas for help to the other deer that might be around. Once again, an unfamiliar feeling overtook Nathaniel, and he couldn't control his actions. He walked over to the fawn and bent down beside it as it peered at him fearlessly. He stroked its head, lightly scratching behind its ears before pulling his hunting knife from the sheath on his hip and sinking it into his throat. The fawn didn't even struggle. It just lay down to die like its mother.

Blood spurted from the blade as he pulled it out, splattering some in his face. It then spilled over his hands like warmed honey. He felt a strange satisfaction overcome him, an eager thrill that rose from his loins to his stomach. He brought his hands to his face and inhaled deeply, breathing in the coppery iron scent.

Just as he was about to stick his bloodied fingers in his mouth to taste the alluring crimson water, the wind stirred once more, carrying the voices with it that he had heard earlier. He was pulled from his elated trance and stared, appalled at his hands so close to his mouth. He quickly wiped the blood from his hands onto his hunting pants, nearly in a tizzy as he thought to himself, *What the fuck is happening?* The blood smeared into the fabric of his pants, and he could feel the sticky residue on the other side touching his thighs. He looked down at the deer that lay side by side, dead, and panicked.

"What did I do? Why?" he asked, truly confused at what he had done. "I never kill the babies. The tenderloin is sweeter and good eating, but I never kill the babies. And I never kill the mama with a baby. What is wrong with me?"

He knew Ozell would suspect something. There wasn't a shot at the fawn at all. All he did was slit its throat. That's alarming to any person who has cleaned deer meat their entire lives. He contemplated cleaning the deer right here or taking it back to Ozell to clean. Afterall, she had been cleaning the deer since they had gotten married. It would be even more alarming to her that he cleaned it himself.

"Fuck it," Nathaniel stated.

Nathaniel strung the carcasses up in trees and grabbed some trash bags from the side-by-side to put the meat in. He picked his hunting blade up from the ground and made one large swipe down the center of their underbelly, making sure not to pop the bladder bag or intestines. He removed all of the organs and then began to slice at the hide and peel it from the skin of the deer. Once he had the hide removed, he began to halve and quarter the deer at their shoulders and hams, placing them in the trash bags along with the rib meat, neck, and tenderloins. After he was finished, he tossed the remains of the carcass into the brush for the scavengers and nature to take over.

He walked back to the side-by-side with the bags of meat and opened the cooler lid he kept on the back of the ATV. He took the cooling beer out, set it aside on the seat up front, and tossed the deer meat into the melting ice. He had every intention of driving home, but instead found himself driving to the edge of the property line where the campgrounds were. The whispers in the wind were heavy, and he could almost make out what they were saying as he pulled his binoculars up from around his chest. He had completely forgotten to put them back in with the gun at the hunting blind.

As soon as he began to watch through the binoculars, the voices were loud in his ears. He dropped the binoculars and grabbed his ears in hopes of stopping them from rupturing his eardrums. He didn't understand what the sounds meant. It sounded like a language, but foreign. One he had never heard before. He gently rocked back and forth in his seat, breathing heavily, trying to hold back the tears of frustration that brimmed in his eyes. The sounds were so loud and piercing to his senses. He balled his hands up and began beating his ears to stop the sounds until blood started to trickle down from inside after his eardrums ruptured.

The voices stopped, and the frantic anxiety that had overtaken his senses and overloaded him was now starting to settle down. He felt the sticky residue of his own blood trickling down the side of his face to his neck. He slowly withdrew his hands from his ears, half-expecting the loud, piercing sounds to re-emerge. Silence filled the area instead.

Something told him to look through his binoculars, so he brought them up to his eyes and resumed whatever his gut had been telling him to do. He saw a little girl and a boy standing at the edge of the tree line, peering into the woods. It was the same two kids who had been in the SUV that passed through earlier. He saw the mother and father chatting with the caretaker, Mikey. He huffed in a smirk tone before once again returning his gaze to the kids. This time, the little girl was staring directly at him, and he fumbled with his binoculars, dropping them.

Nathaniel ducked down below the steering wheel of the side-by-side in hopes that they wouldn't run off and tell their parents someone was watching them in the woods. After a few moments, he picked the binoculars up and looked back where the kids had been standing. The little girl still stood there, almost as if she were in a trance or perhaps possessed. Maybe she had seizures. He didn't know. He just found it odd and was a bit uneasy. Those kids were weird.

He felt a haze befall him, and whispers began in his ear so softly, but this time, he could understand. He was mesmerized by what they were saying in his ear, as if he were the only one who could understand them. The little boy was once again back, trying to get his sister to go with him, when he stopped, and they both stared deeply into the woods where Nathaniel sat. Finally, he pulled her away, and Nathaniel snapped out of whatever he was experiencing.

He shook his drunken stupor off, nearly sober from the whole ordeal, and started his side-by-side up to make it home before dark. Dusk had already begun to settle on the horizon, and these woods got dark at night. The best alpinist could become lost for days in the maze of trees as if nature rerouted the trails herself. As he drove closer to the house, anger flared within, and he had absolutely no reason to feel angered by anything, but he was.

***

From the shadows, a small girl emerged, watching the old man stumble drunkenly from his riding vehicle, up the stairs, and into the house. She was dirty with long, beautiful red hair and wore a white nightdress. A nearly destroyed doll dangled from her hand while she hugged a dilapidated teddy bear to her chest. The old woman inside peeked out her kitchen window and went pale as if she had seen a ghost. Just as she was about to open the door, the small girl vanished back into the woods, dragging her doll behind her.

Chapter Three: 1845

THE COLONIZATION OF THE AMERICAS was the most important part of traveling to the New World. Many claimed that it was to escape the persecution of the church, and for many, that was the case, but to others, they wanted to escape the blade of impending doom that the royals of all European countries threatened their people with. When the Ingrams decided to leave Ireland, they made haste to the ships that sailed west to land unturned and unfarmed.

In 1799, Benjamin Ingram took his pregnant wife and sole son, Adrian, to the New World to make a name for themselves. Along with his family, he was able to afford the tickets of several people who would become indebted to his kindness, the McGradys.

Upon arrival in Virginia, the Ingrams and McGradys set out to find land that had yet to be settled and build a plantation, as many had planned for survival among the newly discovered vastness of what would become the 13 Colonies of the United States. It took several years to grow acclimated to the new land in Virginia. The winters were harsh, and the summers were brutal. They were warned of these misfortunes and stayed close to the mainland until Moira Ingram gave birth to another bouncing baby boy, whom she named James.

Upon the close of winter, the family traveled over two hundred miles to settle in undisturbed land. They had picked up several workers along their travel to what would be their new home, so upon arrival, they set out to clear-cut the area for farming and building a cabin to live in.

The area they had chosen was quite strange and had an eerie energy. After several weeks of work, Moira brought it to Benjamin's attention that she hadn't seen nary a rabbit nor a squirrel come through the area. Benjamin had noticed the same and assumed the area had been hunted out and abandoned by Native American tribes of the area.

Once they had everything built and the plantation growing, the Ingrams flourished on the fertile grounds of what would become Franklin County in later years. The red clay mud was nutrient-rich and perfect for growing corn, tobacco, and other vegetables and fruits. Their boys grew tall and healthy alongside their bountiful plantation. Since they had the cabin to live in, Benjamin began the slow build of what would become Ingram Manor.

Over the years, more and more people made their way out through Virginia or up the coast into what would become the other states of the eastern shoreline. By the time James had reached the age of maturity, other people had popped up their own plantations on the lands that bordered what they had claimed as theirs. The Ingrams became friendly with those around them in hopes that their boys would find young women to settle down, marry, and have children with. Benjamin had long been prepared to parcel out his land to his children upon marriage in hopes that the father of the lucky lasses did the same and the families would become stronger together.

It was 1820 when James met Anne Hodges, and the long, drawn-out build of Ingram Manor came to completion. Just as Benjamin had hoped, the families got along great, and soon, James and Anne were married, with her father giving a dowry of twenty acres of his land. James and Anne accepted the land along with the land that Benjamin bequeathed to James as well, and immediately the two began their journey together. They raised a barn beside the cabin his father had given him, that he had been raised in, and planted their fields within a year. They began to remodel the cabin, expanding it into a larger plantation home. By the end of that year, Anne was giving birth to their oldest daughter, Nancy, as their house came to completion.

Time seemed to fly by as they lived their simple lives. Anne gave birth to another girl around two years later, whom she was to name Jane. However, they had their misfortunes as well when Anne grew sick, miscarrying their third child. It was several years later before she became pregnant with a fourth pregnancy and gave birth to their third child, a healthy, bouncing baby boy that they named William in the year 1841. Nancy had already grown into a young teenager, and Jane wasn't far behind.

Three years later, Anne gave birth to her final child, a girl she named Isobel.

Before long, Nancy and Jane had reached the age where they could be wedded and move away from the plantations. Jane found herself a nice young boy from the Robinson family, and Nancy decided to be a teacher, living on her own. This left William and Isobel at home with their parents, along with Anne's mother, who had grown feeble in old age and was unable to care for herself after the passing of Anne's father.

It was 1821 when Anne's brother, Jeremiah, announced his claim on the land their father had given as her dowry, which was denied in court. It soon turned into a spew of hate and anger from Jeremiah directed at James and Anne, with many empty threats that they ignored.

Before Isobel was to turn five, Elga, Anne's mother, passed away in her sleep, which left Anne distraught, depressed, and withdrawn. Jeremiah once again brought them to court to try and convince the judge that the land had been given to her under duress. Once again, the judge denied his claim, and once more, Jeremiah made his threats. However, this time he sounded more sincere than the last.

James was never a drinker of spirits and instead drank mostly herbal teas. He took his tea with a cube of sugar and sat in his chair to enjoy his time alone. However, Anne noticed a shift in his personality and demeanor that chilled her to the bone whenever he would drink the teas he had traded for. It started with nausea and vomiting that quickly shifted to heavy sweats. He soon became angry and bitter with horrid mood swings, constantly complaining about Jeremiah and how he was a no-good, dirty, greedy dog that needed to be put down. Oftentimes, he fell feverish, and with the fevers came the things only he could see. She often found him staring at his reflection in pools of water, touching the reflection of his face in the water, and then touching his actual face to see if he felt a difference between what he saw and what was actually there.

It wasn't long before there was empty air between James and Anne, and not much longer after that, Anne brought in a bed of her own to sleep in. Between his deepening, altered mood and his descent into madness, Anne didn't even know who her husband had become. They would argue over his need to see the doctor or even the medicine men who welcomed the pale faces troubled by the supernatural. James refused, saying his tea was all he needed.

There was a notable strain on their marriage and a heaviness in the air whenever James was in an episode of lunacy. It didn't take much to set him off on angry-filled rants or abusive behavior. Whenever he would break free of whatever ailed his mind, he would always apologize to Anne, claiming he wasn't himself during those times. Several times, he would try to clear his mind by solely drinking spring water, only to find himself begging for more herbal teas because of the headaches from caffeine withdrawal. He would then fall back into his odd demeanor of hatred and anger and take it out on everyone in the house.

Anne had noticed that James' mood would come and go depending on when he would go to the local medicine woman in town to get the herbal teas he drank. She began to switch them out with teas she would get from a local vendor, and soon, his rage and temper slowly subsided. He started to become the man she had once known and fallen in love with. Just as quickly as his mood had changed back to normal, it shifted once more, and she didn't understand why. It wasn't until she happened to look out of her window one afternoon and saw James speaking with the local medicine woman, Gini, that she understood where he had been getting the herbs from.

Gini lived in a shack on the edge of town in the valley below. She was a Cherokee medicine woman and the only one left in the valley. According to her mother-in-law, Moira, the Siouan Native Americans and the Cherokee did not get along so well. However, it was the Cherokee who had granted them safe passage into the area to make sure the Siouan tribe did not harm them. The Siouans had staked their claim in the land after the Cherokee had abandoned it sometime before Virginia was ever colonized.

Once Anne knew that James was still getting the herbs from Gini, she met with her to explain why he couldn't take them. Gini laughed and said the herbs she gave him were not mind-altering herbs, but your average herbs used for tea, and shouldn't be the cause or reason for his temper flares. Although Anne was skeptical, she believed the medicine woman and continued to allow James to get his herbs from her. She had bigger problems than James' temper to deal with, as she was still having issues with her brother, Jeremiah, over the land her father had given her as dowry.

It was over twenty years later, and he still held his grudge over the fact that the land their father had promised him was given to her instead. Even with the family feuding between them, Jeremiah still came by with his wife, Ketia, to spend time with Lizzy and William. She would often see them out in the fields playing and foraging as Jeremiah taught them the ways of the land.

William was the first one to fall mysteriously ill. Anne had called for Gini to come and see him as the local doctor didn't know what was wrong with him, and there weren't any plagues in the area as there had been in Europe. Gini came by daily to treat William as he grew sicker and sicker.

"I'm sorry," Gini told James and Anne as they stood by William's bed. "There is nothing more I can do for him. This sickness has invaded his soul, I am afraid."

Anne clasped her hand to her mouth and buried her face into James' chest.

"What can we do for him?" James asked.

"I'm afraid he will pass tonight," Gini replied.

"Our daughter," Anne began through choked words. "Lizzy is sick, too."

"Maybe her sickness isn't as bad as his sickness, and I can heal her before it gets too bad," Gini offered.

James and Anne walked Gini to Lizzy's room and opened the door. Lizzy lay in her bed, staring out the window at the falling rain.

"Is William going to die?" Lizzy asked, pulling her gaze from the window and staring at her parents.

A stifled cry caught in Anne's throat, and she couldn't answer her.

"Am I going to die too?" Lizzy asked, looking at Gini.

"We hope not, little one," Gini replied as she sat down on the bed and began to examine her.

Gini smiled at Lizzy as she looked her over. She stood from the bed and walked over to her parents and spoke in hushed tones to them about her findings. "She has the same thing he does," Gini stated gravely. "I am afraid she won't be able to fight off whatever this is, just like young William."

"You have to do something for them!" Anne cried. "We have money to pay you. Please!"

"I'm afraid none of my herbs will work on them," Gini replied. "I tried many remedies with the boy, and he just worsened. Have either of them eaten anything?"

"No, he just vomits whatever we feed him back up," Anne replied, wiping her nose. "Lizzy can keep broth down at the moment, but nothing more."

"If she doesn't get her appetite back, she will not be strong enough to fight whatever this is. It is early for her, but I am afraid that it will take her just as it has taken the boy. It would be best if you made preparations for the two of them," Gini solemnly spoke.

Jeremiah and Ketia walked through the door of the house and nodded in their direction. Gini quickly glanced at them and then away.

"I must go," Gini stated.

James reached into his pocket to pay her, but she waved her hand.

"I cannot in good conscience take your money when I am not able to cure their ailments," Gini said. "If you need anything else, please come find me. I will help as best as I can."

Gini quickly exited the house, and Jeremiah approached his sister.

"What does she say?" he asked.

Anne closed Lizzy's door and broke down into sobs.

"She said William will pass tonight," James replied. "And Lizzy has whatever William has."

"And she can't do anything more for them?" Jeremiah asked.

"No, she cannot," James replied. "She told us to make preparations for them."

"I just don't understand what is wrong with them," Anne cried. "It's not a cold or another type of sickness."

"Perhaps it's cholera," Ketia offered. "I have heard the townspeople speaking about how it's a deadly thing sweeping the nation."

"That very well could be it," Jeremiah added.

"The kids haven't gone anywhere to contract it, and we are both fine," Anne replied. "We would have been sick before them."

"Maybe you are immune to it, and their immunity just isn't strong enough," Jeremiah offered. "Do you need help with William's burial?"

"Don't speak as if he were already dead!" Anne hissed. "He is still alive, and there is still a chance he will pull through this!"

"May I see him?" Ketia asked.

Anne nodded her head, and Ketia brushed past her and entered William's room, closing the door behind her.

"I don't mean to upset you, Anne," Jeremiah began. "But if Gini said there is no hope for him, then there is no hope for him. I have seen her cure ailments that the local doctors could not cure with her medicine."

"He is right," James said. "Gini would have been able to cure him if he were curable."

"Much like she said, your teas don't cause you ailments of your own?" Anne hissed.

"This is not the place nor the time to bring up such nonsense," James replied heatedly. "Come, Jeremiah. We will prepare the grave out near the heart tree."

As James and Jeremiah left the house, Jane walked through the door.

"Has the medicine woman come to see William?" she asked as she tugged her bonnet from her head.

"Yes," Anne replied with tears. "She said William will not make it through the night."

"What did she say was wrong with him?" Jane asked.

"She doesn't know," Anne replied, walking to the kitchen.

"Did you tell her to look at his nailbeds like I suggested?" Jane asked.

"No, I forgot. I was too distraught once she told me he wouldn't make it through the night, even to think to ask anything," Anne replied.

"Is anyone with him right now?" Jane asked.

"Yes, Ketia is visiting with him," Anne replied as she cut up vegetables for dinner.

"Mother!" Jane hissed. "I told you not to let her see him anymore!"

"There's nothing more she can do to him than what is already done, Jane!" Anne exclaimed in frustration.

"What if the medicine woman is helping Jeremiah and Ketia?" Jane questioned out loud. "What if she is purposefully letting William die?"

"That's foolish nonsense," Anne huffed.

"Is it?" Jane pleaded. "It is no more foolish than the teas you believe she gives to father that strikes his temper."

"Jane, I do not have the strength to have this conversation with you," Anne remarked. "Go sit with Lizzy and keep her company."

Jane sneered and turned on her heel, heading into Lizzy's room. When the door closed, Anne dropped her knife and sobbed into her hands. William was four, and Lizzy was six. They were babies. They hadn't even experienced life yet, and here they were, dying for some unknown reason, and Anne could do nothing to help them.

William passed that night just as Gini said he would. Jeremiah helped James bury him beneath the tree they had dug his grave. Everyone stood around the grave for a small funeral. When it was just James, Anne, and Jane left, Jane began to ask questions.

"Did they tell you how he died?" Jane asked.

"The doctor didn't come to see him," James replied as he tipped his jar of tea back for a drink.

"They were poisoned!" Jane insisted. "And if you don't get Lizzy help, she will die as well!"

James reared his hand back and struck Jane across the face.

"I am tired of hearing this nonsense about your uncle and aunt and even Gini!" he hissed and stalked off.

Jane clutched her cheek as Anne tried to remove her hand to look at it.

"I told you he has a temper," Anne stated. "Today of all days was not the day to provoke him when he buried his only son."

"Mother," Jane pleaded. "We have to get Lizzy help!"

"I don't know how!" Anne hissed. "None of the doctors here know how to treat her and your father..."

"What about father?" Jane asked.

"Nothing," Anne replied.

"We can take Lizzy to Roanoke!" Jane offered. "They have better doctors there!"

"Your father won't let me take Lizzy anywhere," Anne replied quietly. "I already asked about Roanoke, and he said the only doctor Lizzy needed was Gini."

"Gini is evil!" Jane hissed. "The tribes have told me that she is evil."

"I cannot help your sister," Anne replied coolly. "Please, stop begging me to."

"Then I will take her," Jane said. "After you and Father go to bed tonight, I will steal her away and take her to be treated. Father won't be angry with you for disobeying his orders then."

"You will face his wrath if you do so," Anne warned.

"I do not care about his wrath!" Jane cried. "I care about my sister and her life!"

Anne quickly glanced around to make sure no one was within earshot of her. "Take her tonight!"

Jane nodded. They made it through dinner, and Jane went to sit with Lizzy as her parents prepared for bed.

"I am going to take you to a doctor," Jane whispered to Lizzy, stroking her hair.

"Am I dying, Jane?" Lizzy asked. "Mother and father won't tell me."

"If I cannot get you away from this house and away from the people who are hurting you, yes, you will die," Jane whispered.

"I don't want to die, Jane," Lizzy cried. "I miss William. He didn't need to die either."

"I will do everything I can to make sure that doesn't happen," Jane replied, kissing the top of her head. "I will be back shortly once mother and father have gone to bed. And then, I am taking you away from here."

Lizzy nodded as Jane stood from the bed and exited the room. She pretended to pull down her blankets in preparation for bed until she saw the light of the candle snuff out in her parents' room. She quietly slipped from her room and outside to the barn to prepare her carriage and horse for the ride to Roanoke. She came back inside quietly, making sure her parents were indeed asleep, then entered Lizzy's room. She helped Lizzy from the bed and wrapped her in a blanket. She picked her up and clutched her to her chest as she quietly opened her door and looked up and down the hall. Everyone was still asleep.

Jane quietly shuffled down the hall and to the front door, closing it quietly behind her. She ran as fast as she could to the barn while Lizzy held onto her neck as she bounced. Jane arrived in the barn and put Lizzy up on the seat of her carriage. She ran to the other side and climbed up into her seat. As quietly as possible, she snapped the reins to signal her horse to move. No sooner had the horse begun to walk from inside the barn than her father appeared at the barn doors.

"What are you doing, Jane?" he asked, slowly walking up beside the carriage. "Lizzy shouldn't be out of bed, most especially at this time of night."

"I'm taking her to a doctor in Roanoke," Jane stated. "You won't stop me either."

With a forceful snap of the reins, Jane's horse lurched forward with the carriage. As she passed by her father, he reached up and grabbed her from her seat and threw her to the ground. The carriage came to a stop, and Lizzy whimpered as James walked around and picked her up from the seat.

"She will die!" Jane screamed. "She will die!"

"Then so be it," James replied.

Jane ran up to him and tackled him to the ground. Lizzy rolled away from them and sat huddled under the blanket, crying. Jane began to beat James's head into the ground repeatedly, breaking his nose and bloodying his forehead. She quickly got up and ran toward Lizzy when he grabbed her by her foot, tripping her. With one sweep of his hand across her face, she was dizzied.

"You will never try this again," James coolly stated.

A few days later, Lizzy died…

It was maybe a week after the children had been buried that Jeremiah came by for dinner as he usually did, joined by Ketia. Jane was also still staying with her parents. They all sat quietly at the table as they ate their food.

"With Lizzy and William gone, things aren't the same," Jeremiah said, breaking the silent dinner.

"Mhmm," Anne hummed as she poked around at her food.

"Since you now have no heirs to leave the land to, you might as well sign it over to me. You and James find another spot on his father's land and build another home," Jeremiah added.

"Why would you even say that?" Jane hissed. "They have heirs. I am their heir. Nancy is their heir. And this is not the time to be speaking of such matters. Your greed will be your downfall and land you straight in the pits of hell!" she cursed.

"Jeremiah, you will not have this land," James stated vehemently. "This is not just the land your father gave as her dowry, but this is also the land that my father left to me. I will not hear of this discussion anymore, and if you bring it up again, you will no longer be permitted to visit with us."

Jeremiah banged his fists on the table and stood from his seat, with Ketia latching onto his arm.

"You will regret this decision, old man," he spat, then left the house.

Chapter Four

IT WAS NEARLY NIGHTFALL when the sound of a backfire echoed from the field and into the house. Ozell stood from her rocking chair where she sat, knitting a dreamcatcher. She laid the dreamcatcher in her knitting basket and walked to the kitchen, quickly stirring her vegetable stock and then setting the ladle down on its drip pan. She heard the motor shut off, and he started to climb the back steps when she peered out the kitchen window. It let her view their property, and she saw the smoke trail that his side-by-side had left as it hung in the humid dusk air.

As she glanced around the backyard, her heart nearly stopped. There was a little girl dressed in white standing at the edge of their woods. She quickly ran to the back door as Nathaniel threw it open, stumbling in and pushing past her. When she got outside, if there had been a little girl outside, she was now gone.

"What the hell are you doing?" Nathaniel slurred as he nearly toppled to the floor.

"I thought I saw something outback, you ole drunk," Ozell replied, helping him to a kitchen chair.

Ozell glanced down and saw he was dragging some black trash bags along with him.

"Whatcha got in the bag, Nate?" she demanded to know.

"Deer meat," he hiccuped out.

"Deer meat? You normally bring the whole thing back with you for me to clean," she replied as she began to dig through the bag. "You cleaned and quartered it already?"

"Yep," Nathaniel replied. "I was pretty hard on ye' earlier, so I thought I'ad do something nice for ya."

"Uh-huh," she replied. "Or your drunk ass missed your perfect shot and had to cover it up, so I wouldn't know. Like I would care either way anyway."

Nathaniel started to kick his boots off and take his socks off as Ozell took the meat to the kitchen island to put into freezer wrap. She wrapped up the shoulders and hams when she noticed there were smaller ones included as well.

"Nate, did you shoot Bambi?" she asked, holding up the itty-bitty tenderloin from its back.

"Yeah, I got trigger-happy and accidentally got them instead of the buck. They walked right in front as soon as I pulled the trigger, and the bullet traveled through the little'un into its mama," he replied back.

"Aw, that poor little thing," she sniffled.

"Chop it up, and we will eat it tonight," he demanded.

"I will not eat Bambi the same day you killed him!" she exclaimed. "I will throw the neck of the mother in the stew pot, and we will have meat and potatoes."

Nathaniel rolled his eyes, and Ozell pursed her lips as she stared at him. His eyes were glassy, and she knew he was three sheets to the wind. He normally doesn't get piss drunk from the shine they had been getting lately.

"Nate, where'd you get the liquor from?" Ozell asked as she hacked at the neck meat.

"I, uh, I," Nate began. "I don't know. It was just there."

"Just where?" Ozell demanded as she cut strips of meat off and chopped them into cubes.

"Where my liquor always is," he replied. "In the barn. I thought Dale dropped it off like he usually does, and you told him to walk it down."

"Dale hasn't been by for weeks," Ozell remarked. "Where the shine come from?"

"God dammit, woman. I don't know!" Nathaniel hollered.

"You ask God for forgiveness right now, mister," Ozell said. "Ain't no point dragging his name into our business. I am only asking because you look copper-sick. Your nose is red, and you're drunker'n usual."

"I ain't drunk," he slurred.

"Then what do you want to call it?" she asked. "Slightly inebriated?"

He hiccupped. "Well, yeah."

Ozell gave a hearty chuckle. "You damn alcoholic."

"Listen here, sassy pants," Nathaniel said as he tried to climb to his feet. "I ain't no alcoholic. I am a drunk. I 'on't go to them AA meetings."

Ozell snorted. "Go to bed and sleep it off until dinner is done."

"Get the fire going," he slurred as he stumbled to their room. "It's freezing cold in this house."

"Nah, you're just hitting the point of being drunk where your body feels freezing while everyone around you is quite normal," she replied.

"It's cold, ya old bat!" he yelled.

"Then put some damn clothes on!" she yelled in return.

"Keep that shit up, and I'm, and I'm," Nathaniel breathed heavily as he slumped down on the bed.

"You're gonna what?" Ozell asked.

"I'ma beat that ass is what I'ma do," he slurred as the room began to spin.

Ozell laughed, walked to the room, and bent over. "Then get to spanking old man."

Nathaniel shooed her away with a hand as his eyelids grew heavier and heavier. The rage and anger he had felt while driving home had somehow dissipated when he walked inside. As Nathaniel drifted off to sleep, Ozell finished chopping up the meat and tossed it into a pot of salted water to boil the gaminess out of it for dinner. She heard the gentle snore of sleep come from Nathaniel in their room. He had been acting so strangely lately. Normally, Nathaniel would run the stragglers that came in the wrong way off back onto the road with his gun. His letting one go through was very odd to her. He hated the tourists and hated the campers even more.

As she stood at the boiling kettle, the steam around her made her sweat terribly. She wiped her brow as it perspired. She had asked Nathaniel several times to fix the auxiliary fan above the stove so she wouldn't suffocate as she cooked. As normal, he ignored her and did everything he wanted to do, down to even cutting the grass with shears to get out of doing repairs.

As she wiped her forehead free of sweat again, a cool breeze settled around her that chilled her to the bone. She rubbed her arms and walked to the back door to make sure it hadn't blown open. There was a heaviness in the air as she tested the doorknob to make sure it was latched. The fire was raging in the hearth, and there weren't any open windows, and yet it felt as cold as a fridge in the house.

"What in the hell," she asked herself. "Maybe Nathaniel was actually cold."

She shrugged and made a note for him to check the underpinning and make sure that the insulation under the house was still intact and didn't need replacing.

"That cold draft is coming from somewhere," she murmured as she walked back to the dinner pot.

A faint smell of perfume blew around the room that Ozell caught a very light whiff of. She stopped in her steps and tried to sniff again to smell it, but it had already faded.

"That's odd," she mumbled to herself. "It almost smelled like black locust blossoms."

She walked around the house sniffing a few more times and was satisfied that the smell was gone. It was probably her mind playing tricks on her or a stroke brewing.

"Oh, the hospital would be a lovely vacation," she chuckled to herself.

She walked back to the kettle and gave the meat a stir as it had come to a boil. It would only take another twenty minutes, and the meat would be ready to add to her stock water. She stirred the kettle, popped the heavy cast-iron lid on top, and then dropped another fire log in under the wood-burning stove. As she stood back up, a face was standing outside her window, peering in.

She screamed in fright. "Nathaniel, if that is you playing tricks, it ain't funny!" she yelled as she ran to the kitchen door.

No one was outside, and when she walked to her room, Nathaniel was soundly asleep in bed, still lightly snoring. An anxious twitch began to grow in the pit of her stomach. She walked back to the window and peered out, wiping off the condensation from the boiling pot. For a moment, she thought she saw someone walking near the tree line. She wiped again to clear all of the water droplets and saw no one.

She rubbed her arms, but not from a chill because the room had already heated back up to its normal temperature. She rubbed her arms as one would when the hairs on the back of their neck and arms would prick up, and goosebumps would riddle their body. That light sense of the paranormal that clung in the air that a normal person would brush off until they experienced just a taste of a spirit lurking in a corner. Ozell gave her arms one last rub before shrugging the feeling off. She walked to her curio cabinet that stood near the back door and pulled out a bottle of black salt. She walked the bottle to the four corners of her house and poured a small pile in each. She walked the jar back to her cabinet and placed it in with all of her other herbs and roots. She grabbed her bag of brick dust from the top shelf, propped open the back door, and put a nice layer down underneath her welcome mat. She placed it back inside the cabinet and shut the cabinet door.

"Nate! Dinner is almost done!" Ozell called.

Chapter Five

"IZZY! JOSHUA! Stop running around!" Carter shouted as he swiped his VISA card to pay for the loaded shopping cart.

They were at the local Wal-Mart in Rocky Mount to buy what they needed to eat for the week. They were not going to blow through their savings dining out at the crap restaurants they had in the area. Plus, the cabin came with a full kitchen and refrigerator stocked with pots and pans as well. They grabbed some cleaning supplies to keep up with the dishes and bought some cheap paper plates and plastic silverware to eat from while there, as well as some red Solo cups.

Carter had spent an enormous amount of time trying to find the right fishing equipment he would need for the upcoming weekend's fishing tournament. They also grabbed some toys and different activities to keep the kids busy when they weren't doing scheduled activities with the camp counselors. Had they had their own cabin on the opposite side of the resort from the parents, it would have been almost like an actual vacation for Carter and Candace and a summer camp vacation for the kids. Carter just hoped the kids played well with the others, and it lasted for more than five minutes at a time, as opposed to how often they played outside at home.

The card machine read payment accepted and printed Carter's three-foot-long receipt. He pulled the receipt, tore it from the machine, and stuffed it down in a random bag in the shopping cart.

"Do we have all the bags loaded?" Carter asked Candace.

She tied the bag in her hands and placed it in the shopping cart. "That was the last of them," she replied.

"Alright, let's go then. Joshua, Izzy!" he called out.

Joshua and Isobel appeared out of thin air beside the shopping cart, and they all headed for the Walmart exit. Carter stopped for a second, and Joshua stepped on the back of his heel. He groaned and tried to walk off the pain while gritting his teeth. Last night was a shit night in the bed at the cabin, so much so that Carter bought a rotating standing fan, an egg crate foam pad for the bed, and earplugs to drown out the sound of the TV that the kids insisted they needed to fall asleep. He was just ready for the vacation to be over.

Just as they made their way to their vehicle, Carter's phone began to ring. Candace took the keys from his pocket as he walked to the side to answer the phone so she could unload the shopping cart. As he glanced at the caller ID, he noticed it was John's number.

"Oh, honey, it's Keith. I'm going to take this," he called out as he slid the answer indicator to answer the call.

"Hello? Keith?... Yes, we made it in yesterday to that resort…the kids seem to like it…I know. I know you said we could stay with you…no, no, the kids need the experience. They already need a TV to fall asleep…exactly in every room, so how do they learn from that?... we're at the

Foxwood Hills Camping Resort… yes, that is the one… do what?... why?..."

Candace slammed the hatch shut on the vehicle and motioned for the kids to get in the back seat.

"Buckle up, you two," she ordered. "Carter," she called.

He held up his pointer finger to her and then waved for her to come over. She walked over, rolling her eyes.

"What?" she asked.

"Hold on, Keith, and let me switch you over to speaker." Carter pressed the speaker button on his phone and made sure it switched over properly. "Hello? Can you hear me?

"Oh, hey. Yeah, I can hear you. Be careful where you are staying. That place has lawsuit after lawsuit coming out its ears. Not too long ago, they had this major incident where some teenager died. Heard their maintenance man was letting them party or something without telling his boss and just pocketing the money," Keith replied.

Carter and Candace exchanged glances.

"Now, don't let the story freak you guys out. I am sure things will be fine this week and weekend. The owner did a lot of revamps to the place to ensure it didn't happen again, but if you want to, my guest house has four bedrooms and its own jacuzzi. Just say the word," Keith chuckled.

"That is a no-can-do. It's nonrefundable and was too expensive to just go to waste," Carter replied.

"Come on, a jacuzzi," Keith replied.

"Everything will be fine," Carter replied. "We will see you Saturday."

"Well, check in with me every so often so I know you haven't died," Keith said.

"No can do. There isn't any reception in the campground. The only reason you got me now is because we went shopping to buy food for the week."

"Alright, alright, I won't twist your arm. See ya Saturday."

Carter made sure the call ended before putting his phone back in his pocket. He stood there for a moment, thinking about everything John had told him.

"No," Candace said.

"Huh?" Carter asked.

"No, we are keeping the cabin and camping," Candace replied.

"What?"

"We are not going to Keith's!" she shouted.

"I wasn't even saying anything," Carter defended.

"You didn't have to! You were thinking it. I could hear it in your voice and see it in your face. We are not squandering away what we paid for that cabin just because you want to drink beer and play pool while watching the football game. Blame it on your kids all you want, but that is you," Candace fumed.

"You heard John! Lawsuits, Candace! People almost died!" Carter defended.

"You're a doctor and know damn well that accidents happen. We don't even know the whole story," Candace said, pushing her point. "Now, we are getting in this vehicle and driving back to the campgrounds and staying the entire week and weekend like we agreed to before going on vacation. I don't want to spend my week having to act like someone else to impress someone you know and put up a façade with his wife when you know damn well that woman is a bitch."

"Oh, do you honestly think this was a ploy to make you act above your *pay grade* for the week and pretend to like people?" Carter asked, irritated.

"Look, I don't care if there are Satanists at the campgrounds planning to sacrifice a goat to the

Dark Lord. We are staying right where we are at. I had to talk you into camping instead of living another week at another house where you get to cut loose, and I have to look like I am not an ass by helping her with the damn dishes," Candace spat. "End of discussion."

"I didn't *have* to bring anyone," Carter muttered. "I could have been here at Keith's for a medical convention and left you all at home. But I asked you to come. I can take you back home and come back myself."

"Sure, be my guest. Take us home. Go on your vacation. And when you get home, we won't be there," Candace yelled. "That way, the family you never want to spend time with or the family that you never want to take anywhere or let them do what they want for fun or the family that isn't your kind of fun or the family with the wife that doesn't like snobby rich people won't be your fucking problem anymore!"

She ripped the door open on their vehicle and nearly slammed it into the shopping cart return. She sat in her seat and slammed the door shut. She reached into her purse, pulled out a cigarette, and immediately lit it, drawing in a long drag.

Carter opened his door, muttering, and looked over at Candace, hotboxing her Marlboro.

"I thought you quit?" he asked, annoyed.

"I did," she hissed.

He rolled his eyes as he started the vehicle and glanced in the rearview mirror. The kids sat there staring straight ahead, unaffected by their spat.

He scoffed, "So, kids, where do you want to stay? Do you want to stay at the cabin or in Keith's guest house? They have TV and video games."

"What the fuck are you doing?" Candace asked, pissed.

"Asking them what they want to do since I never do what y'all want to do."

"That is not what I meant, and you know it," Candace hissed.

"Well, careful what you wish for," Carter replied smugly.

He returned his attention to the kids again. "Well, where do y'all want to stay?" he asked again.

The kids exchanged glances and answered in unison. "We would like to stay at the cabin."

Candace let out a "ha" and said, "Oh, you do? Well then, that is what we will do then."

She smirked at Carter as she buckled her seatbelt. Carter gripped the steering wheel and gritted his teeth. *The one fucking time they don't want to watch TV and play video games,* he thought to himself.

The silence that settled in the vehicle on the way back to the campground was astounding. When they arrived at their cabin and parked in their spot, Candace immediately hopped out of the passenger door to unload the groceries from the hatch. Carter sat in his seat, watching her through the rearview mirror as she unloaded the bags and walked them inside. The kids had long climbed out and had gone to play with the other kids for the afternoon.

After Candace got the remaining bags out of the hatch, she closed it and walked inside, still not speaking to Carter. He sighed and opened his door to go inside and apologize for overstepping in the conversation.

Joshua and Isobel stood on the outskirts of the field the campers played in and watched them kick the ball back and forth in a game of soccer. Truthfully, the kids never would invite them to play, and they were the loaners of the game. Since they had arrived, they hadn't been welcomed into the games to play. Isobel's behavior had also started to worry Joshua. She was acting strangely and unusually, even more than normal. Ever since they arrived here, it was like she had taken on a different persona. Most of the time, both inside the cabin and outside, he had found her staring off into the woods in her own little world.

The previous night, as they lay in bed, Isobel told him that she had been hearing the whispers of the woods and they belonged to children who had once lived there. As always, whenever she would start her crazy story, the hairs on his skin pricked up as his body went into alert mode, sensing the area for energy.

"There's no such thing as ghosts, Lizzy," he whispered in response. "Now go to bed."

Even as he spoke the words, he wasn't sure if he believed them anymore. He always felt a creepy and odd sensation around the trees, as if someone was in there watching their every move, just like the day they had arrived.

As he stood and watched the other kids playing, Isobel wandered back over to the trees and peered down at them. One of the kids pointed and began to laugh as if they had jokes about her already. Joshua rolled his eyes and glanced over at Lizzy, annoyed.

"Get over here, Lizzy," he hissed. "They're making fun again."

He returned his attention back to the kids who had resumed playing the game. He waited for her to appear at his side, but when a few moments had passed, he glanced over to where she had been standing, and no one was there. Panic, adrenaline, and nausea all rose in his chest and back of his throat as he ran to the side of the field where she had been standing a few minutes beforehand.

He squinted his eyes and placed his hand over the top as a shield from the sun so he could see better into the darkness when he caught a glimpse of her hair and the red hat she was wearing. He tore through the thicket, shouting her name. He knew for sure he would be in trouble if she wandered off and got lost. It was his responsibility to keep her safe at all times.

"Lizzy!" he yelled as branches scratched at his face. "Lizzy! Stop!"

As if she had heard her name called for the first time, Lizzy stopped and turned around to her brother, who ran up behind her. He bent over, breathing heavily, and placed his hands above his head to catch his breath.

"What are you doing? What were you thinking running off like that?" he asked.

"The whispers told me to follow them. They knew of a place that we could go and play since the other kids were mean to us," she replied.

"The whispers?" Joshua asked, still breathing heavily from running. "Do the whispers have a name?"

"Yes! They told me their names right before you called my name out. The boy's name is William, and the girl's name is Isobel! Isobel is my name! She even goes by Lizzy like I do!" she exclaimed.

"Lizzy, no one here goes by them names," Joshua replied. "Come on. Let's go before Mom and Dad realize they can't see us anymore, and we both get in trouble."

"Why don't you believe me, Tuck?" Isobel asked, wounded.

"Because what you're saying don't make no sense," Joshua replied. "There aren't any kids in the camp with those names."

"That's because they aren't kids from the camp. They live here!" she retorted. "They said they lived here when the Indians did!"

"That doesn't even make sense either!" he exclaimed. "From what I remember in social studies, the Natives in Virginia were driven out and moved to reservation camps. There ain't no reservation near here, and there certainly aren't any Indians running wildly through the woods."

"Well, that's what they said, and they have no reason to lie to me, Tuck," she replied. "They were leading me to a special tree here in the woods where they played with their mother. They want us to play with them there. Let's go!" she insisted.

"No! Mom and Dad are already going to be mad that we ran off. They won't be happy if they have to form a search team to come looking for us just because you want to play with your imaginary friends that only you can hear!" he shouted. "Now, let's go!"

"Well, that's what they told me. And they have a special tree that they played with their mother that they said has a heart in the middle of the tree! Come on, let's go to the tree!" Isobel begged. "Please, Joshua. They said it's just a few more feet in, and we will be there," Isobel pleaded with a pouty face. "I want to see the tree."

Joshua knew why adults got gray hair now. He sighed heavily. "Ok, just for a few minutes and then back to camp."

Isobel strangely led the way as if she knew exactly where to go. Joshua kept an eye out for the scenery and surroundings for snakes or bears. No sooner had they started on their way than they came to an old fence in a clearing. It was barbed wire at the top and pig wire below, but it had long rusted and collapsed from the fence posts it had been tacked to. A no-trespassing sign hung from a post, and Joshua began to get uneasy about being down in there.

"I have a strange feeling that that fence belongs to that crazy old man we asked for directions when we first got here," Joshua claimed. "This isn't a good idea. Let's head back before we get hurt."

"It's just right up here, though!" Isobel protested and stepped over the downed fence wiring. "And Lizzy and William said old man Nathaniel was at home."

Joshua followed Isobel, grumbling under his breath. He just felt like something bad was going to happen. There was a sense of impending doom that clung to the warm air. He followed Isobel when they walked around the bend, and just as she said, a tree stood there with a heart in the middle of its trunk.

"How did you know this would be here?" he asked.

"I told you! They told me it was here!" Isobel exclaimed.

As if queued for an appearance, the breeze picked up into a gentle wind, rustling the dead leaves around Joshua and Isobel. Laughter echoed in the corners of the clearing and seemed to bounce from one place to another as if kids surrounded them that they couldn't see. Joshua's heart began to pound as he heard more whispers as if they were right in his ear, trying to tell him a secret, and then everywhere at once. Isobel started to giggle.

"Why are you laughing? What's so funny?" he asked, looking around, frightened at the sounds that surrounded him.

"Oh, nothing," Isobel replied. "Lizzy thinks you're cute, is all. I told her that's gross and boys are ew."

"Yeah, whatever," Joshua replied nervously. "It's time to go."

"We just got here, though!" Isobel protested.

"You wanted to see the tree, and now you saw the tree. It's time to go back," Joshua replied firmly.

"But," Isobel protested again.

"Now, Lizzy! I'm not getting in trouble for you. Not again," he remarked.

"Ok, but can we get the surprise out of the tree first?" she asked.

"What surprise?" Joshua asked, irritated.

"They said they have a surprise for us in the tree. It's a bag full of things."

Isobel pointed to the heart-shaped hole that he had noticed on the tree when they first arrived. He looked at the hole and jumped, missing the hole completely.

"It's too tall for me," he replied.

"Stand on my back then. It should boost you up enough for you to reach it," she offered.

Joshua rolled his eyes and climbed onto Isobel's back. He stole glances around to see the imaginary friends she spoke about, but there wasn't anyone but them there. He held onto the tree by grabbing the hole and then reached his hand inside, feeling around to see if there was anything in there like Isobel claimed. He grabbed onto something that felt like a bag and quickly removed it from the tree. His eyes caught the glint of a reflection, and he looked around to see what it was. Through the thicket, he could see the sun reflecting off water. It must be the lake that Mikey had referred to.

He could feel Isobel begin to shake from the weight of his body and quickly hopped off her back so she could stand.

"You ok?" he asked, making sure he hadn't injured her back.

"I'm fine!" she exclaimed. "Whoa! It was there! It was really there! Open it! Open it!" she squealed.

"You're not going to be squealing in joy if a snake or spider crawls out of it," he joked.

He carefully opened the top, but instead of reaching inside the bag, he dumped the contents out on the ground. A teddy bear, a porcelain doll, a ring, and a necklace fell out. The porcelain doll had seen better days with its smashed-in skull and ragged dress. The teddy bear was an old, raggedy doll-type bear made out of socks and some sort of grain.

"Oh! Gimme gimme!" she squealed, reaching for the doll. "Isobel said I could have the doll, and William said you could have the bear."

Joshua scoffed, "I don't play with toys anymore."

"Think of it as a keepsake, silly," Isobel replied.

He pushed the leaves around on the ground to see where the other things had fallen. He carefully picked up the necklace and ring, admiring them before shoving everything back into the bag.

"Mom would love the ring and necklace," Joshua remarked. "Put the doll back in here and let's go."

"No," Isobel said. "We can't take them. We have to put them back."

"Why?" Joshua asked.

"They said we could play with them, not take them," Isobel protested.

"Look, I don't care what your imaginary friends said. Let's go. We aren't coming back here. We are too close to the lake as it is," Joshua replied.

"They said you'll be sorry if you take them," Isobel said in a deep, meaningful voice.

"Oh well," Joshua replied. "Come on before we get in trouble."

"Can we at least look at the lake while we are here?" Isobel asked. "They said it's really pretty."

Joshua sighed in irritation.

"One quick look, and then we are gone! Understood?!" he demanded.

They walked through the bushes that Joshua had seen the glints of light from and stood at the edge of the lake.

"What did Mikey say the name of this lake was?" Isobel asked.

"I think Devil's Claw or something like that," Joshua replied as they stared out across the lake. "It's beautiful."

The sun had started to set in the sky. It was around five or six o'clock, and the soft oranges, purples, and pink hues cast beautiful shadows and reflections off the lake. Birds flew over the top of it, dipping down and catching fish that had come to the top to eat bugs. Joshua pointed to a deer that stood off on the opposite shoreline as it grazed, and a fawn joined it. A fox chased a butterfly further down from it, jumping in the air, trying to catch it with its front paws, and then landing while still gazing up at the butterfly. The water gently lapped at the shoreline, and Isobel bent down, picking a clamshell up.

"I bet there is a pearl in there," Joshua claimed.

"It is so beautiful!" Isobel proclaimed. "We should get Mom and Dad to go swimming here."

Joshua snorted. "Doubt that. Dad has a stick up his-"

"Joshua! Isobel!" Candace yelled. "We have been looking for you forever. What are you doing here?!"

"We went exploring like you suggested," Joshua explained.

"This lake is dangerous to be by yourselves at!" Candace hissed.

"We weren't going in," Joshua protested. "We were just looking and coming back to ask you if we *all* could go swimming tomorrow."

"So what have you been doing, then, huh? Playing twiddly winks?" Carter hissed.

"No, we found an old sack in a tree and were looking at the contents," Joshua explained.

"Why are you in the woods to begin with?!" Carter demanded. "You don't know what is in these woods. Snakes, bears-"

"Dad, we were careful!" Isobel interjected. "Besides, Joshua shouldn't be in trouble. I ran into the woods, and he came to get me back out."

Carter and Candace looked at Joshua. "Is that true, Joshua?" Candace asked.

"Yes, it's true," he sighed. "I wasn't going to tattle on her, though," he replied, eyeing her and shaking his head. "The kids… the kids here don't play with us, and Lizzy got bored."

Candace's face fell. "Honey, why didn't you tell us that the kids weren't playing with you?"

"Because then you would want to leave, and we like it here," Joshua replied. "It doesn't matter if they play with us. I like the place here, and so does Lizzy."

Candace tousled Joshua's hair and looked at the bag.

"So, what's in the bag?" she asked.

"There's a ring, a necklace, an old doll, and an old teddy bear," Joshua replied.

Carter took the bag from Joshua and began pulling the items out. "Where did you say you found these?" he asked.

"In a tree right over there," Joshua replied. "They don't belong to anyone."

"Can we keep them?" Isobel asked.

"I don't see the harm in keeping them," Carter replied. "This lake is gorgeous!" he remarked, staring out over the lake.

"Can we come back to go swimming?" Joshua asked.

"Or for a campfire with smores!" Isobel asked.

"Yes, to the swimming," Carter told Joshua. "And I will ask about the campfire," he told Isobel.

"How did you find this place?" Candace asked.

"Lizzy and William showed me," Isobel replied.

"Oh, there's another little girl here with your name?" Candace asked. "I thought the kids didn't play with you?"

"They're not real people. They are her imaginary friends that only she can hear and see," Joshua replied.

"Oh!" Candace replied, nodding her head as if she understood. "Those are special friends," she told Lizzy.

"It still doesn't explain how she knew the things were in the tree, though," Carter replied, scratching his head. "Alright, let's get back to camp. Your mother has dinner in the oven, and we don't want it to burn down the cabin."

Once they trekked their way back to the cabin, Joshua and Isobel ran off to their room to watch TV before dinner while Carter and Candace stood in the kitchen getting the rest of dinner made.

"Imaginary friends," Candace mused.

"Yeah, I remember my first imaginary friend. Mother fucker stole my damn ice cream, and I ain't seen him since," Carter joked.

"This is a bit more serious than a thieving imaginary friend," Candace laughed. "Do you think…"

"She is *fine!*" Carter insisted. "Many kids go through imaginary friend phases. It's nothing to worry about. I promise."

"How many imaginary friends know the exact location of a bag full of items?" Candace asked, hand on her hip.

"Maybe they are part bloodhound?" Carter offered.

Candace snorted. "Should we let them keep those god-awful toys? I mean, the doll looks smashed," she said, pulling the items out of the bag.

She dumped the ring and necklace on the counter and picked them up, examining them. The ring was simple and old-looking, with silver as the metal, and a single diamond topped it. She also clasped the necklace around her neck before tossing the burlap sack in the trash.

"What do you think about going swimming tomorrow morning like the kids asked?" Candace asked Carter.

"Mikey said it could be dangerous," Carter reminded her.

"That was because they don't have a lifeguard, and we all know how to swim in deep water. We took the kids to the ocean, to lakes, to pools. They know how to swim in all kinds of water, and it looked pretty calm there," Candace retorted.

"Then I don't see the harm, honey," Carter replied, irritated. "Like everything else around here, it will probably have old crazy people waiting to shoot us in the water," he muttered.

Candace rolled her eyes and pulled her lasagna from the oven while Carter grabbed the plates and silverware to set the table.

"Kids! Dinner is done!"

Chapter Six

NATHANIEL SAT QUIETLY in the barn as he puffed on a hand-rolled cigarette. He had stopped buying them from the store years ago and grew his own tobacco in his garden. He could most likely be heftily fined for it, but no more than the marijuana that grew alongside it. Even with the new legalization, the amount of plants he grew was still over the legal limit. Of course, it was to stop illegal sales from drug dealers. Hell, they even put a limit on how much you could have in your possession to smoke on, but he only grew it once a year during the summer to last the entire year, so he wanted to make sure he had enough.

He wasn't all fancy like the younger generations with their grow lights and tents and chemicals and Sour Diesel or Bubblegum Blitz or whatever they called the strain they were smoking. He scoffed, thinking about it. The sun and natural compost were all it needed to grow in the red clay mud of Virginia. Sometimes, he could even get Ozell to smoke with him. There was nothing better than sitting on the screened-in balcony of their room in their rockers, smoking some reefer and drinking some shine before bed. It was one of the few times that the two of them didn't bicker.

He had walked out to gas up the side-by-side to do some night hunting when he realized he was holding an empty can in the gas tank.

"Maybe that wasn't a cigarette," he laughed to himself. "I need to be careful, or I will end up lost in the woods one night."

Nathaniel shivered as he hopped into his coveralls and Carhart coat. It was cool out tonight, and the barn was even colder than outside, which was unusual for this time of year. Being October, it was normally blazing during the day and around sixty degrees at night, but he swore it felt in the forties instead.

The hairs on the back of his neck pricked up, and a cold chill ran straight down his spine as if the holy ghost had touched his very soul, or rather, the devil had. All night, he couldn't get the thought out of his head of killing that fawn by slitting its throat ear to ear.

Nathaniel remembered when his father slipped into early Alzheimer's and began to deteriorate mentally. The rage was what came first, and it made Nathaniel uneasy, knowing he had been angrier lately than normal. Of course, he was always rude to anyone who used the driveway just to get back at the Ingrams. This was different, though. He knew he had been harsher with Ozell lately. They had calmed down in their older age and weren't as theatrical as they had been in their 20s with guns and knives.

His sixth sense kicked up a notch once more, and he quickly turned around to see if anyone was watching him to cause the feeling of paranoia that crept up his spine. *What a way to go out,* he thought to himself. *Losing my damn mind and going schizophrenic all at once. Someone just shoot me now!*

He carried an extra gas can to the side-by-side just in case he ran out, as well as loaded his cooler, gun, and emergency kit. Ozell didn't like it when he went night hunting and always made him take a first aid kit, flares, and a satellite phone in case he got really hurt out there. He made sure his hunting knife was strapped to his side in its sheath before climbing into the side-by-side. He pulled out his tiny map and looked to see which direction he needed to go to find the deer den he had been looking for. He had seen a young ten-pointer run off into the woods from his garden earlier in the day and wanted to see where he was nesting. It would be a pretty nice rack up on his wall of trophy hunts.

Or you can mount that loser, Patrick. Poor Patrick Ingram, whose parents locked him away because they swore he was losing his mind. Your rich childhood friend who inherited King Solomon's fortunes and didn't bother to help you come up in the world as he had always promised, he thought to himself.

He stopped himself mid-turn of the key and sat back in the seat.

"What was that?" he wondered out loud. "That wasn't nowhere near talking to myself. I mutter under my breath so Ozell don't hear me, or I talk myself through things, but I ain't never had that type of inner voice telling me things."

He felt his forehead with the back of his hand, but it did no good when his hands were freezing fucking cold. He was about to head inside and ask Ozell for the thermometer when he caught a glimpse of a shadow walking by the barn door. He hopped out of the side-by-side and dashed to the open doors to see it disappear in the thicket near the trail.

The sun had already settled into dusk, so there was nothing to go on other than a moving shadow that was about as tall as him, if not taller. He looked up to see Ozell standing on the porch, a bit frightened.

"Did you see it, too?" she asked.

"See what?"

"The dark shadow that moved across the barn and into the woods. It was fast as lightning," she replied.

"I saw it, and I will take care of it," he answered.

"Be careful. That shadow… it didn't feel human," Ozell shouted. "Make sure to use the satellite phone if you get hurt."

"I know, I know," he huffed with a wave of his hand. "Quit mothering me, woman!"

Nathaniel fired up the side-by-side and headed toward the gravel driveway to make it to the trail he needed to take to canvas around the property before he went into the woods to hunt. An icy cold draft filled the space around him, and steamy condensation hit the air as his hot breath mingled with the cold draft.

Images began to flash through his mind that looked like his surroundings, but were somehow different. It was more forested and looked as if there hadn't been anyone living in the area for a while. He definitely knew now that it was indeed reefer instead of a cigarette he had smoked earlier. He was stoned off his ass and hallucinating.

Once again, he caught a black shadow moving out of his peripheral vision on the edge of the clearing and quickly bolted across the trail. The headlights caught a glimpse of brown and white as it jumped across the headlights, and Nathaniel slid his side-by-side to a stop, barely missing it. It was the buck he had seen in the garden earlier.

Nathaniel struggled out of his coat and pulled his coveralls off so they wouldn't hang him up while running, pulled his rifle and night vision goggles from his bag, and took off quietly through the thicket the buck had run through. He threw the strap of the gun over his shoulder as he donned the goggles and turned them on. The darkened forest sprang to life, and Nathaniel nearly ran full steam into an old oak tree in front of him. He dodged around it and zipped through the foliage of the woods until he saw a clearing up ahead. He had reached Devil's Claw Lake and popped out of the woods right onto the shoreline, nearly toppling into the high tide.

He gave the area a once-over and saw the deer he had been chasing drinking from the lake. It stopped in mid-drink and looked up at him, fully aware of his presence, and then returned back to the task at hand of drinking water. A doe appeared at his side, along with a fawn. They were all aware of his presence, and none were frightened.

"That just takes the fun out of hunting," he remarked, and was beginning to turn around to walk back to the side-by-side when the cold air blew up his back.

Nathaniel was overcome with the sudden urge to slaughter every single one of the deer that stood there, acknowledging him as a non-threat. It made a rage boil beneath his skin that these lowly creatures were not afraid of him, the hunter. They should be terrified of him, and yet, it was as if they scoffed at him in the dark.

He pulled his rifle up and trained the scope on the ten-pointer. He placed his finger on the trigger and trained the gun to shoot through the heart. With a loud pop, the deer gently lay down where he stood, looking over in the direction that Nathaniel was standing and staring at the old man as it bled out. He had fully expected the mother and fawn to take off at the sound of the gun, but like the two earlier in the day, they just stood there as if offering their lives as a sacrifice to him. Two quick pops, and he downed the baby and the mother.

He walked over to his kill and watched them all gasping for air to stay alive, breathing quickly in and out as if it would keep their hearts beating. He couldn't watch it any longer and pulled his knife from its sheath and slit all three of the deer's necks ear to ear. The warm blood oozed over his hands, and he soon found himself intrigued and enthralled with the sticky, warm liquid that pumped furiously from their throats once more.

Nathaniel lifted his hands to his face and breathed in the warm, coppery smell of his fresh kill. He soon was overcome with an adrenaline rush and urge to hack open the chest of the buck and rip its heart from the cavity. His hands worked quickly, maneuvering the knife through the chest cavity and cracking the breastbone. He put his knife down and reached his hand into the deer while holding its body, giving his one hand a quick yank and tearing the heart from the deer's muscles.

Nathaniel held the heart up to his nose and breathed in deeply again, taking in the coppery, sweet smell of the blood that called to him like a siren's lullaby. Before he realized what he was doing, he brought the heart up to his mouth and took a large bite of the organ. Blood spattered his face, and the organ quickly began to deflate as he squeezed each drop of blood into his mouth.

Once he was finished with the heart of the buck, he moved onto the doe and then the fawn, repeating himself, cutting the hearts out, and then eating them like a wild animal. He was hands deep into the guts of the buck when he snapped out of whatever blackout trance he had been in to find his hands shoved in elbow deep, playing with its entrails, then quickly backed away from the carcasses.

He thrust his fingers down his throat and gagged and coughed up the blood that he had been eating, as well as the bits of meat from the hearts he had eaten.

"What the fuck!" he shouted. "What the fucking fuck!!!"

He quickly scrambled to the side of the lake and began scrubbing his hands together, trying to get the stain of death from his skin. He brought the water up to his face and scrubbed at the coppery scent that clung to his skin. He reached an impasse and began to scramble out into the frigid waters of the lake. He dunked under the water and scrubbed himself before emerging to the top and then dunking back under.

He stumbled out of the water, drenched and shivering from the cold water and the unusually cold air of the night. He trudged back to the side-by-side so he could strip off the soaking wet clothes and put on the spare clothes he kept in there just in case of an emergency. After dressing, he put his coveralls and coat on, hopped in the side-by-side, and drove it down the trail that led to Devil's Claw. He was not toting three dead carcasses back to the side-by-side where he had initially parked it.

Nathaniel drove up right next to the bodies and began to load them onto the side-by-side to tie them down. When he reached for the baby fawn, he panicked. Ozell knew he didn't kill the fawns and had already made a remark about him killing Bambi last night. There was no way he could bring another one home and her not start to prod about what happened when he fully didn't understand what had happened.

Instead of putting the fawn in with the rest of his bounty, he took two tree limbs and sharpened one into a stake point that he drove down through the fawn's mouth and out the other end as if he would roast it over an open fire pit. He pushed the staked wood down into the ground and then drove the other limb that he quickly whittled into a point into the back of the fawn so it wouldn't topple over.

"What the fuck is wrong with me?" he asked out loud.

He heard a twig snap and looked over to see a shadow quickly shifting out of his view, and then the sound of little children's laughter filled the air. Nathaniel swallowed hard and slowly walked to his side-by-side and put it into gear to drive back down the trail back to home. During the entire ride back, it was as if he passed by the same kids laughing and whispering, and he floored the side-by-side to get home quickly.

As he pulled the side-by-side into the driveway, Ozell peeked out the curtain of the back door. He gave a small wave to her, and she went back to where she had been before he arrived. He untied the deer from the top of the side-by-side and let their bodies hit the ground. They looked like wolves had been tearing at their bodies.

He began to think about the warm, bloody juices that had dripped down his face, and even though his reaction had been to gag once he realized what he had done, the bloodlust had taken his soul. That distinct flavor of blood, like when you order a rare steak and push down on the meat with a fork, and the juices just ooze out, that is what it had been like. Bloody deliciousness.

Ozell stepped outside to help with field dressing the deer when he waved her away.

"Another night off, dear," he said as she looked at him, slightly confused. "I'll gut em and cut em up for ya. Just go on back in there and relax."

Ozell shrugged and walked back, but not before stealing a glance at the carcasses he had brought back and the large gaping holes where their hearts had once been.

Part 2: The Diary of Patrick Ingram

AFTER MY PARENTS' DEATHS, I decided I needed to do more with the land they had left me. I was left with the remaining parcel of the land that equaled about 100 acres of woodlands, including Devil Claw's Lake. I built Foxwood Hills Resort with half of my inheritance. Families all summer long come down to rent the nice cabins I have set up. We provide a lot of entertainment and fun for the summer and all the way through to winter.

The McGradys, who had traveled to the Americas alongside my ancestors, remained at Benjamin's side as they migrated to the land of

Franklin County. Just as my ancestors had to create a new title for themselves to live peacefully under the Church of England, the McGradys had to as well. According to Moira, their name was originally Boggs and changed to the McGrady surname. Benjamin not only gave them some of his land, but he also helped build their house, as well, so they didn't have to starve or freeze in the looming winter quickly approaching. Benjamin understood the perils of the new world as he had heard the stories in the ports of how those who had come to America a century before had died in its harsh elements.

Somewhere along the lines, the McGradys married into the Ingrams. Their last surviving heir was my cousin and also my maintenance man for the resort, Mikey. A lot has changed in the world since my ancestors arrived. We lived in the age of sex, drugs, and rock n roll. I missed most of the happenings being locked away at Gaebler's, but Mikey didn't miss out on anything. Mikey was roughly fifteen years older than me. He was old enough to be my brother but not old enough to be a father. However, if it weren't for him and Nathaniel Willard, I would have been totally isolated more than I was as a kid.

Prior to the first asylum where I was officially diagnosed as insane, I was allowed free range to roam and do normal boy things on the property. Nathaniel and Mikey would often meet me in the woods, and we would go exploring the vast valley, swim at Devil's Claw Lake, and stay out until it was dinner time. I often invited Nathaniel to dinner at my house, and Mikey was always welcome to come by and eat whenever he felt like it. However, no matter how many times I offered, Nathaniel always declined. I asked him one time why he always declined to eat at our house. I knew Nathaniel was hungry. His family was poor, and even though "boys will be boys," it always looked as if he were dirtier than normal. "Skin and bones" is what my mother used to say about him. His reply… "That house scares the shit out of me."

During our outings as children, all three of us had happened upon the old homestead that nature had overtaken in the woods. We often played pretend colonials and made up stories about the place as to why it had fallen into ruins. When I asked my father about the place, he told me that one of our ancestors had lived there and had gone insane. In the end, he died alone. What he described chilled me to the bone because, quite often, the nightmares I had in my sleep had been about a family and how the father had murdered them all. Even though I scoured every single journal Moira had left, there wasn't a single mention of them in her journals.

As time passed, Nathaniel was no longer allowed to play with Mikey and me. His father didn't want him to have anything more to do with the Ingrams. It was just Mikey and me from then on. Mikey took me fishing and hunting in the woods. He taught me about trees and plants. If I ever needed to live off the land, I knew exactly how to do that because of Mikey. But as I said, we lived during the age of sex, drugs, and rock-n-roll. It didn't take long for Mikey to fall right in with the local people. He met a local girl who got him into partying, and soon, he was doing lines of cocaine while downing jars of moonshine. It turned into an addiction, and soon Mikey was a drunk, just as my father was. However, he was never a mean drunk, and he was never drunk around me.

The resort needed help, and Mikey needed work. So, I hired him on as my maintenance man so he could feed his addiction. During our off-season from December to April, the resort was closed like many other state campgrounds. Even though we were privately owned and could open and close as we pleased, I felt it was much safer to close down during those months. The weather was so unpredictable during winter in Virginia, and I didn't want to be held responsible if anything were to happen. We had only been open for a few years, and I was still trying to build the reputation and credibility of the place. I couldn't have local papers talking about the resort.

Mikey often told me how we could make so much money if we let people hunt the land during the offseason by paying for permission. I declined. If it were to snow, the valley would become treacherous for the hunters, and they could fall through the ice of the lake since the snow pretty much covered it. Even though people knew about the lake and knew where the lake was, it had some power that drew people to it, much like Nelly Roderick. Unbeknownst to me, Mikey went behind my back and would be slipped money by hunters and teens alike to be able to go out into the woods to hunt or party.

By this time, I could no longer live in the manor and left it hidden within the woods to rot away, along with the memories of everything that had occurred in my childhood. It was nothing more than a nightmare to me, and I wanted no part of it anymore. I have never been able to articulate exactly what it was I felt when I went down into those woods. The feeling you get when the hairs stand up on the back of your neck as anxiety rolls through your adrenaline-beating chest when you're scared is what I had always felt in those woods. It was a heavy, oppressive energy that made your chest feel like rocks were sitting on it, and your face would feel numb. It had always been a sense of foreboding when I was younger. I would go by myself for walks in the woods, but once those feelings started to trickle to the surface, I always hauled ass back up the hill. I tried to avoid that part of the valley.

That part of the property where Devil's Claw Lake rested was what had initially jump-started my schizophrenic episodes. I would hear the whispering and see the leaves move. There didn't even have to be any wind to speak of for them to start dancing through the air. Sometimes, I would hear another child laughing, almost as if they were standing right beside me, and see the branches of the tree move as if they were running through the woods. The ground would indent as if someone were going through the leaves right in front of me. Other times, I would hear the sound of a man, infuriated with rage, yelling, or a woman sobbing in the wind.

The water would ripple, and you could see bodies swimming in the water that weren't real. I assumed it was the souls of those the lake had claimed as its own. If you listened close enough, you could hear the song the water had to offer, beckoning you to come in out of the heat and cool off. You never did alone, and I never swam in that water unless Mikey was around. All of my parents' parties had proven that the lake did not discriminate against social class and status and would eat whoever dared to venture within the murky depths alone.

It was New Year's Eve, the night an eighteen-year-old boy drowned. I was barely a few years older than him. I often think that if I had stayed longer in the manor after my parents had died, I would have been able to stop everything that occurred from happening. It felt like it was my negligence for abandoning the property. Instead of feeding from the Ingrams, it was feeding from whoever graced its forlorn soil. Spilled blood was what it yearned for, and it wasn't being satiated. Even though much of my youth had been spent hunting and fishing with Mikey, we hardly ever brought home any animals to clean and eat. It was as if they had avoided the area entirely. Animal instincts are much more attuned to nature than humans are, and they can sense danger better than we can. It was almost as if they could smell the energy that Foxwood Hills oozed like a cancerous tumor.

The way Foxwood Hills affected the area didn't stop at just nature. It seemed like the tendrils of its malevolent core seeped through the surrounding area like a willow tree's roots seeking water. The entire area of Doe Run was a run-down wasteland of drug addicts and alcoholics that made the slums and projects of the big cities seem like small potatoes. Since I was no longer held prisoner within the manor, I could come and go as I pleased and explore the world that extended farther than the land I was tethered to. Most of the staff had long since been let go while I was at Gaeblers, and the few that had remained were hitting retirement age. After my parents passed, I let them go with a hefty severance package that could last them and possibly even through to their grandkids for years to come.

I was learning a world that I had been hidden away from. I had never been to town to shop or even eat at the local restaurants, as my parents had wait staff that did all of that for them. The decadent and lavish Southern cooking filled our dining hall table as a feast set for a king. Mother had chosen some of the best cooks to fill our kitchen, and we had the experience of food from all parts of the South. Soul food rich with fried chicken, collard greens, and mashed potatoes with brown gravy was always on the table, along with fried squash, fried okra, cornbread, and various other vegetables dripping with butter. My favorite nights were the nights that Camille worked the dinner shift. She was Creole all the way from Louisiana and would fill the table with gumbo perfectly cooked with smoked sausages, corn on the cob, and rice, as well as a seafood boil with red potatoes, large single-serve ears of corn, lobster, shrimp, sausage, and the perfect blend of Cajun seasoning.

I, on the other hand, was not a chef by any means and had no idea how to recreate any of the dishes I had eaten as a child. Those first few months of solitude after my parents had passed were months of hunger. I scraped by on beanie weenie cans, canned spam, tuna, and ramen noodles. Once I had put an ad out in the paper about needing a chef for the resort, I received a surprising answer. Camille's granddaughter, Amarette, lived in the area and was interested in taking over the chef spot. I immediately hired her for the resort, even though it had yet to be built, and paid her to cook my dinners until the resort was up and running.

I learned a lot about the area as I began my quest for truth and understanding about the history and modern living of Franklin County. Much to my dismay, the current state in which it existed put it into the threshold of being a poor county with only a couple of factories really keeping it afloat. This led to poverty-stricken neighborhoods, and it worsened the further out you got from the town of Rocky Mount. Teen pregnancy, teen addicts, girls selling their bodies for drugs, you name it, and the area was blighted with the maddened energy of Foxwood. Addicts would break into people's houses to steal their things to get their next fix. I came across a story where a boy that Nathaniel had mentioned to me that he had gone to school with was shot in the face when he broke into an older man's house to steal and pawn his things for drugs.

Even the churches weren't proven to be above the malignancy of evil that Foxwood Hills possessed. Greed, the deadliest sin, had pervaded the institutions, and when people came looking for help, they were turned away, even if they were long-time standing members of the church, raising their children within the walls of the religious institution, and being turned away when their power was being threatened, or they were losing their house to foreclosures. If anyone in your family had sinned, they cast that sin upon the whole family, and the family was deemed tainted with the inability to be cleansed.

The state of affairs within my county was what really pushed me into opening the resort. It didn't matter if you were white, black, rich, poor, hedonist, atheist, heathen, or Christian. All walks of life were welcomed at the resort. There were many times I had discounted stays for families so that they could have a nice time and not go broke doing it. I started anonymous charities and donations to the local food banks, as well as helped create the local warming shelter for people experiencing homelessness, so they didn't have to sleep in tents in the middle of the woods. I funded the local angel trees for kids at Christmas time and really gave back to my community in hopes it would cleanse my soul of the tainted wealth my family had accumulated over the years, casting our name as wicked in the eyes of the public.

I never thought in a million years that Mikey would take advantage of my giving hand the way he had when the resort began its second season of business. I never thought he would risk the safety of others so he could have cash to get his next fix of alcohol or drugs. In truth, he acted as if he were still a teenager instead of a man in his thirties. When a bunch of freshly turned eighteen-year-olds wanted to go out of the old year and into the new year with a big bang, they knew exactly who to come to and ask. Word around Doe Run was that Mikey was able to set it up, and he did. They slipped him a couple of hundred bucks, so he attested, and he allowed them to venture into the resort to party and cut loose. Cocaine, meth, weed, alcohol, you name it, and they were partying with it. I'm not absolutely certain if Mikey partied with them that night or not because none of them would ever answer the question, including Mikey, when both the cops and I questioned them about what had happened. Silence filled the air instead of the truth, but my gut told me Mikey was there with them when the drowning occurred.

They were all sloshed, high, and not in their right minds by the time the cops arrived. I had been called first. Mikey telephoned me at my house, and I jumped in my Denali as quickly as I could and arrived just moments before the cops did. Upon my arrival, Mikey was bent over the boy doing CPR, trying to resuscitate him. The party had moved from the resort's campgrounds down to Devil Claw's Lake. They were all swimming and having a good time. The boy had climbed up on one of the boulders on the side of the lake to cannonball into the water. The medical examiner said it looked as if he had hit his head and lost consciousness beneath the waters. However, the others had a different story and said they watched him return to the surface, laughing and carrying on as they all were when he was yanked beneath the water. They swam out to save him, even grabbing onto his hand, but no matter how they tried to pull him to the surface, it was like someone, or something, was holding him beneath the water. They watched as the last air bubble escaped his lungs in one large air pocket, and he stopped thrashing. Just like that, they could pull him to the surface.

I don't know who carried him out of the woods. I assume Mikey had, and he laid him down and began to try to breathe the life back into him. The boy was pronounced dead on the scene and tucked away into a body bag that was carried away by an ambulance with its lights and siren turned off. After that night, Mikey changed. He was no longer the partying kind. He even suggested we put in a gate at the entrance of the camp and a fence that wrapped around the area so no one could sneak in, and another accident wouldn't happen. I agreed and paid to have one installed around the entire camping facility. Even Nathaniel agreed that one should go up around the area behind his house, granted he still had access to it.

That was such a long time ago, and thinking back on my childhood and emergence into the world as a fresh, new adult, it's hard not to relive the harrowing moments I experienced at that place. It's one reason I don't often come here and leave it to Mikey to manage. The quiet rage my father kept within him was quite similar to the one my grandfather had, as attestation by my grandmother. I often heard her calling him by my grandfather's name because he acted in such malice and menace as his father had. In a way, I felt sorry for him just as much as I felt sorry for myself. He had grown up with the same type of mistreatment I had from his own father, who berated and belittled him. He never spoke about my grandfather, and I have very few memories of him alive. He passed when I was quite young, and my father inherited the house upon his passing. My grandmother preferred to live in a rest home instead of the manor. She didn't like the way it made her feel. I have often wondered if the same spirits that were able to take over my body had also influenced the other men in the Ingram family. I guess I will never know since I am the last living heir.

Chapter Seven

IT WAS EARLY MORNING Wednesday, and Candace jetted around the kitchen of the cabin, preparing breakfast for the family. She had put on bacon, eggs, sausage, gravy, and popped biscuits in the oven. Carter stood by the coffee maker on the counter, watching it drip by drip, filling the coffee pot with his liquid adrenaline.

"After breakfast, we should all get ready to go swimming like we promised the kids," Candace reminded him.

Carter waved her off. "No conversation before I have my coffee, please," he requested.

"I bet you are a joy at the office when Starbucks is slammed," Candace joked with a laugh.

"Ha ha, ha ha," Carter mimicked while rolling his eyes.

A knock came to the door, and Carter left his watch guard spot by the coffee to answer it. He opened the door to find Mikey standing there, bright-eyed and bushy-tailed.

"Mornin'," Mikey spoke loudly.

Carter felt his head start to pound. He and Candace had spent the previous night drinking beer and smoking some weed after the kids had gone to bed, and he was still a bit drunk.

"Morning," Carter replied back. "What can I do for you?" he asked.

"Well, you are my last stop!" Mikey announced in a chipper tone. "As you know, we offer activities for the kids as well as the adults, and from around six pm today until after dark, I have all kinds of things planned for the youngens to do. After dark, since it is Halloween and no one really takes their kids trick or treating while vacationing, I usually take them down to the lake and build a nice fire to roast marshmallows and tell ghost stories."

"Is it safe after dark down there?" Carter asked. "You had warned us how it was a bit dangerous."

"Oh, we won't be swimming or that close to the shoreline for the kids to get hurt. It's just easier to bring buckets of water to douse the campfire when we are done," he reassured. "Plus, the adults usually throw themselves a nice little get-together with alcohol and all, while the kids are away. It would be great to mingle."

"What do you think, Candace?" Carter asked, turning so she could see his eyes say no.

"It sounds like a wonderful idea!" Candace remarked while setting the table for breakfast and completely ignoring Carter's silent signal. "The kids were just asking yesterday to do smores at the lake. This saves us the hassle!"

Carter quietly groaned as he cussed Candace in his thoughts.

"Sounds like we are all in on the festivities," Carter said, sounding sarcastically excited.

Mikey's smile twitched a bit at the tone of Carter's voice. "If you don't want to do the adult gathering, it's completely optional. Nothing is mandatory."

"Oh, we won't miss it!" Candace replied, enthused.

"Mikey, have you ever been married?" Carter asked.

"I am divorced," Mikey replied honestly, nodding his head.

A moment passed where Carter stood there with a dumbfounded look as he squinted and nodded with Mikey.

"Well, do you still have the attorney's number you used?" Carter asked loud enough for Candace to hear.

Mikey's eyes shifted nervously from Carter, who stared intently at him, to Candace, who now stood with her hands on her hips and a death glare.

"Well, everything starts at six," Mikey replied, changing the subject. "I'll stop by and get the kids personally. The adults will be up in the main event lodge. The boss man supplies the refreshments, and the cafeteria lady is making everyone dinner on us."

"Will there be s'mores and a fire for us as well?" Carter asked, playing his poker face. "Ghost stories?"

Mikey laughed nervously. "I'm sure you all have horror stories of your own you can share. Like your kids sleepwalking or staring blankly out in the field as if they see ghosts."

"We will be there, and the kids will love the nature walks and activities," Candace interrupted, walking up behind Carter and jabbing her pointer finger into his ribs.

"Ow, that hurt," Carter replied, rubbing his side.

"Thank you, Mikey, for stopping by and inviting us," Candace said with a smile. "He hasn't had his morning coffee yet," she whispered.

Mikey nodded, and a smile formed. "Well, I won't take up any more of your time. Nice chatting with you, fine folk... ope my phone is ringing," Mikey stated.

"I don't hear anything," Carter replied, leaning against the door frame.

"It's on vibrate," Mikey replied, pulling it from his pocket. "Ope, it's the boss. Need to take this. Y'all have a nice day!"

Mikey abruptly turned around and walked as fast as he could to his Jeep, pretending to answer his phone as he hopped in.

Carter closed the door as Candace walked back over to finish putting breakfast on the table.

"What was all that?!" Carter asked.

"What?" Candace asked in return.

"You know what! I gave you the signal. My eyes said no!" he retorted.

"The kids need to have some interaction with the other kids. And it would do us some good as well to mingle with the adults instead of being lone wolves, which they see as snobby, stuck-up assholes," Candace replied, removing the biscuits from the oven to cool.

"I don't mind being thought of as snobby and stuck-up. Hell, everyone knows I am an asshole!" Carter shot back.

"Fine. You can stay here while I go mingle, and when people ask about you, I will just tell them how you're an asshole and don't care if anyone knows it," she said as she put the biscuits in a large bowl and set them on the table. "Kids, it's breakfast time!"

Joshua and Isobel came bounding from the other side of the cabin and raced to pick a seat at the table.

"It's about time!" Joshua exclaimed. "The smell of cooking food has been starving me this whole time!"

"Well, eat up! You have a big day today. We are going swimming as promised, and then this afternoon, there are some planned activities for the kids that Mikey invited you to," Candace explained. "And then tonight, he's building a fire, and you're going to be making smores and telling ghost stories and all!"

"That sounds like super-duper fun!" Isobel exclaimed.

Carter mimicked Isobel silently with his mouth and rolled his eyes. He walked over to the coffee pot that had finally finished brewing and poured himself a cup of coffee. He lightly blew on the steaming cup and took a sip, savoring the taste.

"Better?" Candace asked.

"Not better enough to where I want to go to a mixer with a bunch of people I don't know in hillbilly hell," he replied with a snarky smile.

"Sit down and eat so we can go swimming," Candace barked.

They all sat at the table chatting quietly amongst one another. The kids ate a hearty helping of their breakfast food, and Candace was surprised when they asked for seconds.

"Hungry, are we?" she asked as she refilled their plates.

"Starving!" Isobel exclaimed. "Feels like I haven't eaten in days!"

Carter laughed. "Might have a tapeworm from all the germs here," he joked.

The kids finished up their second plates, and Candace began to clear the table.

"Get your swimsuits on!" Candace called as the kids went running to their rooms.

Candace went to her room and began to undress and slip into her bikini. Carter walked into the room behind her. He pulled her into his arms and kissed her on the neck.

"I'm sorry for being a dick," he whispered into her ear. "You know I am not a people person."

"I know," Candace sighed. "I just want to step out of our comfort zone for once and meet some new faces."

Carter's hands glided down the sides of Candace's body as he gently kissed her shoulder blade. Candace giggled and shooed him off to finish putting her bikini on. She pulled her sun robe on over the bikini and topped the ensemble off with a big sun bonnet and flip-flops.

"Gorgeous," Carter whispered.

"You get your trunks on, and I will wrangle the children," she said.

She left him in the room to get dressed and walked to Isobel and Joshua's room. Joshua was sitting out in the den on the couch, ready to go.

"Where's Lizzy?" she asked.

"In her room," he replied.

Candace walked to Isobel's door and went to tap on the door when she heard Isobel giggle and whisper to someone.

"What else did you do to the kids to scare them?" Isobel asked in hushed tones.

Candace opened the door to find Isobel sitting on her bed, dressed in her bathing suit, with nobody else in the room.

"Who were you talking to, Lizzy?" Candace asked, checking behind the door.

"I was talking to Lizzy," Isobel replied.

"Oh, so your friend has the same exact name you do, huh?" Candace asked as she leaned against the door jam.

"Yes," Isobel replied. "Her name is Isobel Ingram."

"That's a pretty name!" Candace remarked. "Does she have any siblings? A brother? A sister?" she asked.

"She has one brother and two sisters," Isobel replied.

"Where are her parents at?" Candace asked, amused.

"They're both dead," Isobel replied solemnly. "Her father murdered her mother, and he died in a fire."

It felt like the air was sucked out of Candace's lungs. She stood there, stunned at what Isobel had said, and didn't know how to reply.

"That's awful," Candace said.

"It's not too bad," Isobel replied. "Lizzy is dead too, so they are together."

Candace grew a bit concerned about the tale that Lizzy was spinning. She had never heard her spout stories like this before. It was uncharacteristic of her to do so.

"Well, are you ready to go swimming?" Candace asked, uneasy.

"I sure am!" Isobel exclaimed, jumping down from her bed and running to sit beside Joshua on the couch.

"Let me go see if Daddy is ready," Candace stated, walking back to her room.

She opened the door just as Carter was about to come out of the room.

She began to whisper to him. "The imaginary friends of Isobel…"

"Yeah," Carter asked. "What about them?"

"She told me they are all dead!" she exclaimed quietly.

"What?" Carter asked, confused.

"Yeah, she said her friend's name is Lizzy, like her, and her father killed her mother and all kinds of weirdness!" Candace hissed. "Where did she hear that story?"

"I have no idea," Carter replied. "Maybe one of the kids here told a ghost story of some sort."

"It doesn't make it any less creepy," Candace retorted.

Candace walked to the bathroom, grabbed some towels, and grouped with everyone waiting outside.

"Let's go!" she exclaimed.

Instead of taking the weird way the kids had gone to find themselves at the lake, they took the designated path to it this time. Carter and Candace walked ahead of the group while Joshua and Isobel hung at the back.

"We need to get the ring and necklace from Mommy and put the stuff back in the bag and in the tree by tonight," Isobel warned Joshua. "I told you not to take them, and now Lizzy says if they aren't in the tree, bad things will happen tonight."

"Lizzy, nothing bad is going to happen," Joshua huffed. "Your friend Lizzy isn't real. William isn't real."

"Yes, they are!" Isobel retorted. "They said tonight is a scary night. It's a full moon on Halloween. It's been three hundred years since everything happened to them. The darkness walks in the woods tonight!"

"What are you rambling on about?" Joshua asked, exasperated.

"The darkness is what killed all of them," Isobel explained. "I don't even want to go to the campout Mikey is doing tonight. It's too risky. They said the safest thing for us to do is to stay inside."

"For the last time, Lizzy, none of that is real! Nothing is going to happen!" Joshua fumed. "Now, quicken your pace. Mom and Dad are far ahead of us right now."

They all arrived at the lake and set up some lounge chairs. Candace had brought a bag that had sunscreen and bug repellant and began spraying everyone head to toe. Joshua and Isobel donned swimming goggles and snorkels.

"Alright, be careful swimming!" Candace warned as Joshua and Isobel ran to the water, splashing in.

Joshua dove under the water and gave a look around before coming back to the surface.

"There's all kinds of trees and everything down there!" he exclaimed.

"Yeah, this used to not be here," Mikey said, walking up beside Candace and Carter.

Candace yelped, startled, and then grabbed her chest.

"You caught us off guard. We didn't hear you coming," she laughed.

"Sorry about that. I saw y'all head down this way and wanted to make sure everyone was safe," he replied with a friendly smile. "I also brought these," Mikey said, holding up scuba tanks and wetsuits for diving.

"So, what did it used to be?" Joshua asked as he floated.

"It used to be all land. Just land. Plantations all around," Mikey replied. "Then they had to flood the area to keep Smith Mountain Lake from washing out the area again, which it too wasn't always a lake either."

"Again?" Carter asked.

"Yeah, since it was a man-made lake, whenever we would get too much rain, it would flood all the way to town," Mikey replied.

"So, they just made another path all the way to here and let the lake bleed off into it?" Candace asked.

"Pretty much. There's a whole town under that lake," Mikey replied. "Government people try to deny that it ever happened, but everyone around here talks about how they wiped out the town of Monroe after taking the twenty thousand acres of farms and all to build the lake. Then, the power company bought it out and made the dam. This area here was a bit similar, minus the power company buying it out. There are old houses and stuff under the water. It wasn't as drastic as Smith Mountain Lake, so a lot of things were preserved as it slowly filled with the water."

"So, they made both of these lakes?" Candace asked.

"Yes, ma'am," he replied. "Except they didn't destroy the little town of Rocky Mount to do it with this one. They piped it over."

"That is *so* fascinating!" Candace remarked.

"So," Mikey said, holding the scuba tanks up. "You want to go for a dive, Carter?" he asked.

"Hell yeah!" Carter replied enthusiastically. "I want to see what's under there. See if you're yanking my chain or not."

Carter and Mikey slipped into the wetsuits and flippers while helping each other put the oxygen tanks on.

"These masks are special masks. You can talk to me in them," Mikey said, holding one of them up.

"Oh, that is fan-fucking-tastic!! Where did you get this stuff?" Carter asked, snatching the mask out of Mikey's hands and adjusting it for his head.

"I don't have much family or much to do here, so I don't have nothing else to spend my money on," Mikey replied.

"You mean you don't spend all your money on beer?" Carter asked, raising his eyebrow. "At least that is the whispers we have heard since we arrived."

Mikey chuckled. "No, I actually quit drinking a few years ago. So instead, I buy stuff I will probably never use."

Mikey fitted his mask to his face and turned the oxygen to Carter's tank on, and Carter did the same for him.

"You ready?" Mikey asked as he pulled his mask down.

"Ready as I'll ever be," Carter replied, pulling his down as well.

The pair walked into the water and waded out until the water reached their chest, then dove under. There wasn't much to see as they descended under the water.

"How far under do we have to swim?" Carter asked.

"It's not that far of a swim, but it is a deep swim," Mikey replied.

Mikey led the way, with Carter trailing behind. There were dead trees that Carter saw the tops of as they swam outward away from the shore. Schools of fish frantically swam away from them as they paddled further out. The trees cleared, and houses came into view.

"Were these houses bought out like the ones for Smith Mountain Lake?" Carter asked.

"There wasn't any need. All of these had long been vacant. Some of them date all the way back to the 1700's. The historical society maintained the upkeep, and it used to be like a sightseeing attraction for the town. However, that all tapered off, and they felt as if it was more money to maintain than what it paid off," Mikey replied.

"Aren't they paid by like the government to keep stuff up and going, though?" Carter asked.

"And there is your million-dollar question with the million-dollar answer already answered by the question," Mikey replied. "The government is what bought the land out for Smith Mountain Lake. It was already government-owned. It just wasn't protected under the historical landmark because it had never been filed."

"Shady mother fuckers," Carter sneered.

"These houses are the old town of Rocky Mount before they settled the larger one later on. A lot of them are general stores or medical offices and such," Mikey stated as they swam overhead.

"Why did they name it Devil's Claw?" Carter asked. "What's the story behind that?"

"It wasn't always named that. When they first built the lake, it was called Franklin Lake after the county. After so many people kept drowning in the lake, the townsfolk said that it was a haunted lake and the devil himself was dragging people's souls to hell," Mikey replied. "It was officially renamed Devil's Claw Lake in the mid-70s."

As they neared the end, Carter saw a place far off from the rest of them.

"What's that?" he asked.

"Well, that depends on if you listen to the legends," Mikey replied.

"What legends?" Carter asked.

"Back before all of this was settled, this was Native American land. Not a pale face to be seen. Something spooked them all away. They left their things behind as if they left in the middle of the night," Mikey stated.

"What does that have to do with the house, if you can call it that?" Carter asked.

"According to the locals, there was a Cherokee woman named Gini who didn't leave with her tribe. She stayed behind and lived in a hut. The townspeople built her a sturdier shelter. She was their local medicine man, so to speak. She gave them herbs for their ailments and made herbal teas for them and all that good shit," Mikey replied.

"What happened to her?" Carter asked.

"No one knows for certain. One day, she just vanished, and they never saw her again," Mikey replied. "Want to go inside? It's pretty cool in there."

"Why not? You only live once," Carter replied.

The two began their descent down to the dwelling. Mikey led the way through the door as Carter cautiously followed.

"There aren't alligators or anything in the waters, are there?" Carter asked nervously.

Mikey chuckled. "There aren't any gators or crocs in these parts."

Once Carter entered the house, his eyes widened.

"Everything looks pretty much intact down here. How is that even possible?" he asked.

"No idea. I have found a lot of things in this place that I have brought back as souvenirs, though," Mikey replied.

As they swam through the old building, Carter stopped in front of what looked to be a painting, but weird looking.

"What's this?" Carter asked.

"That is a Cherokee painting on buck hide," Mikey explained.

"Well, I am not a smart man, but I gathered that much. But what *is it*?" Carter asked again.

"After I saw that, I went through Cherokee lore for days on Google. That is apparently what the Cherokee call a Raven Mocker," Mikey replied.

"What the hell is a Raven Mocker?" Carter asked as he studied the painting.

"It's a ghost spirit or witch, so to speak. They feed on the dying and eat their hearts for everlasting life," Mikey replied. "This is actually part of the ghost stories that I tell the kids on campout night."

"You are one seriously fucked up dude, you know that?" Carter laughed. "Telling kids this shit. I love it!"

"I never expected you to be as…. Cool as you are," Mikey laughed.

"Why? Do I look like I have a stick up my ass?" Carter asked.

"Yeah, yeah, you do," Mikey laughed.

"I just don't like change in plans and all. It irritates me more than anything else in this world when the plans that I spent months planning fall apart. It makes me moody," Carter explained. "What's this?" he asked, pointing at bottles floating around in the water.

"I'm not sure. When you look closely, it looks like some sort of cactus preserved. But that doesn't make sense because cactus is definitely not a plant that grows anywhere near here," Mikey replied.

"Interesting…" Carter said.

Carter felt something woosh behind him, and he turned around as fast as he could.

"Was that a fish?" he asked.

"I didn't see anything," Mikey replied.

There was another woosh in the water, and Mikey turned around quickly, this time to see what it was.

"I felt it that time. We can head back up if you want," Mikey offered.

"That sounds nice," Carter replied a bit nervously.

They began to swim for the door when Carter gave one last look behind him and scrambled into Mikey.

"Did you fucking see that?" Carter yelled.

"See what?" Mikey asked, turning around.

"It looked like one of them ugly creatures in that painting. It was just standing right there!" Carter yelled, pointing to the corner of the house.

"Well, whatever it was is gone now. And we should go too before you have a panic attack under here," Mikey warned.

"You don't have to tell me twice," Carter replied, pushing past Mikey and out into the water.

As soon as he was out the door, it felt like something snagged him by the foot. "Hey, let go of me!" Carter demanded.

"I'm not touching you," Mikey defended. "You're caught on some brush. Hold on, and I will get you loose."

"Well, hurry up. Because that panic attack is going to be a real thing in a minute," Carter hissed.

Mikey tugged on the flipper stuck in the underbrush and got it loose when a huge catfish swam past them.

"We need to leave now," Mikey stated calmly. "That fish is big enough to eat us. So, no sudden movements. No jostling around in the water. When its back is turned to us, we get moving."

Carter stopped flailing and remained immobile in the water until the catfish began to swim around the other side of the house.

"Alright, go!" Mikey warned.

Both Mikey and Carter swam in an even diagonal formation back to the shore as Mikey watched behind them for the catfish.

"We can't ascend too fast, or we will get the bends, so keep swimming in this formation. We will hit the trees first, so be careful and watch where you are going. Also, keep an eye out for more of those catfish," Mikey explained.

They soon hit the trees, and Carter dodged tree limbs and tree trunks as they slowly swam upward.

"Stop moving!" Mikey yelled.

Carter immediately halted and carefully looked behind him. The catfish was right behind Mikey. It was the size of a pontoon boat.

"What do we do?" Carter asked.

"We just wait for it to leave," Mikey replied.

"Then what do we do about the other ones?" Carter asked.

Mikey looked around him, and there were at least a dozen more catfish the same size slowly making their way over to them.

"I am going to slowly reach into my wetsuit. I want you to stay perfectly still while I do this," Mikey calmly replied.

"What are you getting?" Carter asked.

"Bug spray. Catfish hate DEET," Mikey replied.

Carter kept an eye on the fish surrounding them while Mikey slowly unzipped his wetsuit and fished out a container of bug spray. He rezipped his suit slowly and stopped moving altogether.

"Now what?" Carter asked.

"I am pushing the button," Mikey replied as the bug spray began to pool around them and float upward toward the circling fish.

The fish immediately turned nose and began to swim away.

"Go!" Mikey yelled.

Carter and Mikey swam as furiously as they could through the thicket of trees while Mikey held the can's spray nozzle depressed, leaving a trail of DEET scent behind them. As they neared the shore, Carter gave one last look behind him to see the one catfish sitting in the water staring at them as they breached the water's surface. None of the other fish stayed around, but that one acted as if the DEET didn't even bother it.

They hit the sandbank, and Carter clamored out of the water, splashing water everywhere as he struggled to remove his mask. Candace stood with the kids off to the side, a bit frightened by how he was acting. As he pulled the mask off, he took in a deep breath of air and looked around.

"Where's Mikey?" he asked as he looked behind him, and the water was empty.

"You were the only one to surface," Candace replied.

"Shit," Carter hissed as he went to jump back in the water.

Just as he was about to resubmerge, Mikey popped up from the water.

"What the hell, man!" Carter yelled. "I thought you were fish food!"

"I saw something in the water and went to grab it," Mikey replied, holding up a bead necklace.

Carter sighed heavily and thrashed out of the water. He took off his wetsuit and laid it on the beach while he sank onto a towel that was lying there.

"What happened?" Candace asked.

"We were almost fish food to some huge catfish," Carter explained.

"Is it safe for the kids to swim?" Candace asked.

"Yeah, they won't come close to shore," Mikey replied.

Mikey, Candace, and Carter chatted quietly amongst themselves about the diving adventure while Isobel and Joshua jumped in and swam around.

"I bet there is treasure under here!" Joshua exclaimed to Isobel. "Just like the necklace Mikey found."

Isobel had waded over to the shallow part of the lake and stood staring at Joshua.

"You should get out," she said to Joshua.

"Why?" he snarked. "Are your ghost friends going to get me?"

"No," Isobel replied and pointed. "She is."

Before Joshua could turn around to look, a hand grabbed his ankle and yanked him under the water. He looked down to see a woman dressed in a white dress with long black hair dragging him down. He kicked at her hand, and she let go long enough for him to break the top of the water and quickly yell for help before being dragged back down by her.

Hands were quickly around him, and he felt her hand let go again and watched her descend back down to the murky depths of the water as he ascended. When he reached the top of the water, he gasped for air.

"Joshua!" Candace screamed frantically. "Are you ok?"

"Thank you, Mikey, for jumping in after him," Carter said, sticking his hand out to shake Mikey's.

"It wasn't no trouble at all," Mikey replied, panting.

"What happened?" Carter asked Joshua.

"There was this woman!" Joshua recalled. "She was all in white with black hair, and she grabbed my ankle and pulled me under!"

"There hasn't been anyone, but us come down here and go in the lake," Carter refuted.

"Dad, there is a lady in the water, and she is evil!" Joshua insisted.

"His leg most likely got caught on a tree branch in the current," Mikey offered as comfort. "It's why I warned the danger of the lake."

Mikey eyed Joshua and the necklace he held in his hand. "You want this? I have plenty back at my cabin."

"Sure," Joshua replied, taking the necklace from him. "What is it?"

"I am fairly certain it's a Cherokee tribe necklace," Mikey replied.

Mikey picked up the wetsuits that had been taken off and grabbed the scuba gear. "Y'all have a nice rest of your day. I'm going to head back and get ready for this evening," he called out over his shoulder. "See you kids at six!"

"Yeah, we are leaving too. This is too dangerous," Candace stated, packing up her bag and capsizing her lounge chair.

As they started back up the trail, Isobel nudged Joshua and asked, "Believe me now?"

***

Just as scheduled, Mikey showed up at six to get Joshua and Isobel for their activities. They joined the troop of kids waiting in line at the edge of the woods. Once they were all together and the talking had died down, Mikey held his finger to his lips and began with instructions.

"Before we descend into the dark of night within the woods, we need ground rules. Absolutely no one is to stray from the group. You are to pair off with a buddy system. If you do not know where your buddy is and do not see them with the group, you are to tell me. Do you understand?" Mikey asked.

All the children nodded in compliance. Isobel grabbed Joshua's hand, claiming him as her buddy.

"It is easy to get lost in these woods at night, and that is not fun at all. We all would have to stop our campout and return to camp while the adults search for whoever is missing. So, no stragglers and no walking off. I mean it!" he reinforced.

Once again, the children nodded in compliance.

"Alright!" Mikey excitedly exclaimed. "Hi-ho!"

Mikey led them into the woods, and all of the kids followed hand in hand with their buddy in a two-by-two-line formation while Mikey sang the hi-ho song they all knew from scouts. They trekked down a worn-out path that Mikey had undoubtedly used for years to take campers or the grand campout.

It took about fifteen minutes before they reached a cleared-out area with large tree trunks carved down into benches surrounding a stone circle. Inside the circle was firewood to be used for the night.

Isobel glanced around nervously as the canopy of trees above them muted the sun enough to make it dusk dark in the woods.

Joshua watched her, acknowledging that she was truly frightened of what was to come of the night. However, no matter how frightened Isobel was, he knew they couldn't go back to their parents because they, too, were having an outing with the other adults at the campgrounds.

The feel of the woods had a darker vibe than when Joshua and Isobel arrived. The air felt stagnant, as if it had stopped moving. There weren't any sounds of the forest, like squirrels or raccoons traipsing through the underbrush. A musty, death-like smell lingered in the unmoving, humid air that was stifling. It was an all-in-all creepy feeling that wasn't due to Mikey's efforts. As Joshua looked around at all of the other kids' reactions to the area, he immediately knew that they did not feel the same unease he and Isobel felt in this place.

Joshua took Isobel by the hand and led her to one of the tree logs to sit down. Her hand tightened nervously around his, not wanting to release the grip that made her feel safer. The other kids, two by two, took their seats around the fire pit as Mikey began to get the fire going for them. Joshua and Isobel were left alone on their own log as the other kids chatted amongst themselves.

As Mikey stoked the small fire to get it to gain momentum, he smiled at Joshua and Isobel and gave them a wink. He knew that the other kids were leaving them out on purpose, and he intended to get the whole group to act as one unit tonight. He knew what it felt like to be the odd man out growing up, and these two kids didn't need to feel left out in a strange place where they didn't know anyone.

"How many of you are returning campers this year?" Mikey asked as he stood from the now roaring fire.

All of the kids glanced around at one another to see who would raise a hand. None of them raised their hands to acknowledge the answer.

"Well, I absolutely love new campers. I have been the recreational park's camper activity attendee for quite some time," he stated as he smiled at them all. "Every summer, I organize a huge campout every single week for the kids. I bring them down here, and we make s'mores like I promised your parents," he said, holding up a bag of chocolates, a bag of marshmallows, and a box of graham crackers. "We sometimes roast hot dogs, or we go fishing and cook up the trout we caught. But it always ends in ghost stories!"

The kids around them clapped happily as Joshua and Isobel sat solemnly listening.

"This campout is a bit different. Does anyone know what today is?" he asked.

"It's Halloween!" one little girl exclaimed.

"That is right! It is Halloween!" he reiterated. "Do you know what else makes tonight special?" he asked. He waited for someone to answer, and after nobody spoke up, he answered his own question for them. "Tonight is a full moon!"

"What makes it so special?" one of the kids asked.

"Well, a full moon on Halloween is extra special. During hunting season, the Native Americans would use the moons of the month to know special things about the month ahead. They called October's full moon the Hunter's moon or Blood moon because it was when hunting season had arrived."

"Well, what makes Halloween important?" another kid asked.

"Halloween is a special holiday to many different people. To most people, it's just a day where kids dress up and get candy like you are used to doing for Trick-Or-Treating. To many other cultures, Halloween came from the holiday called Samhain. Most cultures had similar beliefs that this day was the one day that the veil between the living and the dead was the thinnest, and it allowed those in the spirit realm to walk the earth one more time," he explained.

"Well, what did the Native Americans believe?" Joshua asked.

"I am glad you asked, Joshua. In specific, the Cherokee tribe believed that October was the beginning of the year. They believed that the world was created in autumn during the harvest season. They called their October moon the Harvest moon." Mikey began to walk toward a mound of stones off to the right of the campfire. "This land that we are on is Cherokee land. A long time ago, a Cherokee tribe lived and hunted in these woods. This is one of their grave markers."

"Why did they leave?" Isobel asked.

Mikey held up a finger and walked to his backpack, opening it slowly. He pulled a mask from within and held it up for all of them to see.

"Legend has it that the Cherokee tribe thrived well here and had plenty to eat. However, what they called Asgina came in the night. An Asgina was an evil witch spirit. In particular, a Raven Mocker plagued their tribe," he replied.

"What is a Raven Mocker?" one of the other kids asked.

"A Raven Mocker was a specific kind of evil spirit that lived among them in secret. They took the form of an elder woman so the children would not fear them. Whenever someone was dying, the Raven Mocker would sneak into their home and feed off of their heart unseen by those that stood around their body. The heart of a person would give the Raven Mocker more years to live on in immortality," Mikey explained. "I found this mask years ago preserved and had it authenticated. It is one of the masks the Cherokee used to thwart the Raven Mocker away from bodies, similar in the fashion of wearing a Halloween costume, so other spirits would think you are one of them as well, like in Celtic lore."

"Where did you find it?" Isobel squeaked.

"There are remnants of an old house from long ago on an adjacent property. I found it tucked away in an old box," he replied. "I also found this."

Mikey reached down into his bag and pulled out an old book made from the skin of a deer. The pages inside the book were also buck hide with strange writing on them.

"What is it?" one of the other kids asked.

"This is a magic spell book of a Cherokee Witch," Mikey replied. "According to legends in the area, a woman by the name of Gini Raven lived here when the property was one huge lot of land instead of parceled out. She lived in a hut on the outskirts of the town, and even though townspeople feared her, they would go to her for herbs and cures for their ailments. This was where she wrote her recipes down and other things."

"What all does the book say?" Joshua asked.

"We will get to that in a little bit. Let's all get some s'mores going and some campfire tales, and we will come back to it," Mikey replied, placing the book back in the bag.

Isobel leaned in close to Joshua and whispered, "He shouldn't read from that book. It's not a good book." Her voice cracked as she looked at Joshua with pleading eyes.

"Somehow, I think you're right," Joshua replied in a whisper.

"We should leave," Isobel persisted once again.

"We can't," Joshua replied.

"We're going to die in these woods," Isobel said in a whispered voice. "Lizzy warned us, Joshua. We're all in danger..."

***

"I just don't understand why we *have* to go," Carter huffed as he and Candace walked through the field up to the main event lodge.

"You *never* want to do anything unless it involves one of your buddies," Candace huffed. "We can't go to dinner unless it's a double with a friend. We can't go on vacation unless it has to do with a friend. I tried to get you to go with me to the dispensaries because you like to smoke weed. Did you want to go? No! Why? And I quote, *'No one I know will be there,'*" Candace mimicked. "All I am asking is a night for us. Is that too much for me to ask? Or shall I just sit and be mute the rest of the vacation and give your friends something to talk about when we live about how stuck up your wife is?"

Carter groaned and rolled his eyes upward while pinching the bridge of his nose. He ran his hand through his hair, exasperated. "Fine! We will have some drinks, talk to the parents of the assholes that won't have anything to do with our kids, and then leave."

"Thank you," Candace replied with a sarcastic smile.

"You're making me go bald. You do realize that?" Carter asked as he held the door of the lodge open for Candace to walk through.

As they stepped through the door, what was happening in the room was completely unexpected for either of them. A millennial mixtape blared Eminem's "The Real Slim Shady" in the background while the people in the cabin to the left of them did Jell-O shots off the body of the woman who was in the cabin adjacent to their right. Another of the interesting parents ripped a bong with a couple of college kids who were in the cabin in the bend.

"Oh," Candace murmured. "Is…is this what you call a swinger's party?" she asked, looking at Carter.

Carter's face was pure shock and awe. He felt a tug at his shirt and looked to his side. An old couple sat at the entrance with a grinder, rolling tray, and joint papers, rolling joints to pass out to everyone as they walked through the door. The old lady smiled as she thrust the joint up to Carter, and he gave a half-hearted smile as he carefully took it from her hand and gestured a thank you with it.

"Be careful with that one," the old man offered. "It's called the Holy Ghost, and it will *fuck* your world up."

"Why is it called the Holy Ghost?" Candace asked.

"Because when you smoke it, you think you're going to meet Jesus," he replied, laughing.

"Thank you," Candace smiled as she snaked the joint from Carter.

Candace rummaged around in her purse before her hand emerged with a light. She carefully lit the end and toked a couple of puffs from the joint before exhaling and handing it over to Carter. Carter scowled at her.

"It's legal here, Carter!" she whined. "Live a little and stop being a doorknob."

Carter caved and took the joint from Candace and puffed the joint a few times, held it for five seconds, and then let it loose with a deep gruntled cough.

"This shit is lit!" Carter remarked back to the old man, who raised a glass of beer in response.

The lodge was bumping and jiving, and after about ten minutes of loosening up with a joint, Carter was vibing with the rest of the party. Carter offered the joint to the old lady.

"Name's Carter," he said as she took the joint and drew a puff from it. "This is my wife, Candace."

"The name's Joy," the elderly woman replied with a nasal tone as she tried to hold the smoke in her lungs. She exhaled like a pro, handing it off to her husband sitting beside her. "This is Bill."

Bill nodded as he drew a toke from the joint, immediately going into a coughing fit as if he had collapsed a lung. Joy reached into her bag beside her and pulled out an inhaler.

"He has asthma," she said, hand clasped around her mouth as if she didn't want the whole room to hear—as if they would have heard them over the loudspeaker.

Candace quickly grabbed a cocktail from the open bar and returned to Carter's side as he finished hitting the joint again and handed it off to her. Soon, a small circle began to form where everyone passed around the joints that were rolled and handed out. Everyone talked amongst themselves as they passed the joints, while Carter and Candace stood quietly listening with attentive ears to the names.

The college kids were Kevin and Jimmy. Both were going to Virginia Tech on football scholarships, and by looking at them, they were not starting points. They were really lanky. Down from them in their small cul-de-sac in the campground were the two hillbilly rednecks, Bobby and Carl. Carter kept feeling eyes creep on them as he toked his joint, and when he looked up, all eyes were on him and Candace. He slowly exhaled and handed the joint over to Candace, who took it calmly and slowly brought it to her lips for a drag. She held it up in the air.

"Are you guys waiting on this one?" she asked nervously.

Everyone silently stared until Bobby broke the silence. "We all watched y'all pull in with your vehicle and get the presidential cabin. We thought you might be snooty or higher class than the rest of us. Y'all were the *last* ones in this campground we ever thought would be potheads," he said.

Laughter erupted around them, and Carter and Candace embarrassingly laughed along with them.

"See, hun. They heard your whining all the way here," Candace laughed.

Carter rolled his eyes, sighing heavily.

"Yeah, this was a complete surprise," Evette said. "We didn't think you would be down for the whole atmosphere we got going on in here."

"Not going to lie. At first, we thought we had walked in on an orgy," Candace laughed nervously.

Evette and the rest of the group cackled with laughter.

"You would have never guessed that a classy resort like this one would throw these kinds of adult parties, but the owner is pretty cool," Carl said. "I guess since they legalized marijuana, they couldn't fight the fate of the campers blazing up. And then we thought we were busted when you two rolled up in here," he laughed. "VIP clients and all. Name's Carl," he said with one hand holding a joint and the other extended out to shake.

"Oh, I wish, Carl. But, alas, we are just normal non-rich people who got saddled with the wrong campground when our other one caught on fire from a pothead employee," Carter replied as he shook hands.

"Smith Mountain Lake Campgrounds?" Bobby asked.

"Yeah, that's the one, sons a bitches," Carter replied.

"That explains it. The owner likes to treat the guests who have to settle for this resort like royalty. They give them the best cabins with a discounted price so they'll return the next year.

Besides, with all the bad publicity and rumors of this place, they need all the help they can get to keep it afloat."

Candace blinked a couple of times, recalling the conversation they had with Keith the day before. "What do you mean by rumors? And bad publicity?" she asked.

"Well, there was the incident with a drowning that was the most damaging. They normally have the resort shut down during off-peak season because there's just not enough staff to make sure it runs smoothly due to inclement weather all the time," Bobby replied.

"What happened with the drowning?" Carter asked, concerned.

"Well, the official story is some kids snuck onto the resort to have themselves a party for New Year's Eve. Had a bunch of drugs and alcohol with them, and thought it was a great idea to go swimming. One of the boys smacked his head on the lakebed when he dove from a boulder and drowned," Bobby replied.

"What's the unofficial story?" Carter asked.

"Mikey was selling cabins on the side when the park was closed to get extra money for his own alcohol and drug problem. The kids paid him, and even though no one outright said it, he was partying with them. Rumor has it he was the one who pulled the boy's body from the water and tried giving him CPR," Bobby replied.

"Oh, that is awful," Candace murmured.

"To keep it out of the papers and to keep it from going against the resort's reputation, Patrick, that's the owner, ponied up money in a quiet settlement. The families had no proof it was the fault of the resort, but it wouldn't stop them from filing a wrongful death suit against Patrick, especially since it could have very well been Mikey partying with them," Carl added.

"As far as reputation-wise and lawsuits, Yeah that's it," Bobby Joe replied. "Unless..."

"Unless what?" Candace prodded.

"Depends on you and whether you're willing to believe in ghosts or not," Carl laughed. "Mikey can rattle on about some Native American ghosts and the family that originally owned this place back in the 1800s like he was there when it all happened."

Bobby laughed along with Carl. "That drunk bastard will spout off some crazy shit at times. Sometimes, I think he smokes too much weed or is dipping into ole Nathaniel's stash down the ways."

***

"How do you know so much about this area? The people who lived here and all?" Joshua asked.

"Along with this book here, I found other books. Journals of the people that lived here in the 1800s on a plantation they formed," Mikey replied.

"Who were they?" Isobel asked.

"They were the Ingrams," Mikey replied. "The father was James, the mother Anne, and the two younger kids were William and Isobel," Mikey replied. "They had two older daughters as well, named Nancy and Jane, who had already come of age and moved out."

"What happened to them?" one of the kids asked.

"Well, no one is sure of what happened to James and Anne. Other than the family feud between her and her brother, there were no reasons to explain how or why they died," Mikey explained. "However, there were rumors in town that Jeremiah could have possibly murdered them."

"Do you know what really happened?" Isobel asked.

"According to the county's record office, a death certificate was issued stating that James and Anne had died in an accidental fire that had burned their house down to the stone foundation," Mikey explained.

"But do you know what *really* happened?" Isobel asked.

"Yes, Isobel. I do know," Mikey replied. "James kept a journal, and for a few weeks, he was completely grief-stricken after William and Lizzy had passed away from what they were told was cholera. He blamed Jeremiah and Jeremiah's wife Ketia, along with Gini Raven."

"What happened to the kids? Did they really die of cholera?" one of the children asked.

"Not according to their older sister, Jane," Mikey replied. "When her mother sent for her, Jane arrived without hesitation to find both Lizzy and William really sick. When she examined them, she noticed that they had evidence of poisoning in their fingernails. However, none of the doctors knew what arsenic poisoning looked like then, so they didn't know how to treat them properly. They expected Gini would, since she was a native."

"So what happened after the kids died?" Isobel asked.

"Strange things began to happen. Animals began disappearing everywhere, both wild and domesticated. At first, no one noticed and thought maybe the wildlife was migrating because of their presence. However, hunting started becoming a problem, and people's cattle, goats, chickens, and such had been disappearing more than here and there. So, the county sheriff got involved and began investigating."

"Who was doing it all?" one of the kids asked.

"Well, the sheriff had spent weeks tracking down every lead that he was given from townspeople. There wasn't anything concrete to go on. The last person he needed to speak with was James. It had been a while since he had checked in on him after his children had died. So, the sheriff stopped by their house and was deeply disturbed by what he witnessed."

"What?!" the kids shouted in unison.

"The house had been burned to the ground, and all around the outside were animal heads on stakes. The missing cows, goats, deer, everything, all staked down," Mikey explained.

"And James and Anne had been in the house when it burned down?" Joshua asked nervously.

"They found James and Anne both inside the house with both of them missing their hearts," Mikey replied.

"How did the kids die?" Isobel asked

"Well, they dug up their bodies and performed an autopsy. They found two different things. One, the kids had been fed arsenic like Jane had thought. Most likely, they had eaten pokeberries, which look like elderberries but are poisonous."

"And what was the second thing?" Joshua asked while gulping.

"They were missing their hearts," Mikey replied.

"So, a Raven Mocker stole their hearts?" one of the kids asked.

"That's what Jane Anne believed," Mikey replied, holding up another journal. "Jane had it in her head that Ketia had been poisoning the children, and Gini knew of the poisoning and continued to let it happen. Once she asked around about the kind of person Gini was, she sought out Cherokee natives to speak about what kind of evil Gini could have been. They told her that she was a raven mocker."

"What happened to Jane Anne?" Joshua asked.

"They sent her away for being crazy and believing in the natives' myths and accusing Ketia of witchcraft," Mikey replied.

"Do you believe what she said was true? Do you think it was a Raven Mocker?" Isobel asked.

Mikey stared intently at all of the kids before replying to them.

"It's a ghost story, guys," he chuckled. "Who is ready for some s'mores?"

All of the kids cheered as Mikey began to pass out the bags of chocolates and marshmallows. He handed out sticks for them to use to roast the marshmallows on. He then helped them prepare their graham crackers with their chocolates.

Isobel nudged Joshua while Mikey was busy making their s'mores. "We need to leave now!" she hissed in a whisper.

***

"You mean to tell me, Carter, that you knew what story he was going to tell and didn't think it was a bit too much for kids to hear for ghost stories?" Candace huffed, crossing her arms. "Isobel is six and is already going on about an imaginary friend's family burning alive."

"I didn't see anything wrong with the story. They watch horror movies, for God's sake!" Carter retorted.

"The story has some legitimacy to it. Mikey did serious research on the area. He has been using the story for campouts for years now. No one has ever had a problem with it," Carl replied.

"Well, I do. What kind of idiot tells a story like that to little kids? It would cause nightmares!" Candace fumed.

"Chill your motor," Bobby replied reassuringly. "He will make sure he tells them it isn't a real story. Most of the kids have fun with the ghost stories."

"Did he ever find out the names of the family members that perished?" Carter asked.

"Yeah. The father's name was James Ingram. His wife was Anne, and his two children were Isobel and William," Carl replied, taking a swig from his beer.

"Wait," Candace said, holding her hand up and shaking her head. "Did you say Isobel and William?" she asked.

"Yeah," Carl replied.

Candace was quiet for a moment. "You told them the story about earlier, didn't you?!" Candace demanded of Carter.

"What story?" Carter asked, confused.

"Isobel's imaginary friends," Candace huffed. "Those are the names of the imaginary friends that our Lizzy told us about earlier. She even mentioned everyone dying in a horrible fire."

"You're kidding, right?" Kevin asked. "Because that's some freaky ass shit right there. You're just pulling our leg. Ha-ha, they thought we were stuck up, so let's get them back. Hardy har har. Let's make them think our kids' imaginary friends are ghosts."

***

"So, it is close to midnight, and the moon is highest in the sky," Mikey said as he pulled out the spell book. Who wants to see if we can summon a Raven Mocker?"

None of the children raised their hands. They all sat quietly amongst themselves, too afraid to speak out against it.

"I want to go home," Isobel sobbed quietly. "She will kill us like she did them."

Mikey opened the book and began to speak in the Cherokee language as he raised his hand to the sky like he had done so many times. The wind began to blow, and lightning crackled in the sky as all of the kids began to scream.

"Joshua, we have to go! Lizzy and William told us to run!" she said.

Mikey continued to recite from the book, oblivious to nature around him. The wind blew harder with whispers trailing on it. And then an eerie laughter began to drift in the woods.

"Come on! Let's go!" Isobel pleaded, standing up and pulling on Joshua's arm.

Her grip slipped, and she stumbled backward, tripping on a tree root that jutted from the ground. She landed with a thud, tearing open her hand and knee. She cried out, and Mikey stopped reading and ran to her side to see how badly she had cut herself. The ground began to tremble as the sound of a raven echoed in the trees above them. The sky began to cloud, and the bright moon that drifted above them was soon covered, canceling out what little light they had to see around the campfire.

"Let's get back to camp before it pours the rain," Mikey said, helping Isobel to her feet.

All of the kids clambered to their feet, frightened, and ran to Mikey's side, ready for him to lead the way out of the woods. As the lightning struck, it illuminated Mikey's face, and Joshua saw that Mikey was just as scared as the rest of them were.

"What did you read!?" Joshua demanded.

"Nothing! It was just a prayer for peace!" Mikey replied as they hurried out of the forest.

Isobel whimpered as the sound of the raven crackled through the air like thunder. "She is here. And she will eat our hearts as we lie lifeless among the dead."

Chapter Eight

JOY AND BILL CONTINUED rolling joints on their rolling tray, passing them out to the parents, who lit them up and partied on them. A small tremor shook the lodge they all sat in. Everyone stared at the ceiling as the lights swayed back and forth from the strings that held them in place.

"I can't just sit here anymore. Does anyone know exactly where Mikey does that campout? It's late, and the kids need to get in bed," Candace asked.

Carter lit up one of the joints and passed it to her. "Just relax, babe. Everything is fine. You don't have to worry about the kids."

Everyone laughed around her, which just pissed her off even more.

"I am so glad that their father is worried about them. Lord forbid he have any excuse to go see his kids other than sit around and get stoned and drunk," Candace fumed.

"You're a bit bitchy tonight," Carter laughed.

"Take a chill pill and relax. Mikey should be bringing them back soon," Evette offered.

Lightning struck outside, and thunder boomed through the night sky.

"That's it. I am going to get them. It's about to storm," Candace huffed as she opened the doors to the lodge.

As she peered outside, she could see Mikey herding all of the kids to the lodge while carrying Isobel in his arms.

"Kids are coming! Put that shit out!" Candace hissed.

She ran out to meet them and noticed Isobel had been crying and saw the blood on her leg and hand.

"What the hell happened to her?" Candace demanded as she snatched Isobel out of his arms.

"She tripped and fell," Mikey replied.

"How did she trip and fall? Weren't you watching her?" Candace hissed.

"I have twenty kids with me tonight, and only one got scratched from falling. Cut me a break," Mikey sneered.

Candace glared at him and turned to Isobel. "What happened, sweetie?" she asked.

"I got scared, and it was dark, and I tripped over something," Isobel whimpered.

"Of course, you were scared. He was down there all night telling you a bunch of scary stories like a complete and utter imbecile," Candace replied. She stood and faced Mikey. "Did you really think those stories were appropriate for little kids?"

"Your husband didn't object to them when I told him the same stories and said it's what I tell them at the campout," Mikey snapped back.

Candace turned her glare to Carter, who now huffed and stared at the ceiling, waiting for her to attack.

"Yeah, and he is an ass too!" she hissed.

"Yes, and like Carl said, he always reminds them it's *just a story!* No wonder people think we have sticks up our ass or are stuck up," Carter seethed back at her. "Now, instead of lashing out at everyone, why don't you go get a bandage for her knee and hand?"

"Where's the first aid kit?" Candace asked Evette.

"There's one over here in the office," Evette replied and led Candace, carrying Isobel away from the crowd.

The kids ran to their parents and huddled closely, grabbing whatever they could to cling on as if their lives depended on it. Carter turned to Mikey while pinching the bridge of his nose.

"You told them the same story you told me, right?" Carter asked, annoyed.

"Yes, only difference is I showed them props. A mask I made and a book I created to make it feel authentic," Mikey admitted. "When it started thundering and lightning, it was right at the end of the campout when I was reading to them."

"What were you reading to them?" Carter asked.

"To make the experience more creepy and scary, I looked up a Cherokee prayer. I recite the prayer to the campers, and they think it's an evil spell," Mikey replied. "Look, I didn't even know it was supposed to rain tonight. The thunder and lightning spooked them. Most kids love it. Their parents bring them here for Halloween, and some of them even attend the campout. There is nothing out of the ordinary with what happened tonight except for the storm."

"Let me see the book," Carter demanded, holding his hand out for it.

Mikey dug through the backpack and pulled out the buck hide spell book he had created. He handed the book over to Carter, who immediately began to look through it.

"Nice rendition of the Raven Mocker in here," Carter complimented. "It looks almost identical to the painting we saw when we went diving."

"Diving?" Carl asked.

"Raven Mocker?" Jimmy asked.

"Mikey paints?" Bobby asked.

"What's a Raven Mocker?!" Jimmy demanded.

Just as he spoke the words, the caws of a raven sounded around the lodge as if one was swooping around the building and over its roof.

"A Raven Mocker is a Cherokee fable about a witch that only medicine men can see," Mikey began. "They wait for the sick or dying to be left alone so they can come in and eat their hearts. The only way to kill one is to figure out that they are a Raven Mocker."

"Well, if they look like that, it won't be too fucking hard," Jimmy replied.

"They don't look like that," Mikey said. "They look like you and me. They used to take on the shape of the elders so people would trust them."

"How do you know so much about all this?" Carl asked.

"I go to the library in my spare time and read," Mikey replied.

"Shit, Mikey, you know how to read?" Bobby laughed.

"Mikey, what's this say?" Carter asked, pointing at the Cherokee words.

"That's the Cherokee prayer I was telling you about," Mikey replied.

"Who gave it to you?" Carter asked.

"Why, Ozell did," Mikey replied.

"You mean that old coot's wife down there gave you this?" Carter demanded.

"She's not at all as bad as you think she would be. I ran into her one day at the library, and she apologized on behalf of Nate being a dick to me all the time," Mikey said. "She even apologized for what happened to that camper when it snowed that year because Nate had run him off."

"How does she know what this says, though?" Carter asked.

"Her mom was a Cherokee princess," Mikey replied. "She grew up learning the Cherokee language alongside the English language."

"And you are absolutely sure that the prayer she gave you is an actual prayer," Carter asked again.

Mikey looked around among them all. "I don't know. I put my faith and trust in her."

"This has the word Asgina in it," Carter stated, showing Mikey the part of the prayer. "You said *Asgina* means witch, right?" he asked.

"Right, this prayer is a protection prayer. It's Halloween, and I don't know about you, but I believe in all the legends of Samhain. The dead walk the veil tonight, both good and evil," Mikey replied.

"Someone pull up one of those Google Translate things on their phone," Carter said. "Or Google Cherokee translations."

"Alright, I have something pulled up," Jimmy said, holding his phone up.

"*noir Asgina manger oyohusa gavldi Udanvdo alisdayvdi Ama gvindi Igohidaquu gesv Agilvgis Adayotaedi Ayolis Udanvgalvda Unilohisdi Nulinigvgv Strenuous Itsula Alenidasdi Nulisdv,*" Carter read and spelled to Jimmy.

Jimmy dropped his phone to the ground and pointed at it, frightened. "That ain't no prayer."

Joy reached down and picked up the phone, adjusting her glasses to read what was on the screen. "Black witch eat While dying sleep heart is food I live forever Sisters Share Children pure Gather strength We live soon…"

Evette emerged with Candace from the office and led the children off to a corner to keep them from hearing anything else from the rest of the adults.

"That is not a prayer, you dumbass!" Candace shrieked. "That is a summoning! A summoning that you read on a powerful day during a full moon!"

Candace yanked the book out of Carter's hand and flipped through the pages, landing on the painting of the Raven Mocker.

"You said you saw this painting?" Candace asked, turning to Carter.

"Yeah, when we went diving at Devil's Claw, we found a house that had a painting in it of one. It was the house that was Gini Raven's, the local medicine woman back in the 1800s," Carter replied.

"And you said that Raven Mockers can take the face of anyone to pass off as normal, right?" Candace asked Mikey.

"Yeah, that's what legend says," Mikey replied.

"What if… what if it wasn't Ozell you spoke to at the library and instead it was… I can't believe I am asking this… What if it was a Raven Mocker?" Candace asked. "Had you ever spoken to Ozell before then?"

Mikey hesitated. "Well, not really. But it's just a legend. A myth. I didn't think they were real."

"Until today, we hadn't heard of it, let alone believed in it," Candace groaned.

"I think we should kick his ass," Jimmy yelled.

"Yeah," some of the parents chimed in.

"I have read this, I don't know how many times, to the kids on this day, and nothing has ever happened," Mikey refuted. "All there is is a bunch of lightning and thunder of an October storm. They aren't that unusual here. For God's sake, Carl, you live right up the damn road!"

Carl nodded. "This isn't unusual weather at all."

Carter began thinking and shushing everyone around him. He paced around piecing everything together from the last couple of days.

"We need to go back to that place underwater," Carte said.

"It's too dark to do that. We would be live bait for every single one of them, pontoon boat size catfish that we ran into last time," Mikey refuted.

"We felt a tremor not too long ago. What if that tremor broke something open?" Carter asked.

"Well, we can't necessarily shove whatever came out back in!" Mikey protested.

"But what if we could find whatever it was that trapped them in there, to begin with?" Carter asked.

The wind stopped blowing, and an eerie quiet settled across the valley. Everyone walked to the lodge's front porch, then out into the grass and peered up into the sky. The full moon was out from behind the cloud coverage and was the color of blood. An eerie laughter could be heard as if it were coming from everywhere at once, and then the sounds of the raven swooping down and cawing echoed throughout the night like a megaphone.

Wolves howled in the distance, and the leaves on the floor of the campground kicked up into the air like a tornado was trying to funnel right in front of them. The sounds of nature sprang to life as the wildlife cried out in the night.

A burst of electrostatic energy sent everyone standing, toppling to the ground. As Carter landed on his back, the air was knocked from his lungs, and he gasped hard to breathe. Everything grew hazy in his eyesight, and it was like a bomb had gone off because all he could hear was a ringing in his ears.

Finally, he was able to breathe in deeply and sat up carefully as everyone rushed to Bill's side. Carter sluggishly climbed to his feet and made it to the circle that was around the old man. Bill lay on the ground, clutching his chest and gasping for air.

"He must have had the breath knocked out of him like I did," Carter mumbled.

"My heart," Bill groaned. "I think it's a heart attack."

The screeching and cawing sound of the raven was loud and circling the group.

"I don't think it's a heart attack," Carter whispered.

"It's the Raven Mocker!" Joshua yelled from the door of the lodge. "It's eating his heart!"

A loud, raucous roar echoed through the valley, and then all fell silent.

"Bill?" Joy cried. "Bill?!"

Carter turned back to see Joy shaking Bill. Bill wasn't moving or answering her. Carter knelt beside him and placed his fingers on his carotid artery to see if there was a pulse. He sighed heavily and hung his head.

"I'm sorry, Joy," Carter said. "He's gone."

"No!" Joy cried out. "No!"

She stood to her feet and glared at Mikey. "This is your fault!"

She pounded her fists on his chest as she heaved sobs. Mikey grabbed her by the wrists to stop her from striking him and then pulled her into his chest and gave her a bear hug.

"This isn't Mikey's fault," Isobel said.

Everyone turned, surprised that the children were here to see the dead body lying in the grass.

"Honey, go back inside with the rest of the kids," Candace sweetly said.

"This isn't Mikey's fault," Isobel said. "It's our fault."

"What are you talking about?" Carter asked.

"We are the descendants of the Cherokee tribe that Gini Raven attacked," Isobel replied.

"We are her unfinished business, and my blood released her."

"How do you know this, honey?" Candace asked.

"Because the Chief of the tribe was our great great great great great grandfather. He told me. The Raven Mocker terrorized their village until they left after losing many of their people."

The ground began to tremble again, and trees started to topple everywhere.

"She is a spirit Raven Mocker!" Isobel yelled out above the roaring winds. "We have to destroy what binds her here!"

"Everyone, get inside!" Mikey yelled as he turned to run in the opposite direction. "It's a tornado!"

"Where are you going?" Carter hollered back.

"To get help!" Mikey replied.

Mikey ran off toward the property line that led toward Ozell and Nathaniel's house.

"Everyone inside! Now!" Carter yelled.

"What about Bill?" Joy cried, refusing to leave his side.

Carter pried her from his body. "We can't help him, Joy."

Everyone scrambled to the lodge as the winds picked up, and Carter dragged Joy kicking and screaming behind him. He began to struggle with each step until they made it inside the building. It took all of the men's force to shut the doors of the lodge as the wind howled and swirled around the building. The wooden slats of the roof began to rumble, and a few here and there were kicked off and picked up by the twister outside.

"We're all going to die!" Evette screamed.

The lights began to flicker on and off until everything went dark.

***

Emergency lights kicked on in the lodge, and everyone looked around to make sure all were still there.

"Is everyone ok?" Carter asked.

The storm had passed, and the kids hunkered with the adults, whimpering and crying in fear.

"We are all ok," Bobby replied.

"Good, now let's get the fuck out of here," Carter said as he opened the door to the lodge.

Their eyes swept across the campgrounds, and everyone gasped. Vehicles were tumbled across the fields with trees and debris covering them. The whole camp was one huge wreck.

"That's going to be pretty hard to do," Bobby murmured.

"Is there an emergency kit here with lights or something?" Carter asked Evette.

"Yes, one second," Evette said, running off to the back of the lodge. She returned shortly with a box.

Carter opened the box and handed out lanterns to everyone. Everyone lit their lanterns, and the room lit up brighter than what the emergency lights offered.

"Bobby, Carl, let's try and find a vehicle that the storm didn't flip," Carter said. "Everyone else, stay here."

The three of them left the building and began maneuvering through the campground to see if there were any vehicles that the tornado hadn't harmed.

"Isn't that your truck, Bobby?" Carl asked, pointing across the field.

"Yes, it is!" Bobby chuckled in delight.

The three of them began to jog down to the truck that didn't have a single scratch on it. Bobby jumped in the driver's seat and hit the switch on the truck.

"What the fuck?" Bobby asked.

"What's wrong?" Carter asked.

"The fucking battery is dead!" Bobby exclaimed.

"Pop the hood," Carter replied.

Bobby popped the hood, and Carter handed his lantern off to Carl so he could get the latch open. He grabbed his lantern back once he had the hood propped up and just stared.

"Either you have a massive rat problem or..."

Bobby jumped out of the driver's seat and ran around the front of the truck to see what Carter was talking about. Under the hood, the cables were slashed, and there was a huge claw mark through the motor. Oil and water dripped from the holes.

"Son of a bitch!" Bobby hissed.

The main lights for the park tried to come back on.

"At least the power is coming back," Carter stated, relieved.

One by one, the dusk-to-dawn lights exploded in sparks.

"I sure hope Mikey gets some help," Carter murmured.

Chapter Nine

"RAVEN MOCKERS!" Ozell screamed out in her sleep, bolting awake in a cold sweat.

She looked around her room, breathing heavily as if she were still caught up in the nightmare she had been trapped in. Growing up, her mother had taught her the ways of the Cherokee. Her grandmother was full-blooded Cherokee, making her a quarter Cherokee, and she knew that the dream was an omen.

Ozell reached over to wake up Nate, but her hand met an empty bed. Still groggy and sleep-ridden, she threw her legs over the side of the bed and stood carefully so she wouldn't topple over. She donned her night robe over her sleeping gown and walked to the restroom to relieve herself. Her breath hung in the air of the cold house, and as soon as she was done with her business, she made her way through the house to get the fire going again.

She checked around in the house to see if Nate had passed out drunk somewhere, but each room she walked to was empty, without another soul to be found. She walked to the fireplace and tossed some wood pieces in on the burning embers. She picked up the bellows and gave it a few pumps under the wood toward the embers, and the fire breathed to life, crackling and popping the newly furnished wood.

She warmed her hands above the fire and looked up to the mantle to see that Nate had left a note. It stated that he couldn't sleep, so he went night fishing down at the lake. She rolled her eyes and huffed loudly. He was always sneaking out at night to go hunting or fishing, saying he couldn't sleep. The grandfather's clock in the hall began to chime, and she counted each time to figure out that it was midnight.

Ozell walked over to her grandmother's old rocking chair, picked up the shawl from the seat, wrapped it around herself, and sat down. After her nightmare, there was no way she was able to go back to sleep alone in the house. It felt so real. Her mother had told her about the Cherokee stories of why her people fled this land. It was one reason she was so eager to purchase the property when it came up for sale many moons ago. It was her rightful heritage. She felt at home in these woods.

But something didn't sit right with her tonight. It felt off. She couldn't put her finger on it. Nate's strange behavior lately, paired with the nightmare and the eerie feeling in the air, it was as if magic was afoot, and her mama taught her all about magic.

A blast of cold air shivered her to the bone, and once again, she went to the fireplace to poke around with the wood to get it warmer in the house. It was supposed to be mild tonight with a forecast in the sixties, but her thermostat hanging on the wall clearly showed freezing temperatures in the house. She rubbed her arms and picked up the wood poker to move the wood around in the fireplace so it would catch fire evenly. The fire leapt up, and she once again tried to warm her hands above the flames. She lost her balance and caught the metal grate to keep herself from tumbling into the fire, and a sharp pain shot through her hands.

Ozell cursed silently to herself as she quickly released the grate and turned toward the kitchen to run some cold water over her hand. She dried her hand off and reached into the cabinet to retrieve the burn salve she had made from various herbs in the garden. The cooling sensation of the herbs wrapped her hand, and she sighed in relief.

. She walked back to the living room, wrapping her hand in some gauze, and sat back down in the rocking chair to wait for Nate to return from his night out. No sooner had she sat down in her chair than there was a loud crash from the kitchen. Upon investigating the crash, she found that her jar of salve had fallen from the counter and smashed on the floor.

"Now, how did that happen?" Ozell asked herself, placing her hands on her hips. "I could have sworn it was sitting in the middle of the counter so it wouldn't accidentally fall off."

She grabbed a dish towel from the stove handle, carefully got down on her hands and knees, and pushed all of the glass and salve into the center of the floor. She picked it all up in the dish towel and carried it to the trash can, tossing the remnants away.

"I'll have to make more tomorrow, I suppose," she grunted.

Behind her, she heard a clicking noise like nails tapping the floor. She turned around and squinted in the dark of the house. As her eyes scanned each room, she thought she saw a shadow slip behind her bedroom door. She flipped the light switch on in the living room, and the bulb immediately blew.

"Confounded bulbs never last," she hissed as she carefully walked to her room.

She ran her hand on the inside of her wall and flipped the switch on. She gasped as the light illuminated the room brightly before popping like the one in the living room. But that wasn't what made her gasp.

"Raven Mocker," she hissed as she quickly grabbed her oil lantern on the table and lit it with a match.

She adjusted the wick, brought the lantern up to shoulder height, and peered again into her room. It was empty.

"My nightmare must be making me see shit," she muttered.

As she turned around, she caught a glimpse of the long arm with talons as fingers slipped behind the wall that led into the living room. Her breathing quickened, and she swallowed hard as she walked cautiously toward the area.

She heard scratching this time as if nails were being dragged across the hardwood flooring.

As she rounded the wall to enter the room, a taloned hand thrust into her chest, squeezing her heart. Her eyes widened as she came face-to-face with the sinister creature she had grown up hearing about.

"I see you," she seethed. "And you know what that means!"

The creature hissed as it released her, and she fell backward. Ozell began chanting the chant her mother taught her to ward off the Raven Mockers, and a guttural laugh erupted from the creature.

"You cannot kill what is already dead, foolish muddy water," the creature hissed.

"And you cannot kill what sees you!" Ozell yelled back as she continued to chant in Cherokee.

The creature roared and burst into dozens of ravens that squawked and cawed as they swarmed her. Ozell put her hands up to her face so they couldn't claw her eyes out. The birds swarmed above her before fleeing the house, breaking every window as they did. Ozell quickly knelt on the floor and covered her face and head so the glass wouldn't cut her. Silence fell over the house.

She ran to the window and watched as the swarm of birds flew off into the sky, quickly darkening.

"You have to save them," a voice whispered in the house.

Ozell quickly turned to see where the voice was coming from. Two small children emerged from the dark shadows.

"Who are you?" Ozell demanded. "Why are you in my house?"

"You can see us because you have an old spirit. You can hear us because you are of Cherokee blood. You must save the rest of them before the Asginas take their souls and once again roam the earth," the little girl stated.

The kitchen began to freeze with frost as the children walked closer to her. Each of their footsteps left ice in their wake as they walked into the light of the fireplace.

"I have seen your faces before," Ozell murmured. "Where have I seen your faces before?"

"The Asginas took our life force long ago when we owned this land," the little boy replied. "They will kill everyone!"

"How do I stop what is already dead?" Ozell asked breathlessly and frightened.

"Find the one they call Joshua. He has something that belongs to you," the little girl said as they slowly disappeared before her eyes.

Ozell ran to the back door and slipped her mud boots on as well as her winter coat.

"I'm going crazy!" she exclaimed. "I have to find Nate."

As she stepped out the door, the chill of the air hit her face and startled her. She was about to turn around and forget it all, just drift back off to sleep and wake up from the nightmare for real. However, she saw the children again off near the forest line. She knew they wanted her to follow them. She grabbed the outside lantern and quickly lit it before shutting the door behind her and heading out into the cold night.

She took the stairs carefully so she wouldn't slip on the frost and walked through the dewy grass toward the edge of the woods. Her nose burned from the cold winds that hit her like walls of ice. She could feel the evil that drifted in the air as she hustled past the barn in their backyard and into the woods.

The voices of the children were but whispers now that she strained to make out what was being said. All she could do was follow the sound of their voices into the black of the night.

It wasn't long before she heard actual talking and then crying. She saw the glow of a campfire in the thicket and knew it must be Mikey doing his campout with the children. She had run into Mikey a few times at the library and offered her apologies for what had happened to the one camper during that bad blizzard a few years back. She had long been told he was a drunk, just like her Nate, but when she met him, he was sober. The whole incident must have set him straight.

Ozell hurried to the campfire, but by the time she reached the fire, they had left. The caws and shrieks of birds echoed around her. She spun in a circle, trying to see them against the dark sky. The moon had been obliterated by whatever storm was moving in. She didn't have much time to find Nate and get him home before the storm hit.

As she walked, she chanted in Cherokee the warding prayer using every ounce of belief and might in each word. The cries of the birds grew louder above her, and she began to run mindlessly through the thicket of the trees, veering from the paths she was used to. One of the birds swooped down and knocked her lantern from her hand, and it hit the ground with a crash, burning out.

She stopped in her tracks and screamed with all of her energy, "Anagalisgv!" and light erupted around her.

The ravens shrieked and shied away from the light that emanated from her core.

"I am the descendant of Woya Echota Starr! You have no power over me, Asgina!"

Silence befell the woods as the light died and the birds had disappeared.

She quickly returned to her sprint, trying to find some sort of pathway that would lead her to Devil's Claw. Before long, a horrible stench wafted through the air, and she had to stop to catch her breath without heaving up her stomach. As she walked closer to the smell, she could hear the water of the lake lapping the shore and knew she had reached the lake. As she broke through the thicket of the bushes and onto the sandy shore, she gasped in terror. There were animals everywhere, strung up and gutted like some madman had been hunting in the area.

"Nathaniel?" she whispered. "Did he do this?"

Raven Mockers were unable to possess people, so she knew it wasn't the Asgina persuading his strange behavior.

"My poor, Nate," she whispered. "How am I going to fix this?"

Her foot kicked a bottle lying on the ground. She picked it up and gave it a whiff. It was one of Nate's, but it smelled different than his normal hooch. She gave it a small taste, and her eyes grew wild.

"Why is there peyote in this?" she wondered. "He knows better than to take peyote. He learned his lesson many years ago when he thought he would make a mash from my cacti I had growing."

She gave a quick glance around the area, looking for any evidence that he may have been here recently. A shadowy figure stepped behind a tree as she scanned behind her.

"Nate!" she called out. "Is that you? Don't be afraid. It's Ozell!"

She walked toward where she had seen the shadow. A faint voice replied, but she couldn't make it out through the wind that was ruffling the trees. She heard the scurrying of feet through the leaves and saw the shadowy figure dart toward the other side of the lake.

"Nate, you can't swim in these temperatures. It's freezing out, and you will die! The peyote is making you think you are seeing things!" Ozell called out as she tried to track the shadow from the shoreline.

She couldn't let him get in the water. He would die of hypothermia before they even reached the house. Thorny briar bushes reached out from the sides of the shoreline and caught her legs and nightgown, tearing them and shredding her legs with small, stinging scrapes.

"Dammit," she hissed. "Come on, Nate. Let's get home! I have what you need to take to come down off the peyote."

She walked the shoreline, watching for the shadow, when she caught another glimpse of it. It darted out into the water a ways ahead of her.

"Nate! No!" she called out.

She ran up the shore to find something odd. She looked behind her and then in front of her. There was a land bridge that led out into the middle of the lake, where a cabin-type house stood.

"No fucking way," Ozell murmured.

"I am here, Ozell," a voice called from across the lake.

Ozell cautiously made her way across the land bridge and to the cabin that she had never before seen in her life.

"Maybe the peyote dab I had is making me trip?" she told herself. "We are both going to die out here tonight because of that stupid bastard."

Ozell carefully stepped up onto the porch of the cabin and cautiously entered the dwelling. Candles were lit all around the cabin. A painting of a Raven Mocker hung on the wall, and bottles of herbs and concoctions littered the counters and tables. She picked one of the bottles up and took a whiff of it.

"Peyote," she said as she gagged from the smell. "Where the hell did all of this come from?"

Even though the cabin looked as if someone might live there, it also looked like it had been abandoned for years. Spider webs and dust covered every nook and cranny of the place. A raven was mounted on the wall above the hearth.

"That's an unusual mount," she mumbled as she peered closer at the bird.

The bird blinked, and she jumped back, stumbling into the table with all the bottles of herbs. One by one, they dropped to the floor and shattered around her.

A woman began laughing, and Ozell looked around, trying to find the face that the laugh belonged to. The laugh increased in pitch and sounded sinister and maniacal.

"Who are you!?" Ozell demanded. "Show yourself!"

The pitch of the laugh changed from a high to a low, dark, reverberating sound. It was menacing, almost evil.

"Show yourself, Asgina!" Ozell demanded, her voice quivering with fright.

A piercing shriek erupted behind her, bringing with it a torrential wind that sent papers flying around the room. Ozell knelt and covered her ears as the sound surrounded her. She closed her eyes and began chanting her prayer, but it only seemed to make the shriek worsen.

Suddenly, as soon as it had started, it stopped. Ozell slowly removed her hands from her ears and opened her eyes. When she turned around, a young Native American woman with long, flowing raven black hair stood staring at her. The rest of the world had fallen away, and the only sound Ozell could hear was the beating of her own frantic heart.

"Who are you?" she whispered.

The woman opened her mouth to speak, but the only sound that came out was the sound of a flock of ravens attacking prey. A large raven head emerged from her mouth, peeling back the flesh of her face. One taloned hand after another with wings attached to the shoulder emerged, and the body of the woman began to rip in half as the rest of the creature emerged.

"It is you," Ozell hissed. "Gini Raven, the Raven Mocker of Ingram plantation."

"I am reborn from the heart of the old man," Gini garbled through her beak.

"Well, you won't live that much longer, for I have seen your true face," Ozell hissed.

The creature laughed in a deep, garbled tone.

"You cannot kill me, granddaughter of Woya Echota Starr. You do not have what keeps me grounded to this plain."

"No, but I know where it is," Ozell sneered. "And I will put you to rest before you bring any of the other Asginas back with you!"

The creature opened its mouth, and a black hand emerged, shooting quickly into Ozell's face. Ozell held the hand, struggling to keep it from entering her.

"Give it up, muddy water," Gini grunted. "Your blood isn't strong enough to thwart the claw of the Raven Mocker."

Ozell continued to struggle as the hand pried her mouth open and began to slip down inside her body.

"Raven Mockers cannot possess people. You are correct. But as you said, you are not an ordinary person. You are the granddaughter of a medicine man. And we all know medicine men take the shape of spirit animals."

Ozell began to shrink and transform. Her hands turned into wings, and her face transformed into a bird head. Once the Raven Mocker was through, Ozell had become a dove. Before Gini could grab her, she flew out through the door and into the air of the night.

"Run away, muddy water," Gini sneered as she slowly took the shape of an old woman.

Gini walked out of the cabin and to the shore of the lake, peering in to see her new face.

"I wear you well, muddy water," Gini said as she stared at the face of Ozell reflecting back to her in the water.

The Diary of Jane Anne Ingram

May 1, 1845
Dear Diary,

I came home to visit today. After my betrothal to the Robinson boy, Thomas, I moved in with him at his farm and have had very little communication with my family. He feels it is for the best, considering how my uncle tries to force my mom into giving him her land at nearly every dinner. I was beside myself to learn that both William and Lizzie were sick. Mother fears it to be cholera, but one glance at their nailbeds confirmed what I feared. They had been fed the poison berries from the surrounding fields. Mother doesn't allow them to eat berries, and neither does Father. I know it is our wench of an aunt, Ketia, poisoning my dearest siblings. But what can I do? It would be mere accusations, and the sheriff wouldn't hear of the sort since my mother's brother owns the church everyone attends. I sent word by messenger to my husband that I would stay to tend to the children. He arrived by carriage by morning light to assist around the farm. Some days, I can see why I fell madly in love with him.

Mother and Father haven't heard a word from my oldest sister, Nancy. It seems she received a job as the local schoolmarm. Once we left… we never looked back.

May 4, 1845
Dear Diary,

William passed away this morning in his sleep, and I am afraid Lizzie isn't far behind him. I overheard our uncle and aunt fighting about some nonsense this morning. I know for a fact now that they are the culprits behind my little brother's passing. I can hardly bear to look at Lizzie while she lies lifeless in her bed, barely breathing. It breaks me apart inside.

Mother and Father set the arrangements for William's burial. I can hardly contain the heartache I feel from his passing. He was so young, so tiny, so frail. He was only four years old. What monsters take the life of a four-year-old child?!

May 6, 1845
Dear Diary,

I caught Ketia draining blood from a pinprick from Lizzie's finger into a glass. Come to think of it, as I held poor little William's hand as he took his last breaths. He, too, had pinpricks on his fingertips. I didn't think anything of it at the time. I wonder what they need the children's blood for? What kind of twisted perversion of faith have they found themselves in where they would go against the hand of God and smite their own flesh and blood? What evil have they sold their souls to?

May 10, 1845
Dear Diary,

Lizzie passed this morning, and I sobbed quietly beside her bed, holding her weak little lifeless hand. Those monsters not only took my baby brother from me, but they took my baby sister as well, and I cannot bear to think that those sweet little angels are dead while our so-called family members live. I brought my plight to God, and it seems as if he is unanswering. I am wavering in my faith because of those two wretched souls. Thomas has begged me to leave for a few days to clear my head so we can return to our own farm and tend to things, but I have no will left to move on. It is such an unfair set of events to burden my mind. Thomas promises me that justice will be sought and will prevail over the untimely deaths of my younger sibling. I hope to God he is right… because praying to God is now unthinkable…

May 14, 1845
Dear Diary,

The local sheriff just left our farm, and after I regained consciousness, I have completely fallen to pieces. Mother and Father were killed in a fire late last night, but I know it isn't true. Lizzie came to me, whispering to me the secrets of our aunt and uncle. My parents were hanged and murdered, with the fire only being a cover-up for the godless act. I know it is all over the land, and whatever evil they work with to gain control over it. I haven't told my dearest Thomas yet, but I plan to add my family's farm to the adjacent acreage we have. Those inept family members will never have the farm, not until the last breath of life has escaped my lungs. I swear in vain to God they shan't have the land that my father poured blood, sweat, and tears into.

May 20, 1845
Dear Diary,

I must be quick, for they come for me. I found my dearest husband slain in the fields at daybreak. His neck had been slit. My mother's family has told the local sheriffs that I was the one who murdered him and has been hearing voices since the departure of my sister and brother's spirits from this place. It is true. I have heard their voices, but I see them as well. They tell me the things I need to know. Whoever finds this, please bring my family's name justice. I fear it is the only way they can all make safe passage into heaven is to have their murders solved, and their murderers bear the name upon the brow of which they carry their sins. Please, I beg of you!

Chapter Ten

MIKEY SLID IN the gravel as he rounded the bend of the driveway that led to Nathaniel and Ozell's house, thudding to the ground. He scrambled to his feet and breathed through the pain coursing through his ribcage. He made it to their door and began pounding on it.

"Ozell!" Mikey called out. "Ozell! We have an emergency!"

He continued to beat on the door, but no one came to answer it.

"Fuck!" he yelled out as he bent over to catch his breath.

"I need to get to the office and call Patrick," he mumbled.

He turned on his heels and bounded down the steps from the front door and started back up the drive to the resort. His lungs burned, and his muscles ached in his legs, but he pushed through it all. He had to get help.

By the time he made it to the office, his breath was coming in short, ragged gasps. All of the years he spent drinking and partying didn't help his health years after he had stopped. He fumbled with the keys in his pocket and dropped them between the slats of the porch.

"God damn!" he yelled.

He brought up his elbow and smashed the window on the door in with all his force, shattering the glass into pieces. He reached through the window and turned the lock on the door. He pushed the door open and ran to his desk, fumbling with the handset. He tapped the hook switch a couple of times, but no bell tone came on the line. He slammed the handset down on the hook switch and then swiped everything off the desk and onto the floor.

Mikey sat down in his desk chair and rested his head in his hands.

"What the fuck am I going to do?" he asked out loud.

He peered down to see his bottom drawer slightly ajar and sighed heavily, opening it the rest of the way up. At the bottom of the drawer was a bottle of Canadian Mist he hadn't finished. He hadn't touched a drop in years, and his blood called out to the bottle at this very moment. He could feel the warmth of the liquor slip past his lips, across his tongue, and down his throat into his stomach while that warmth spread throughout the rest of his body.

With one swift movement, he heaved the bottle across the room at the wall, and it shattered, spraying liquor everywhere. The wind suddenly started to howl outside, and Mikey raced to the door to push it closed. Rocks and other debris began to pelt the outside of the office as Mikey stood with his back to the door, holding it shut.

"Why are you here?" a voice hissed at him.

Mikey jerked his head toward the dark corner of his office. "Who's there?" he demanded.

Out of the shadows, two little kids emerged.

"I know you," he murmured as he continued to hold the door shut. "I know you from somewhere."

"You have to help them," the little girl said. "The Raven Mocker will eat their hearts and live forever. They are Cherokee blood!"

"What does them having Cherokee blood have anything to do with the Raven Mocker attacking people?" Mikey asked. "She already killed one of the campers on the campground."

"If she killed him, then he has Cherokee somewhere in his bloodline," the little boy said.

"So, there's no telling who she goes after next," Mikey replied.

"Not just she," the little girl replied. "Them. She is awakening her sisters."

"There's more?!" Mikey hissed.

"She can resurrect every single Raven Mocker tonight. What you read, you didn't read by accident. She has been portraying Ozell and talking to you," the little girl said. "You read her spell to give her the power to resurrect them all."

"What can destroy her?" Mikey asked.

"Ozell needs her necklace," the little boy replied.

"What necklace?" Mikey asked.

"The necklace you gave Joshua," the little girl replied. "It's her family heirloom. The same necklace that was given to her ancestor, Woya Echota, from a Raven Mocker he destroyed. That necklace is the key to it all."

"Where is Ozell?" Mikey asked. "I went to her home, and she wasn't there."

The sounds of birds cawing surrounded the building as Mikey held the door shut with all of his strength. Birds began to filter in through the broken window.

"We have to go, or she will take our souls!" the little girl cried. "Get the necklace!"

"I remember!" Mikey called. "Lizzy, William, wait!"

The kids vanished as the last bird flew through the window. Each one of them began to merge and dissolve into one another until a woman stood before him.

"Ozell?" he asked.

The Raven Mocker laughed. "You are such a fool. Even as I appear before you in my natural state, you still can't see past my façade."

She began to pace slowly in front of Mikey.

"That's why you won't be able to destroy me," she gleaned. "Because even knowing me as what I am, you still cannot see my true form because you don't have thick Cherokee blood."

"That also means that you can't hurt me," Mikey chuckled. "You are powerless against me, Gini."

Gini glared at him. "I can't take your life force, but that doesn't mean I can't hurt you."

Something large and heavy hit the door of the office, knocking it from its hinges and pinning Mikey beneath it on the floor. The room spun as he tried to get his sense of gravity back. Gini knelt beside him and smiled as a howl echoed outside.

"There would be no greater pleasure than to see you ripped to shreds by wolves," she mused.

Blood trickled down the side of his face and into his eye as he heard the low growl at the door. He didn't move a muscle as a large wolf walked over the door and stood beside him, teeth bared. One by one, more wolves came through the door and circled him as Gini walked past them.

"It was so nice getting to know you, Mikey," Gini said. "I'm sorry it had to end this way. You would have been a nice friend to have to teach me the ways of humans."

Gini slipped out the door as the wolves snarled and snapped, waiting to dig into Mikey's trapped body. Mikey closed his eyes in defeat and waited for the wolves to tear into his flesh. A piercing squall-like whistle erupted in the air as dozens of snowy owls swooped into the office building and began harassing the wolves. The wolves snarled and bit at the owls as the owls dodged their attacks, pecking and scratching at the wolves' faces.

The wolves began to whimper and run from the office as the birds continued their assault on them. Mikey sighed with relief as he released every muscle in his body. He began to maneuver himself out from under the door he was wedged beneath. Glass cut into his legs as he pulled them free. He propped his body up against his desk and looked over at the pile of glass that was once a whiskey bottle.

"I should have just drank it," he muttered.

A dove flew through the door, and he felt a sense of peace wash over him. It perched beside him on the desk and nudged his head unafraid. He lifted his hand as the bird hopped onto it, and he stroked its feathers with his other hand. Its feathers began to glow with each stroke.

"A little Woya Echota," he mumbled with a smile. His smile faded. "Woya Echota," he repeated. "Woya Echota Starr, Ozell's ancestor." He peered closer at the bird as it nuzzled his hand. "Ozell?" he asked.

"Now, why would you think my wife is a bird, Mikey?" a gruff voice asked, interrupting the quiet

"Nathaniel?" Mikey asked. "Is that you?"

"It seems the wolves failed. Now, it's up to me," Nathaniel huffed as he walked closer to Mikey.

"Nathaniel, you have to get out of here. There's a..."

"A Raven Mocker?" Nathaniel asked. "Yeah, I know. Who do you think sent me?" he asked.

With one swift movement, he raised a shotgun in his hands and brought it down against Mikey's temple, knocking him out instantly. The dove flew at Nathaniel, pecking at him and trying to run him away. Nathaniel gave a hard swat and sent the bird careening against the wall. It hit the floor with a thud, Nathaniel presuming it was dead. He reached down and checked Mikey's pulse just to make sure he hadn't killed him with the blow to his head. Once he felt the pulse and could see he was breathing, he hoisted Mikey up from the floor and threw him over his shoulders, carrying him out of the office.

"Put him down!" a voice demanded.

Nathaniel turned around to see Lizzy and William standing behind him.

"Now, why would I go and do a thing like that?" he asked.

"Why are you helping her, Papa?" Lizzy asked.

"Because she's bringing your mother back tonight," he replied. "We are going to be a happy family again."

"We are dead, Papa," William replied. "Let mother rest in peace."

"What about my peace?" he seethed. "I deserve peace. I deserve my family!"

"Papa, you didn't mean to do anything that happened to us," Lizzy replied.

"But I did it," Nathaniel cried. "I killed her. I killed you! I have to make it right. You deserve to grow up. You deserve to live!"

"It's not right switching our spirits with anyone else's," Lizzy hissed.

"Hush, now," Nathaniel replied, walking toward the woods. "Tonight, your mother will be back with us, and we can live happily ever after..."

Chapter Eleven

WHILE THEY ALL WAITED for Carter, Carl, and Bobby to return, the adults all rummaged through the utility closet, pulling out cots for the children to lie down on and try to sleep. Candace curled up on the cot with Lizzy and stroked her hair as the child lay there silently, sucking her thumb. A million things raced through Candace's mind from the night's experiences.

She glanced over at Joy sobbing in the corner and felt a pang in her heart. Joy and Bill had been married for forty-five years. Yesterday was their anniversary, and the happiness was ripped right away from her with Bill's death. As if

Isobel knew what she was thinking, she rolled around and faced Candace.

"Mommy, does it hurt to die?" she whispered.

Candace was a bit taken aback by the question. "I don't know, sweetie. I guess it depends on how you die," she replied.

"Did it hurt that man to die?" Isobel asked.

"I'm not sure," Candace replied with a heavy sigh. "Why do you ask?"

"Because I don't want it to hurt when I die," Isobel answered. "I don't want it to hurt when any of us die."

"Well, you don't have to worry about that for a very long time," Candace choked out, holding back tears.

A migraine tickled the back of her head as all of the stress and tension of the night began to weigh down on her. The alcohol and weed didn't help the matter. Sobering the way she did always snaps a migraine into place. It was one reason she didn't really smoke and drink anymore. One of the last times she could remember partying like this was when Isobel was a baby. She got strangled on her formula, and Candace nearly had a heart attack trying to get her to breathe right.

Candace rubbed her temples, trying to push the migraine back, when a wave of exhaustion took hold of her. Isobel had drifted off to sleep, and Joshua lay motionless, snoring away on his cot. She quit fighting the overwhelming need to sleep and closed her eyes.

At first, she didn't even know she was dreaming. The colors looked crystal clear, and she could even feel the wind on her cheek. She walked through the woods with the wind pointing her in specific directions whenever she would be going in the wrong direction. She passed by a barbed wire fence and continued through the trees. The area looked similar to what it does now, but different somehow. The trees looked shorter, and there was more wildlife in the woods than she had witnessed during her couple of days of being there.

She didn't understand what it all meant, but she followed the wind wherever it pushed her. Anxiety swelled in her chest as she heard the sound of children laughing and playing off in the distance. She began to run toward the sound, calling out for Isobel and Joshua. It wasn't safe for them to be in the woods, and terror tore through her core, fearful that the creature plaguing them would snatch them up before she got to where they were to protect them.

Branches and thorn bushes tore at her arms and legs, ripping at her flesh and dress. She couldn't remember why she was in a dress in the woods, but that wasn't important to her at the moment. She had to get to the fading sound of the children, or something bad would happen to them.

Before she knew it, she was thundering through the brush and standing on the sandy shore of Devil's Claw Lake, except it was just a bubbling stream of water. The sounds of her children had tapered off to a whisper before fading altogether.

"Isobel! Joshua!" she called out as she ran along the shore, but no one answered her calls.

As she moved up the shoreline, she came across a hut in the middle of the forest with a fire going outside. A woman emerged from within wearing buckskin clothing. Her raven black hair was braided down her back. A raven squalled in the air, and she held her hand out to it, coaxing it down from its flight. It perched on her hand, and she seemed to have a conversation with it as she stroked its feathers. She grabbed it by its throat, removed a dagger from a sheath on her side, and drove it into the bird's ribcage, filleting it open. She brought the bird over to the fire and dug out the heart of the raven, letting the blood pool in the wooden bowl sitting on the stones. She then cut the head of the bird off and placed it in a separate bowl.

The woman set the carcass of the bird in another bowl made from stone and placed it inside the fire. The smell of the burning feathers and molting flesh wafted over to Candace, and she wretched. Once the body of the bird had burned to ashes, leaving only remnants of bones, the woman removed the stone dish from the fire and set it to the side.

A young girl appeared in the clearing and walked over to the woman and knelt before her.

"Are you ready to join us?" the woman asked the girl.

"I have nothing left. They all abandoned me here because I am sick," the girl replied. "They feared the Asginas would follow them."

"They are not your family anymore," the woman stated. "We will be your family now."

The woman picked the head of the raven up and held it above the girl's head.

"With the head of a raven, you will become one with the raven. You will have its strength, its agility, its cunning, and its flight. Never lose this talisman, for whoever wields it will be your undoing."

The head of the bird transformed into a turquoise necklace with a raven charm. The girl bowed her head as the woman placed the necklace over her head and around her neck. Next, the woman picked the heart of the raven up out of the bowl and lifted it above the girl's head.

"With this heart, you will gain everlasting life. The raven is the messenger between the living and the dead, so you, too, shall exist between the living and the dead. Never aging and never dying."

The girl raised her face to the woman and opened her mouth. The woman placed the heart in her mouth, and Candace watched the girl chew and swallow the piece of meat. Then, the woman turned to the burned carcass of the raven and took a pestle to the body, grinding it into a fine ash. She took the dagger she had used to kill the raven, dipped it into the blood she had set aside, and then dipped it into the ashes of the carcass.

"With these ashes serving as the dust of our body and the blood serving as the life force of our soul, combined, they shall set you free." And then she began to chant, "*noir Asgina manger oyohusa gavldi Udanvdo alisdayvdi Ama gvindi Igohidaquu gesv Agilvgis Adayotaedi Ayolis Udanvgalvda Unilohisdi Nulinigvgv Strenuous Itsula Alenidasdi Nulisdv,"*

The woman thrust the dagger through the girl's heart, and she hit the ground dead. Not long after, her body began to convulse and mutate. Her arms turned into mutated wings, with her hands and fingers turning into talons. Her feet turned into the feet of a raven while her face morphed and shaped into half a raven's head and half her head.

Once Gini rose from the place where she died, the older woman spoke again.

"Ashes burned in your vicinity can harm you if they suspect you as a Raven Mocker. You must never let them find out who you really are or let them obtain your talisman."

The Raven Mocker nodded her head.

"I am old, and it is my time. I wish I could be with you longer to teach you more of the ways of the Raven Mocker. You are the last of our kind. Feed well, Gini," the old woman said as she raised her hands in the air.

Candace went to run and help the older woman, but a gust of wind began to blow against her, pushing her away from Gini as she thrust her hand into the old woman's chest and tore the heart from within the breastbone, devouring it in minutes. The wind pushed her away from the shore and through the woods to a small cabin. Candace watched the young girl who had been changed into a Raven Mocker walk around an herbal garden, grabbing various things and putting them into a basket. She stopped at a pokeberry bush and pulled the berries off of it. She then handed the basket over to another woman who toted it toward the house.

"No," Candace protested. "That can kill someone."

The sound of two small children echoed from inside, and Candace peered through the window to see a small girl and a boy not much older than her. The woman who was handed the basket walked inside and set the basket down on the table near the hearth.

"Who wants my elderberry pie?" she asked loudly.

"I want pie," the older boy replied.

"Give me a few hours, and you can have a slice," the woman smiled.

Candace looked from the little boy to the little girl's face. Their lips were bluish. Their faces were pale, with dark circles under their eyes from malnutrition. Their hands had sores all over them with darkened patches of skin. Candace had spent some time as a candy striper when she was a teenager, and the only time she had ever seen something like this was when a patient was being poisoned with arsenic by her mother.

Everything shifted quickly to a man and a woman holding the young boy, crying. As if flash-forward were hit, she watched everything zip by. They buried the boy, and not long after, the little girl passed as well. They buried them underneath the tree they had found the bag in.

It came to a slow when the man and woman pleaded with another man as they were strung up in the very tree that was at the children's graves.

"Jeremiah, please no!" the woman pleaded as he placed a burlap sack over her head and the man's head.

With one quick jerk of a rope attached to the bench they stood on, it was ripped from beneath their feet, and they hung their with their feet kicking the air. Their legs straightened and twitched as they slowly died from hanging. The man named Jeremiah removed their bodies from the tree and placed them inside the house before setting it on fire. Jeremiah and the woman who had toted the basket of berries inside stood there and watched the house ignite up into flames.

Gini appeared from within the woods and slowly walked to the burning building. She passed by the two that stood there and entered the home. It was as if the flames couldn't touch her as she walked through the spiraling blaze. She knelt beside the man, thrust her hand into his chest, and pulled his heart from his chest cavity. She did the same with the woman and then began to devour the hearts as the tendrils of flames popped and cracked all around.

Everything erupted into flames, and black, acrid smoke billowed from the house as Gini left it behind, with Jeremiah and Ketia following her into the woods. Candace collapsed to her knees in tears as everything she saw repeated over and over in her mind. Sadness and despair consumed her as she felt every single spirit Gini took wail in the great beyond. The heat and smoke filtered into her lungs, and she began to gasp and cough as it burned her lungs. She clawed at her throat, trying to inhale a fresh breath of air.

Candace bolted upright from her sleep, still choking and gasping for air. She glanced around to see that everyone had drifted off to sleep, and she quickly checked to make sure

Isobel and Joshua were ok. She tried to stand from the cot, but she was disoriented and weak. She crawled to the doors of the lodge and pulled the handle down with all of her energy just to prop it open for a breath of fresh air.

Everything was quiet outside. Carter hadn't returned yet, and she had no clue where they were or where Mikey was. The cool air felt like heaven on her face. After gulping down fresh air for a few moments, she stood from her place at the door and walked back over to the cot Isobel slept on. She curled up beside her, the migraine still thumping in the back of her head, and sleep immediately came once again with the sound of gentle children's laughter echoing in her ears.

Chapter Twelve

CARTER, BOBBY, AND CARL made their way back through the carnage of the night, checking various vehicle batteries to see if they would work on his truck.

"Hopefully," Carter started, breathing from all of the walking, "this one is the one that finally works," he grunted as he struggled to put the battery up on the truck's front end. "Because these mother fuckers are heavy, and I am not carrying anymore!" he huffed as he took the last battery out they had tried and popped the new one in its place.

Carter attached the battery cables, made sure the alternator line was fine, and double-checked the ground. "Alright, Bobby. Hit the switch," he said, praying silently that it would work.

Bobby turned the switch, and nothing lit up. He pounded the steering wheel before hopping out of the truck, slamming the door shut, and kicking the shit out of the door.

"God damn stupid piece of mother fucking shit," he seethed.

"Calm down, Bobby!" Carl yelled.

Bobby muttered and walked to the back of his truck. He opened the cooler lid and humphed. "Beers still fine," he said as he cracked a cold one and drank it down in five seconds.

He picked another up and offered it to Carl and Carter. Carter smiled his appreciation but refused, while Carl quickly grabbed the beer and guzzled it as Bobby had. Carter sighed and bent over, trying to quell the burning in his lungs from all of the walking and carrying in the rapidly cooling temperatures outside. He slowly sat down on the dewy grass and gave up.

"What now?" Carl asked, exasperated. "I mean, no one has a vehicle to get out of here. We can't go anywhere to get fucking help. We are sitting ducks in this place and are being hunted by a mythical creature out of a Native American storybook!"

"Did we even have a real plan?" Carter asked. "I mean, what were we going to do once we got a vehicle running?"

"We were going to run for the hills!" Carl replied. "Find help."

"And what exactly would we tell the help?" Carter asked. "Excuse me, 911? An evil raven mocker witch out of Cherokee mythology is stalking and killing me and a bunch of campers over at Foxwood Resort. Can you please send a medicine man to drive it back to death?"

"We would have figured that out when we got there," Carl replied.

"We need to go check on everyone else back at the main lodge," Carter stated as he stood back to his feet. "See if Mikey made it back from Ozell and Nathaniel's place yet or something. We need a game plan."

"All of them tours I did in Vietnam, and ain't a damn one of them teach me how to fight off a mystical entity," Bobby muttered as they began to walk back to the lodge. "All the rice paddy guerrillas I took out. I even won a Purple Heart. But I have no idea how to fight this thing."

"It's just like those guerrillas, too," Carl replied. "Hiding in the shadows, and no one can see them. How we 'sposed to fight something we can't even see? Why can't we just leave this to be someone else's problem? Ride the night out and leave in the morning?"

"Because," Carter began, "we don't know who it will come after next."

They arrived back at the lodge and found all the kids tucked away, sleeping with their parents. Carter stood at the door and watched Candace, Joshua, and Isobel as they inhaled and exhaled in their sleep.

"What about the phones at the office?" Carter whispered. "Aren't they on a landline?"

"Yeah," Bobby replied.

"Well, the power wouldn't affect the old ones that plug straight into the phone. Do they have those, or are they all cordless?"

"I am pretty sure they are the old ones that don't have caller ID," Carl replied.

"Maybe we can get in touch with the property owner," Carter suggested. "I'm out of ideas, and just calling 911 won't work. They'll think it's a joke."

"Do you think they will be safe if we leave them here to go find out?" Bobby asked.

"I don't know," Carter mumbled. "But what else can we do?"

The other two remained silent, unable to offer any type of ideas.

"Alright, it's settled," Carter answered himself. "Let's go."

The men headed toward the office, carefully watching the woods for any type of attack the witch may have planned. When they arrived at the office, it was a mess. The door had been knocked from its hinges. All of the glass was busted out of the windows. There was blood beneath the door, as if someone had been there.

"What the fuck happened here?" Bobby asked, poking his head around inside of the building.

They noticed the smashed bottle of whiskey against one wall, and the desk was swept clean of everything that had been on it.

"That's Mikey's desk," Carl replied. "Looks like he was here and wasn't too happy about anything."

"Hopefully, he didn't drink that bottle before smashing it to bits, or we are all fucked," Bobby replied.

"I told y'all. Mikey doesn't drink anymore," Carter said. "You can smell the liquor on the floor from the busted bottle."

"Why do you believe what he says?" Bobby asked. "He's a fool. A drunk."

"Because not only did he save my life earlier today or yesterday, whatever you want to call it. He saved my son's life, too, when we were down at Devil's Claw. Those reflexes weren't the reflexes of a drunk," Carter replied. "Mistakes are human nature. And when Mikey made that huge mistake with those campers, it changed him."

Carter picked the phone up and hit the hook switch a couple of times. "Dead," he said as he put the phone back on the hook. "Explains why Mikey got so mad he tossed the room." Carter looked at all the damage in the room and furrowed his brows. "It does not explain the rest of the damage, though. Pretty sure something happened here to him."

The wind blew gently, and something moved on the floor. Carter bent down carefully and picked up a black feather.

"Safe to say the Raven Mocker was here," he stated as he held the feather up for Carl and Bobby to see.

As he looked closer at the door, he saw muddy prints all over it.

"Are those wolf prints?" he asked. "I'm not much of an outdoorsman."

Bobby and Carl shone their light on the door and examined it.

"Yeah, those are wolf prints," Carl gulped.

"There aren't wolves around here, though," Bobby refuted. "Coyotes, sure. But wolves? We ain't never had a wolf problem in Virginia."

"Well, we ain't exactly under normal circumstances here, are we?" Carter replied. "We need to find Mikey."

"Mikey is the least of our concern!" Carl shouted. "It's his damn fault this shit is happening!"

Carter grabbed Carl up by the collar of his shirt. "Mikey is the only one that knows anything about this shit unless you want to try the crazy gun-toting loons over the ridge." Carter released his grip. "Besides, we don't know what the witch wants with him, and I sure as hell ain't giving her anymore lives to eat for eternal youth."

"Well, one of us still needs to go for help!" Carl snapped back.

"Fine! I saw Mikey's Jeep parked out front. Go and start it!" Carter hissed.

They all walked outside, and Carl hopped into the Jeep.

"It has interior lights," Carl said. "Battery works."

He checked the ignition, but the keys were missing. He pulled the sun visor down, checked, opened the glove box, and checked the console.

"The keys aren't in it," he said.

Carl shifted his glance between Bobby and Carter.

"What? Oh, Carl's a hick. He should know how to hotwire a vehicle," Carl mocked.

Carter sighed in frustration. "Just look for a freaking screwdriver!"

Carl rummaged around inside the Jeep, checking everywhere. He scooped the trash out of the floorboard, tossing it on the ground beside him before hopping out and getting in the backseat to look. He stopped for a second and turned to Carter.

"What kind of screwdriver?" Carl asked.

"A flathead, you moron!" Carter replied.

Carl returned to rummaging before coming up with a flathead screwdriver. Carter swiped it from his hand and hopped in the driver's seat.

"Hand me one of those large quartz rocks over there near the walkway," Carter asked.

Bobby ran over, picked one up, and jogged it back to him. Carter put the screwdriver in the locking mechanism of the switch and struck it a few times with the rock to break the inner switch. He gave the screwdriver a turn to see if it was broken free and attempted to start the

Jeep. The Jeep spat and sputtered and rumbled to life as the three of them whooped and hollered.

"Finally, something went our way tonight," Bobby laughed.

"How the hell did you know to do that with the screwdriver?" Carl asked Carter as he hopped out of the driver's seat.

"Let's just say there's a sealed court record from my teenager days of joyriding," Carter replied.

"Smoking weed, drinking, partying, now boosting cars?" Bobby asked, laughing. "Man, we really had you pegged wrong."

"Let's get back to everyone else," Carter said as he hopped in the driver's seat. Bobby walked around the front of the Jeep to the passenger side while Carl hopped into the backseat. Carter put the Jeep in drive and was about to pull out when he heard the sound of kids laughing and playing.

"Do you see any kids behind the Jeep?" Carter asked Bobby and Carl.

"No, all of the kids are asleep back at the lodge," Bobby replied.

"So, you didn't hear the laughing?" Carter asked.

"I didn't hear nothing," Carl replied.

"One of you go check," Carter suggested. "I don't want to run over anyone."

Carl got out, walked around the back of the Jeep, and turned around with his hands in the air.

"No one back here, bud," he replied.

The hair on Carter's arms began to prickle as he heard the sound again.

"You don't hear that?" Carter asked as he turned to face Carl.

Carl's face was as white as a ghost, and it looked like he had pissed his pants.

"I hear them now," he whispered.

Carter put the Jeep back in park and hopped out with Carl. The icy wind started blowing again, and the Jeep rocked slowly. Bobby hopped out with the other two, and they all looked around as the sound of laughter grew louder and more sinister. The sounds seemed to swirl around them as if kids were running in between them all.

"You have got to be kidding me," Carter muttered. "Not only do we have this mythic creature hunting us, but there's ghost kids too?"

The laughter turned into screams, and they all held their hands against their ears. The hairs on Carter's arms were sounding an alarm of doom, and dread settled into the pit of his stomach. And as fast as it started, it stopped.

"We have to get back now!" Carter yelled.

They all ran back to the Jeep doors and hopped in, slamming them shut. Bobby hit the door lock, and Carter just stared at him.

"What?" Bobby asked, scared shitless.

"They're ghosts, Bobby," Carter replied, shaking his head.

"Stop judging me and drive this mother fucker!" Bobby hissed.

Carter revved the engine and put the Jeep in reverse, stomping the gas. The Jeep spat and sputtered before a slight knocking sound ended with the Jeep shutting off.

"You have got to be fucking kidding me!" Carter yelled.

He put the Jeep back in park and started it again, yanking the gear shifter back down to reverse and stomping the gas once more. The Jeep died again. He tried several times before shutting the Jeep off and beating the steering wheel.

"God dammit!" Carter seethed. "Is anything going to fucking go right tonight, or should we just offer ourselves up and get it the fuck over with?!"

Carter put his forehead against the steering wheel and breathed deeply, trying to calm himself down.

"The moon is back out," Bobby said, breaking the silence.

Carter stared up at the moon as an orange glow slowly started to pass over the top of it. "Blood on the moon," he murmured.

"What was that?" Carl asked.

"There's blood on the moon," Carter repeated. "Depending on which traditions you follow, some call it a blood moon or hunter's moon. Others call it a harvest moon. It's the last harvest of the year. Tonight is a Harvest Moon night. It all makes sense now. The veil is the thinnest. The full moon on this night. It's harvest time... The harvesting of souls..."

Chapter Thirteen

CARTER SAT DEFEATED in the driver's seat. He had absolutely no clue how to fix anything wrong with tonight.

"Hot damn!" Carl shouted, scaring both Bobby and Carter in deafening silence. "Hot damn! Hot damn!"

"Carl, you scared the fucking shit out of me!" Bobby hissed. "What the hell are you babbling on about?"

"I'm a fucking genius, is what I am babbling on about," Carl replied, opening the Jeep door and jumping out. "The fucking emergency phone!"

"Hot damn!" Bobby reiterated excitedly.

"What's the emergency phone?" Carter asked.

"Remember how we harp on and on about Mikey and that god-forsaken blizzard! Well, thank you, Mikey!" Bobby shouted as he jumped out of the Jeep as well.

They started to jog to the side of the office with Carter trailing them.

"Someone mind filling me in on your grand discovery?" Carter hissed.

"When Mikey fucked up, Mr. Ingram updated the emergency phone. It used to dial Mikey's cabin directly, but he couldn't trust Mikey anymore to handle the emergencies. It dials him directly now!" Carl exclaimed as they hit the back of the cabin and found the box that covered the phone. Carl ripped open the casing, and the handset was perfectly intact.

Carl picked up the handset and pushed the only button on the phone. A dial tone came on, and it auto-dialed the only number it had set for calling.

"It's working!" Carl exclaimed.

The phone rang several times. "Come on. Come on. Pick up, you bastard."

The phone clicked, and a very groggy voice answered the call. "Hello?"

"Boy, am I glad to hear your voice, Mr. Ingram," Carl yapped.

Mr. Ingram rolled over in his bed and checked the time on the clock. "For fuck's sake. Who is this?"

"It's Carl from the resort."

"What kind of emergency is there that Mikey couldn't handle?" Mr. Ingram replied.

"A whole bunch of fuckery is what the emergency is," Carl replied.

"Mikey can handle it," Mr. Ingram replied, about to hang up when Carter took the phone from Carl.

"Mr. Ingram, Carter here. You hang up, and I will hunt you down and gut you like a fish," Carter hissed. "Mikey is missing. Most likely dead. We have one dead camper so far and a shitstorm of unbelievable proportions happening. We are all in danger!"

"What kind of danger?" Mr. Ingram asked, sitting up in bed, alert.

"You wouldn't believe us if we told you," Carter replied.

"Try me," Mr. Ingram huffed, rubbing his eyes.

"Raven Mockers are…" The line went dead.

"Raven Mockers? Hello?" Mr. Ingram asked. Silence answered him. "Carter?" he asked into the phone, but no one answered. He slammed the phone down on his hook switch.

"Fuck!" he seethed.

He jumped out of bed and ran to his dresser, fumbling with the handles to jerk it open for clothes.

He stared at his reflection in the mirror above the dresser as memories flashed back through his mind. The room began to spin.

"Keep it together, Patrick," he said to himself.

But no amount of reassurances that he gave to himself could keep the images from flooding into his mind. He had been dreaming again of the ruins, the graves, the voices in the woods; they all flooded back into his head. His memories of how they died crashed around inside his memories, and a migraine storm struck him. He sat down on the bed and squeezed his temples… the horrors of those many nights locked in the sanitarium.

"It can't be," he murmured.

Lizzy and William flashed through his mind, and the witch.

"They promised me those memories were gone for good," he said, rocking back and forth on the bed. "They told me I was crazy. They fed me those pills. All of that shit should be done with and gone. They promised me!" he seethed.

Then, a new image flashed in his mind. One he had suppressed for so long and had never spoken a word of to anyone. The creature.

"The Raven Mocker," he murmured.

He quickly dressed and fumbled with his keys on his dresser. His hands shook so violently, and anxiety welled in his chest. He ran to his bathroom and vomited in the toilet.

"I can't do this," he told himself over and over. "I can't do this."

He quickly reached for his medicine cabinet and nearly cleared the contents out of it, dropping every bottle into the sink below before he found his anxiety medication. He popped the lid off and dumped two into his hand, and was about to take them when he stopped.

"I can't take these," he whispered. "I can't help them if I take these."

He threw the pills in the toilet and flushed them along with his vomit. He walked back into his room, picked the keys up from the floor he had dropped, and left his house. He jumped in his Denali and backed out of his driveway. He didn't live close to the property anymore. It was going to take him close to an hour to get there from his home in Gretna.

Patrick stomped the accelerator, and his needle jumped from the speed limit to nearly 95 mph. "I can make it there in fifteen. I have to make it there."

The dread from earlier just deepened in the pit of his stomach as he took the curves of the winding back roads. The back tires slid around a curve, and the top-heaviness of the SUV nearly made him total the vehicle. With one swift jerk of the hand, the SUV's tires that had lifted off the ground landed back down with a thud, and he hit the gas harder.

"I won't be any use dead," he muttered to himself. "Plus, I don't know if they're all drunk or if this is a prank or a game to them coddled assholes. I just hope Mikey is ok and not drunk with them."

It was exactly seventeen minutes and 34 seconds from his house to the campgrounds at the speeds he was taking. However, his being here meant nothing with the gates locked and Mikey the only one with a key to open them.

Luckily, he had created an emergency PIN code for someone to use from the outside to access the park. He got out of his vehicle and punched the code in, expecting the gate to slide open. Nothing happened. He punched the code in again, and still nothing happened.

"The power must have gone down to the grid," he muttered.

He walked back to the Denali and hopped in. He put the vehicle in reverse and backed up as far as he could before jamming it in drive and gunning it. He hit the gate and broke it in half, doing minimal damage to the front end. He peeled down the drive to the main office. When he rounded the curve, his headlights illuminated the side of the building, and he saw Bobby and Carl standing there, along with the new guy named Carter, who had registered earlier in the week. He stomped the brakes and slid to a stop before turning the Denali off and hopping out.

"Where is everyone?" he demanded.

"The rest of us campers are in the main lodge sleeping since that was the safest place to be," Carter replied. "We don't know where Mikey is. It appears there was a struggle of some sort, and there's blood in the office. We don't know if he is alive or dead."

"Why didn't you try 911?" Patrick demanded.

"The phones and power are down," Bobby replied. "We couldn't leave because of the locked gate, and all of the vehicles were either trashed by the twister that hit us, or the batteries were dead. This rust bucket wouldn't stay running," Bobby said as he kicked the wheel of Mikey's Jeep.

"What in the fuck!" Patrick exclaimed. "You said someone was dead?"

They all three nodded.

"What the fuck happened to them?" he demanded.

"You wouldn't believe us," Carter replied. "Hell, I didn't want to believe it until all the weird shit started happening."

"Well, fucking try to explain then because I can't handle this shit right now," Patrick hissed as he wiped the sweat from his brow.

"The only thing I can say for certain happened is Mikey did the campout with the kids, read some prayer from the book that he had learned, and some ancient creature emerged from it," Carter replied. "There's also little kid ghosts running around that apparently only my daughter can see and hear unless they want to freak you the fuck out by laughing."

"Mikey has read that prayer every single campout to people, and nothing has ever happened," Patrick retorted.

"Yeah, but tonight was Halloween, and the moon is full," Carl replied. "And Carter's little girl skinned up her arm and leg when it frightened her, and boom."

"We don't know what to do. If we believe this Raven Mocker shit is real, we have no definite way of destroying it because none of us are practicing Cherokee, if you know what I mean. The kids are scared shitless. It's like a scene out of Friday the 13th, except Mothman came to play instead of Jason Vorhees," Carter huffed.

The sound of shrieking birds filled the air off in the distance, and everyone froze still until it died down. As soon as the shrieks had stopped, the icy wind appeared again, blowing gusts against the four of them. Laughter erupted all around them as if hundreds of children stood around them that they couldn't see. Patrick covered his ears and crouched down.

"Stop!" he yelled over and over. "It's all in my head. It's all in my head," he repeated as he rocked back and forth.

"What the fuck is wrong with you?" Carter hissed as he yanked Patrick's hands away from his ears.

"You don't hear it?" Patrick asked. "That laughter..."

"Of course, we fucking hear it! It's what we have been trying to tell you, idiot," Carl said.

Patrick stared off into the distance. "They told me I was crazy. That I was sick. That it was all in my fucking head!"

"Who told you that?" Carter asked.

"Every fucking body!" he squealed. "My parents locked me away because they were ashamed of me and my mental disorder. I spent years in a sanatorium receiving brain shock therapy because they said the voices weren't real!"

"You've heard this before?" Carter asked, bending down in Patrick's face.

"Yes," he whispered.

An eerie quiet settled over the ridge as the laughter stopped. Nothing but the sound of their pounding hearts in their ears and breathing was heard. Their steamy breath left droplets of condensation in the air as it got colder and colder where they stood.

A howl ripped through the silence, and Patrick jerked his head to the trees where a pack of wolves stood with teeth bared and growling. Patrick scrambled to his feet, lifted the hatch of Mikey's Jeep, and dragged out a gas container.

"Quick, find a tree limb or something," he barked as he pulled out an old shirt from the back.

Carter glanced around and saw a sizeable stick a few feet away and bounded over to get it. He returned with it, and Patrick swiped it from his hands, wrapping the old shirt around it. He then doused the shirt in the gasoline.

The wolves barked and snarled and began to run toward the crowd of men.

"Lighter!" Patrick screamed as everyone fumbled in their pockets.

Carter snatched a lighter first and struck the flint. A flame jumped to life, and Patrick held the gasoline-soaked makeshift torch over it, and it exploded into flames. Patrick turned just in time as the wolves were about to leap and swung the torch around, smacking one in the face. The wolf howled in pain, and they backed away from the flame.

Without notice, the wind stirred again, and the sound of thousands of birds squalling rolled across the wind, like a long drawn-out murder, but deeper, darker, more sinister. To their dismay, they heard a loud sound like a transformer building a charge. Bobby grabbed a torch, lit it, and handed it to Patrick.

"Everyone in the Jeep, now!" Patrick yelled as he continued to swing the torch to and fro in front of the wolves, slowly backing to the driver's side door.

Once he saw they were safe inside with their doors shut, he dropped the torch and hopped in the Jeep, slamming the door just as a wolf pounced. Its face was pressed against the side of the door, whimpering for a moment and shaking it off.

"Where's the fucking keys?" Patrick asked.

Carter handed him the flat screwdriver, and Patrick looked at him, dumbfounded.

"Keys are lost. Just stick it in and turn it," Carter instructed.

Patrick did as he was told, and the Jeep sprang to life. He held the brake and gas at the same time as he shifted the Jeep into reverse and let go of the brake, and the Jeep lurched in reverse.

"It's a janky piece of shit, but it's one of the first vehicles I learned to drive in," Patrick said. "Mikey taught me."

Patrick shoved the gear shift into drive and peeled down the driveway toward the main lodge, ramming wolves as he drove. Carter, Bobby, and Carl whooped in glee as they watched the wolves being driven back into the woods. Patrick smiled and sighed in relief, but his relief was wasted. Dread and terror tore through him as debris began to blow across his tracks.

Patrick looked into the rearview mirror to see a twister touching down behind them at the office, tearing it to shreds. There wasn't a cloud in the sky aside from the tornado following behind them. He glanced up at the moon, and it was red.

"Blood on the moon," he mumbled.

Patrick slid the Jeep to a stop in front of the main lodge, and everyone jumped out, covering their faces as debris lashed at their bodies.

"As soon as this tornado is gone, we need to get everyone out of here!" Patrick yelled over the roaring winds.

They ran up the steps as the twister neared, and Patrick struggled with every step to make it to the doors. His feet seemed to slip out from underneath him, and he prepared for the tornado to suck him up and eat him. A hand grabbed him, and he looked up to see Carter struggling to hold him with one hand while holding onto one of the porch posts.

"Hang on!" Carter yelled.

"Just don't let go!" Patrick pleaded.

The wooden post began to crack from the pressure and weight of the two bodies. Carter began to slip from his grip when the porch post completely caved. Just when they thought they were both goners, Carter felt hands on his feet and legs. Bobby and Carl had grabbed him while other campers pulled the two men back into the doors using the walls for leverage with their feet.

With one hard tug, it seemed to snap them out of the current and wind, and they came sprawling inside across the floor as the others shut the doors as quickly as possible behind them.

Chapter Fourteen

CANDACE WAS STARTLED awake when all of the commotion began. She sat up to see Carter holding onto a post, and it fell beneath his weight. She took in a sharp inhale, about to scream out his name when Carl and Bobby grabbed his feet, and other adults had made their way to the front to hold onto the men bracing against the doorframe. With one hard tug, everyone stumbled backward, falling to the floor as Carter was jerked through the door and thudded, rolling across the wooden boards. Another man careened through the door right behind him, thudding the same way.

Carl and Bobby scrambled to their feet to shut the doors as Carter and the other man slowly righted themselves into a sitting position. As soon as Carl and Bobby latched the doors, they ran to Carter and the man's side.

"You ok, Mr. Ingram?" Carl asked and then turned to Carter. "Carter?"

"Yeah, we're alright," Carter breathed. "Has Mikey returned?"

"Unfortunately, not," Evette replied.

Candace let out the breath she had been holding as her adrenaline began to settle. She glanced down beside her and noticed that Isobel wasn't in the bed. She hadn't even paid attention to the beds when she woke up. She turned quickly to look at Joshua's cot, and it was empty, too.

"Isobel?! Joshua?!" she called out in alarm.

Everyone turned to look at Candace. She stood from the bed and started checking around the room and through the office door in the back. She turned around in full-blown panic.

"Did any of you see them?" Candace questioned. "Did you see them get out of the bed?!"

Everyone was quiet as Carter scrambled to his feet.

"They're not here?" he demanded.

"I laid down with them after they fell asleep. I was in the same bed as Isobel," Candace stammered.

"Where are the kids, Candace!" Carter bellowed.

"Don't you fucking talk to me like that, Carter," Candace hissed. "Don't you *ever* talk to me like that or…"

"Or what?" Carter seethed, walking up to Candace's face. "You had one fucking job, and you couldn't even do that!"

Candace brought her hand back and slapped Carter hard across his left cheek.

"Fuck, you," she snarled through gritted teeth.

Candace pushed past Carter and walked to the front doors, unlatched them, and walked outside.

"Where the fuck are you going?" Carter yelled.

"To find my fucking kids," Candace hollered over her shoulder, walking briskly through the grass toward the woods.

Carter turned around to the quiet crowd that gathered behind him.

"Are any other kids missing?" he asked quietly.

Everyone shook their heads.

"It wasn't right for you to talk to her like that," Joy spoke up. "Everyone here went to sleep, and she stayed up way longer than the rest of us to make sure them two youngens went to sleep before she did. You're a dick."

"I know," Carter replied.

"Then stop standing here and go help your wife find your kids!" Joy hissed.

"I'm pretty sure I know where the kids are," Patrick piped up. "I'll go with you, Carter, and help you and your wife find them. Bobby, Carl, you two up to help us?"

They both nodded.

"The rest of you take the Denali back to the main office and get away from the property," Patrick ordered.

Patrick led Carter, Bobby, and Carl out of the main event hall and down toward the woods. The rest of the campers ran up the hill to the main office to look for the Denali.

"Candace!" Carter called as he watched her jogging toward the tree line.

She spun quickly on her heels and yelled, "What?"

He jogged to catch up to her as she stood there with her hands on her hips like she always did when she was irritated.

"I'm sorry," Carter replied softly. "I shouldn't have said those things."

Candace quickly swiped the tears that were running down her face and crossed her arms. "Yeah, well, you should be," she croaked.

Carter stroked her face and kissed her on the forehead. "It wasn't your fault. I should have never blamed you. Not with all this crazy shit happening tonight."

She nodded while squelching her face to hold back the tears threatening to spill as he pulled her in for a hug.

"Patrick," Carter began.

"Yes?" Patrick replied.

"You said you knew where they would have most likely gone. Lead us there," Carter asked.

"Follow me," Patrick ordered as he headed in the opposite direction.

"Where are we going?" Carter asked as he and Candace began to follow him, with Bobby and Carl flanking them.

"To my house," Patrick replied.

"Your house is in Gretna!" Bobby yelled. "We are not walking to Gretna."

"Not that house," Patrick sighed. "That's just where I live. My real home is right here on this land."

They climbed the road that led to the main office, and Candace gasped as they walked past the rubble. Carter looked around and didn't see any other roads except the one that led out from the resort.

"Where is your house?" Carter asked, scanning the area and seeing nothing but trees.

"Through those trees. Hidden away from people," Patrick replied. "I came from a wealthy family. Well, wealthy is putting it lightly. My family was aristocratic. They were the ones that founded this land before it was ever called Franklin County and long before counties even existed."

Patrick stopped at the tree line, staring off into the darkness of the woods. He breathed heavily as the visions of his past poured into his mind, flooding it with pain and anguish.

"Why did we stop?" Candace asked.

"Just give me a minute, please," Patrick pleaded. "When I had freshly turned eighteen, I came home from an insane asylum where I had spent four years being treated for schizophrenia," Patrick began as the others stood around and listened. "I told my parents I saw spirits. I heard spirits. I had visions of the past. The spirits would possess me. And I was met with mockery. I was crazy. I was the family stain because no one else in the family had ever seen the ghosts. The maids knew, of course. The maids came from Louisiana and the Appalachians. They were folk witches and conjurers. My parents even knew what the witches were. But it was like they didn't or couldn't care that I was being plagued by ghosts and pretended it was mental illness since they couldn't see the ghosts themselves."

"What happened… to you… in the asylum?" Candace asked quietly.

"I was tortured. You've heard of Gaeblers, right?" Patrick asked.

Everyone's eyes widened as they nodded their heads.

"That's where I was," Patrick meekly replied. "And one day, it all stopped. And I was convinced it had indeed been all in my head. Even when I came home, the voices weren't there anymore. But," he stopped.

"But what?" Bobby asked.

"The darkness, the rot, the cancerous tendrils of death and decay still lingered in the air of that manor," Patrick replied. "That manor is evil. That manor is the first house where footers were dug, and a well was placed in the ground. That manor broke the sacred ground that the natives had warned my ancestors not to do.

They told them not to disturb the malignant and dormant tumor that rested below the ground they refused to walk on. But they did. And we have paid for it all of these years later."

"Are you sure we should go there, then?" Carter asked.

"Yes," Patrick replied. "I will tell you straight up, it is frightening and maddening in that place. Any protection the maids had put in place has long since run its expiration, so there's no telling what evil has snuck through the doors in my absence."

"What makes you think that's where the kids are?" Candace asked.

"Tell me, Candace. The kids said they were talking to Lizzy and William, right?" Patrick asked.

"Yes," Candace replied hesitantly. "Why?"

"Lizzy and William were the children of James and Anne Ingram. They were my ancestors," Patrick replied. "Lizzy and William have talked to me since I was a small boy, just like they did your kids."

"What?" Candace breathed.

"Yeah, it was more than just voices or apparitions or possessions. I made friends with them. My mother would catch me quite often talking to them while I was alone in my room and would tell me to be quiet before my father heard me," Patrick replied. "Deep down, I believe my father saw them too, and that is why he drank heavily and was influenced by the spirit of their father. When James died, he wasn't in the right state of mind."

"How did they all die?" Candace asked, shifting uncomfortably.

"The children were poisoned and found buried without their hearts. James was found heartless in the ashes of the cabin his father Benjamin had given him as a wedding present, along with his wife, Anne," Patrick explained.

"In my dream, I saw all of that. Along with another woman and a man who had murdered them," Candace said. "There was also a Cherokee woman there."

"Prior to the children's death, James had hired a native woman who was the resident witch doctor to care for them. She was Cherokee," Patrick replied.

"Gini," Carter interjected.

"Yes, Gini," Patrick replied, nodding his head. "How did you know that?"

"Mikey told me the story," Carter replied. "He took me to her shack under the lake when we went scuba diving. I believe that was where she was released. I'm not sure how she was captured and put underground, but I know as soon as there was an earthquake, she was full power and completely released."

"Once we find the children, we bury her for good," Patrick stated firmly.

Patrick still hesitated at the tree line. He had left Ingram Manor so long ago when he could no longer bear living there by himself. He had never set foot back in the manor again once he packed his things and bought his new house. He had hoped that his absence would have quelled the hunger of the land, but apparently, it just made it even hungrier. Mikey hadn't been the only one who had researched the place. He had done his research as well, since nothing his family left in their journals could point him to any answers to the questions he had.

The tribes of the Cherokee had a legend about this land that had been told orally and only modernly recorded with the invention of the internet. Legend had it that long ago, long before England had even set foot on Virginia land, the Cherokee thrived in this part of the area. It was fertile for food and bountiful with animals to hunt. And then a baby was born to the chief and his wife. The baby was sickly from the moment it was born and through the years as it grew. Modern medicine calls it a failure to thrive. Natives believed it to be a sign of malevolent spirits lurking in the shadows.

The habitation began to die around them. It was hard for them to get any food to grow, and the animals started disappearing one by one as the baby grew older. Soon, it was nearly a desolate wasteland. They noticed that the more the land died, the stronger the child had grown, as if she were sucking the life from the earth itself to sustain her spirit.

The elders convened, and the medicine men of the tribe spoke in secrecy away from the chief to discuss what should happen. The land had become a barren pit, and they could no longer feel the vibrations that Mother Earth had to offer. They absolutely had no idea what they should do. Then, one day, the land started to feel alive again, except it was a different type of life. It didn't feel the same as the normal energy the earth provided in other parts of the area. It was stagnant, and it didn't emanate but rather began to drain the life of the tribe members. They began to suddenly age, and one by one, they became husks. All but one.

The baby had grown into a young and beautiful princess. She was healthy and remained youthful, almost frozen in age as the years had passed. And as she remained frozen in her young age, those around her lost their years as if they were bleeding the years from their veins. The elders convened one last time, including the chief. They told him they must leave the area, for it was no longer alive but more like a living dead source of energy that would continue to feed off the tribe. The chief agreed that everyone should pack their things and leave at once. It was the medicine man who told him all, but one could leave. The chief had to leave his daughter, or wherever they went, she would suck the life from the land and turn it into poisonous ground for the others, reversing its natural cycle of radiating energy and turning it into a vampiric type of energy. Mournful, the chief agreed. He took his princess aside and told her that in the morning, the tribe was leaving to escape a raven mocker that had been plaguing their tribe and sucking the life out of the tribe members. He told her to pack her things and have them ready to leave at dawn's first light.

In the middle of the night, while the princess was asleep, the tribe packed their things and left her behind. When she awoke the next day, the ground could no longer feed her the energy she needed. She became sickly again. She sought out the help of an old, native witch who taught her the stories of raven mockers. She agreed to become the last raven mocker to exist and vowed to destroy the bloodlines of the natives that had abandoned her, leaving her behind to turn into a shell of sickly putrefaction. No one knew the name of the princess, and he could only find one portrait of her that had been painted onto a buckskin hide. She looked just like Gini from the pictures the townspeople had taken of the medicine woman that his ancestor had married.

"Is everyone ready?" Patrick asked.

"I'm ready," Candace replied.

"Yeah, me too," Carter responded.

"I wouldn't say ready, but let's get it over with," Carl replied.

"I'm with him. Let's get it over with," Bobby said.

"Ok. Now, follow me, and whatever you see, don't let it mesmerize you. Don't listen to any of the voices. Don't follow anything you hear. Don't stray away from the group. Just stick to me," Patrick said. "Or you will die."

Chapter Fifteen

THE PARTY OF FIVE slowly trekked through the woods toward the hidden manor that only Patrick had known about. With each step he took toward the manor, he could feel it tug at his very soul as if it were eating him while he was still alive. There wasn't a single light to light their way through the thicket of trees, but Patrick didn't need light to know where he needed to go. He had walked these woods so many times as a child that it had been etched into his brain like a living map. The others followed in a single file line, keeping up with the silhouette in front of them.

The group was silent with each step they took, feeling the icy claws of death rip at their necks and claw at their feet. Each step felt like they were walking in quicksand as the ground began to feed from their energy. When the trees started to thin, letting them know there was a break in the forest and a clearing up ahead, static energy clung to their skin like electricity in the air before a thunderstorm. The hairs of their skin prickled and stood on end as the tiny bursts of electrical nodes ignited their pores. Even though it was cold, sweat gripped their bodies from a building humidity that seemed to flush with heat the closer they grew to the manor.

As they emerged from the trees and into the clearing, a blanket of fog covered the area. An eerie red shadow enveloped the manor from the blood moon high in the sky, shining through the tight water particles hanging in the hair. It looked as if the manor had been sprayed in a red mist of dread and doom. Patrick could feel the house calling to him to come inside. He could feel its need to feed from him, the same need he had felt as a child growing up within the walls. He stood there facing his nemesis of decay. The elements completely overtook the walls. The wild grape vines had weaved themselves around the antebellum pillars and through the roofing like they had tried so many years before to do and failed. Spanish moss covered the roof, as well as a green film glinting under the rays of the moon.

Parts of the roof looked as if they were about to collapse due to disrepair and upkeep. The snowstorms and thunderstorms that had rolled through the area throughout all of the years it had been vacant had done their damage to the shingles and even busted the windows out from hail and wind. Hurricane Katrina could have played a part as well, as it had hit the area with a greater force than the locals believed it would have hit, and many had costly damage to their houses from the raging winds and torrential rain.

Patrick could hear the moans and groans of the wood as if he were already standing inside the abandoned and run-down plantation house. Just as he was about to take a step forward, a tickle played at the nape of his neck, and he froze in his place. From the corner of his left eye, he could see the smiling, sinister face of Nelly Roderick. Her skin was rotted, showing bone in places, and looked as if it had been half eaten. Her fingers trailed his skin, playing with his sweat-matted hair. Terror coursed through his body as the adrenaline pumped, screaming at him to run, but he stood still. Nelly hummed a lullaby into his ear as she leaned in and licked his earlobe, nibbling it with her teeth.

"What do we do?" Candace whispered as they all stood motionless, too afraid to move from their spots.

"Just… follow… me," Patrick slowly spoke. "Don't pay her any mind. Don't acknowledge her. Don't look her in the eye."

Patrick picked his foot up, placed it a stride ahead, and slowly began to move away from the actress who plagued his nightmares from so long ago. Each of them walked as slowly and as cautiously as they could past the apparition, making sure not to look at her as Patrick had instructed, while she reached out and touched each of them as they passed by. Candace closed her eyes and gulped as she tried to withhold the shivers that threatened to bring her to her knees in terror.

Carter stared straight ahead, not paying her any mind, when something tugged at his shirt to the right of him and halted in his step. "Patrick," he calmly whispered. "Something has my shirt."

"No one turn around or look," Patrick ordered as he slowly pivoted on his heel to look at Carter.

Patrick inhaled deeply and swallowed hard as he took each step as carefully as he could toward Carter. Beside Carter stood an old Native American. His hair hung loosely past his shoulders, and he had a headband with a hawk feather wrapped around his forehead. Blood trickled down his decayed face where a tomahawk was embedded. He held a spear in his hand, and Carter's shirt had snagged on the tip of the stone blade. Carter breathed heavily as he tried to remain calm. Patrick slowly reached for Carter's shirt and unhooked it from the tip of the spear.

"Move forward," Patrick instructed, and Carter nodded in acknowledgment.

Carter slowly moved past the spirit with Bobby and Carl pacing behind him until they had caught up to where Candace stood. Everyone kept their eyes trained forward as instructed. As Patrick began to slowly turn on his heel, the Native American grabbed his arm. Patrick looked from his arm and up to the face of the dead native. It unnaturally opened its mouth, almost like a snake dislocating its jaw to eat its prey, and let out a deafening screech.

Patrick yanked his hand free of the native's grasp and quickly backed up, bumping into Carl. However, when he turned around, it wasn't Carl.

Patrick shivered and gagged as his father's face, full of maggots and putrefaction, smiled maliciously before grabbing him by his shirt collar and lifting him from the ground. Patrick didn't know what to do. He knew his mother and father had died on the property, but he had no idea that their spirit still roamed the land, lost and taken, instead of moving on into the afterlife.

"I told you," his father garbled and spat as blood and embalming fluid ran down his chin, "to stop telling your ghost stories."

Patrick looked over at the huddled group, scared witless. "Run!" he screamed as he tore his shirt loose from the hand of his father, stumbling backward as his feet hit the ground.

Patrick dug his heels into the ground and pushed off in a sprint, following the group as they snaked and dodged around each heinous ghost of every single person that had died on the land, who leapt in front of them. Maids and servants of his family who had met their unfortunate end while tending the halls grabbed for Patrick. Conjurers who had worked the land with their families rattled bones hanging from a stick at him. People who had drowned in the lake, people who had been killed in hunting accidents, more natives that had died long ago, being left behind by their tribe, every single life that the earth had claimed raged with fury. Hands popped from the earth and grabbed their feet, nearly tripping them as more people crawled from the depths of the soil they had been buried in.

They reached the porch of the manor, and Patrick quickly yanked the door open. On the other side stood the boy who had been around his age when he drowned at Devil's Lake during that New Year's Eve party Mikey had allowed. He was one of the very scant bodies that had been pulled from the lake after it had claimed their life. His face looked down at the ground, and he slowly raised his eyes to meet Patrick. His neck snapped quickly to the side, and a wide, vicious grin spread across his face before he opened his mouth, much like the native had done when it let loose a loud squelch. Water rushed from his mouth as if he were drawing from the lake itself, pushing Patrick and the group back from the door with force and pressure like a fireman's hose. The group was pushed against the railing of the porch as the water dissipated, and thorns from the overgrown rose bush wrapped around them as if they were a sentient bush, tearing into the flesh as they struggled against them like chains.

A voice arose out of the darkness, speaking in a language no one recognized except for Patrick, while shaking something that rattled. Patrick craned his neck around to see who it was.

"Amarette!" he hissed. "Why are you here?"

"My grandmother came to me and told me you needed me," Amarette replied as she continued to rattle her weapon. "I went to your house in Gretna, and you weren't there. I just knew you were here, mon cher."

"Go!" Patrick yelled. "It's too dangerous for you here."

"I have the power of my ancestors coursing through my blood," Amarette called out as bright spirits began to appear by her side. "These things have no power over me."

She continued to chant in the Creole language her grandmother had taught her. The apparitions stopped in their tracks while letting loose a harrowing moan before disappearing, solely leaving behind the ghostly sounds of their departure. The thorns that clutched them in the deathly thorny grip released, and everyone scrambled away from the bush. Patrick ran over to Amarette and embraced her.

"You really shouldn't be here," he murmured into her ear.

"Mon cher, the hounds of hell couldn't keep me from coming here," Amarette replied, kissing his cheek. "Why did you come back here?"

"I had to," Patrick replied. "These people were in trouble. Mikey is missing and most likely dead by now. They had no one to save them."

"You are too kind for your own good," Amarette replied, patting his cheek. "But that still doesn't answer why you are back *here.*"

"Their kids are here," Patrick replied, pointing to Candace and Carter. "The spirits led them off."

"I don't think they are here, mon chere," Amarette replied. "I don't feel anything from inside that house that is alive. All I feel is the deep emptiness of hunger it has for you."

"This land... it has a way of hiding things that you want to find," Patrick replied. "And that house will eat them alive if we don't make sure they're not in there."

Amarette nodded in understanding. She removed a necklace from around her neck and clasped it around his neck. She grabbed his face in her hands. "You come back to me, Patrick Ingram, and you come back to me whole."

Patrick leaned in and kissed her quickly. "You need to go back down to the road and wait where it is safe. This place will suck you dry faster than a juice box."

She nodded and handed him the talisman she had been shaking. "This will drive them back from you. Remember what I told you if you ever had to come back here."

"Yeah, I remember," Patrick replied. "Don't bleed for it, and don't listen to the voices."

"That's my boy," she said, brushing her hand against his face one last time. "Now, hurry in and out. Don't be in there longer than you need to be."

"Yes, ma cherie," he replied as she turned on her heel and ran.

Patrick returned to the group, and Bobby and Carl stared at him.

"What?" Patrick asked.

"How the hell did you land that?" Carl asked.

"Shut up," Patrick snickered. "Is everyone ready to move forward?"

They all nodded.

"What did she give you?" Candace asked.

Patrick held up a small stick that had a globe full of bones attached to it. "It's the creole version of a native wishbone stick," he replied. He lifted the necklace she had clasped around his neck for them to see. "This is a protection amulet, so the spirits can't possess me like they did when I was a kid. Now, let's get going."

Patrick brushed past them and walked to the manor's door one more time. The dead boy's ghost was nowhere to be seen this time. He peered through the door of the manor and breathed deeply, then stepped through the threshold of the door frame. The manor smelled of stagnant mold and dust. The lights of the manor flickered to life, illuminating the interior. The inside of the manor looked as rough as the outside did, with holes in the floors everywhere and rotting floorboards. The walls looked as if someone had taken a sledgehammer to them, trying to look inside for hidden treasure. The main hall chandelier lay on the floor, shattered into pieces, along with pieces of the ceiling and roofing that had collapsed in.

The turntable against the wall started to pop and crackle as music roared to life on it. Patrick watched as the floorboards of the house began to creak and groan as they put themselves back together, restoring the mahogany flooring that had been put in when his grandfather took care of the house. The walls shook and trembled as the bits and pieces lying on the floor were sucked back into place on the walls as they were restored to normal. The chandelier began to tremble and shake on the floor and rose from the ground, with all of the glass pieces taking their original shape, as well as the roofing and ceiling rushing to the top of the house to fix the gaping holes. The chandelier reattached to the ceiling and sprang to life with light.

"You guys are all seeing this, too, right?" Patrick hoarsely asked.

"Yes," Carter replied, stepping in the door and standing beside Patrick on the inside of the house. "We all see it."

Chapter Sixteen

AS CARL STEPPED through the doors of the manor, the last one to walk through the threshold, the doors of the manor slammed shut. Bobby tried jiggling the doorknob, but the doors were locked tight and wouldn't budge. Everyone glanced at one another nervously.

"There's no turning back now," Bobby said, releasing the doorknob.

Patrick caught a glimpse of movement out of the corner of his eye and turned his attention to the doorway of the library. A body lay face down on the ground, but Patrick would recognize the hair from anywhere.

"Mikey!" Patrick hollered as he ran to the library.

Patrick knelt beside Mikey as he twitched and slowly stirred. Patrick rolled him over. There was a huge gash on his forehead with a spreading bruise. Mikey's eyes slowly fluttered open, and he squinted his eyes, trying to focus.

"Patrick?" Mikey asked. "Is that you?"

"Man, are you a sight for sore eyes," Patrick chuckled as he helped Mikey up into a sitting position.

"What are you doing here?" Mikey asked, lightly touching the wound on his forehead and wincing. "You know you don't need to be here after dark."

"I came looking for you," Patrick replied as he ripped the bottom of his t-shirt and wrapped it around Mikey's forehead. "The campers called me and told me about everything that was happening and that they couldn't find you. What happened to you?"

"That evil bitch Gini is what happened to me," Mikey grunted as he tried to stand to his feet. "She called her wolves on me, and Ozell tried to help me in her bird form or whatever the hell you want to call it."

"Bird form?" Patrick asked, confused. "Have you been drinking?"

"You know what, fuck you," Mikey hissed as he wobbled slightly on his feet. "You know I haven't touched a drop of liquor since that night."

"I'm sorry," Patrick replied, catching Mikey before he hit the ground again. "You're just not making sense."

"There ain't nothing about tonight that makes any goddamn sense," Mikey growled. "And then, out of nowhere, Nathaniel cold-cocked me with his fucking gun."

"Why the hell would he do that?" Patrick asked, looping Mikey's arm over his as he helped him hobble into the sitting room.

Patrick dropped Mikey into his father's study chair as Mikey winced again, grabbing his head.

"God, my head is splitting," Mikey replied. "I don't know why he did it. He was going on about Gini sending him to do what the wolves couldn't do or some bullshit like that. I don't even know where the fuckers came from. There ain't no wolves in these parts."

"Yeah, we saw the wolves too," Carl said, shifting uneasily in his place as he glanced nervously around the room.

"Have you been unconscious this whole time?" Carter asked.

"In and out of it," Mikey replied, pinching the bridge of his nose. His face contorted into a look of confusion. "How the hell did the lights come on? There ain't no power here."

"I have no idea," Patrick muttered. "When I stepped through the doors, it was like the manor came alive."

"Have you seen or heard our kids?" Carter asked, changing the subject. "They went missing."

"I'm… I'm not sure," Mikey replied.

"Think hard," Candace pleaded.

Mikey sat for a moment. "I think I heard them, but I heard all kinds of shit in here. This shit hole has always scared the shit out of me, and I never thought I would wake up kidnapped in here."

"You never told me this place scared you," Patrick remarked, sitting in a chair across from Mikey.

"And what? End up like you? Tortured and called insane because I was going on about seeing ghosts?" Mikey asked. "No, no sir-ree. My parents told me to keep my trap shut about all of it. They knew, too. Hell, my family has worked for yours since before the Ingrams even came over to America. We aren't stupid."

"So, your family knew the whole time, too?" Patrick asked.

"Of course, they did. Who do you think took all of Moira's diaries so no one could read about what happened to Benjamin's son, James?" Mikey replied.

"She had more diaries?" Patrick asked.

"Yes, she had more diaries," Mikey replied, shifting in his chair. "And they tell exactly what happened to Gini after James and Anne were found burned in their house with their hearts ripped from their chests. It was also when Benjamin found out that Moira had an affair with one of the natives."

"What did they do to Gini?" Patrick asked.

Mikey remained silent.

"What did my ancestors do?!" Patrick demanded again.

"They buried her alive where her house sits," Mikey replied. "They put her in a pine box, ripped her necklace from her neck, and got a medicine man to enchant her box so she couldn't escape."

"So, this whole time, she has been continuing to suck the life from the land and living off the heirs of Benjamin," Patrick asked.

"Why do you think no one lives long in your family, Patrick?" Mikey asked. "It's not genetics. It's her. Her and this god-forsaken house that was the pride and joy of Benjamin's achievements were built exactly where the natives told him not to break ground. He freed whatever monster Gini had created when she was born and turned this land into whatever it is now."

A giggle startled everyone into silence, and everyone's eyes trailed the walls of the manor, looking for the source.

"Fuck this," Mikey shouted, jumping up from his seat. "I'm out."

"You can't leave," Patrick protested as Mikey walked to the door.

"Watch me," Mikey replied as he grabbed the doorknob and tried to turn it.

"It won't let you leave," Patrick explained.

"I'm not dying in this god-forsaken house to become one of the restless spirits that roam around stuck here," Mikey hollered as he faced the group.

Mikey's face lost all color as he stared at the corner behind them.

"What?" Patrick asked.

All Mikey could do was point. Patrick and the rest of the group slowly turned around.

Looming in the shadowy corner was a figure with its back turned toward them. In its hand, it held a needle. Its body began popping and cracking in abnormal ways as it moved each limb to turn around and face them.

"Mother?" Mikey whispered.

"You forgot to take your heroin, dear," the corpse-like being garbled.

Inhumanly, it began to run full steam at Mikey, and he braced himself for impact, slinking down into a huddle position while closing his eyes tight with his hands. Just as the thing reached him and raised its hand to jab the needle into Mikey's exposed neck, Patrick shook the wishbone talisman Amarette had given him, and the apparition melted into a pool of steaming sludge in front of Mikey. Mikey, with his knees still pulled tight to his chest and his head buried deeply into them, began to rock back and forth, babbling incoherently. Patrick ran over to him and grabbed him, shaking him hard as Mikey let out a howl.

"She's gone!" Patrick yelled.

Mikey slowly opened his eyes and looked around the room, his eyes landing on the bubbling, putrid mess on the floor in front of him.

"Why is she here?" he croaked.

"Because she died here just like my father and mother," Patrick replied, pulling him to his feet. "I have yet to see my mother, though, so maybe we will get lucky with that."

"We need to find Lizzy and Joshua and get the fuck out of here!" Carter interjected. "That thing had an actual weapon. A needle full of god knows what."

"Mikey, think hard," Patrick prodded. "Where did you hear the kids heading?"

Still shaking, with spit bubbling from his lips, Mikey replied, "I think the cellar."

"The…cellar?" Patrick repeated, his voice shaking.

Mikey nodded.

"What's wrong with the cellar?" Candace asked.

Patrick hesitated before he replied. "This place… it caused all of the men to become vicious, mean-spirited drunks."

"And?" Candace prodded on.

"After Benjamin passed, his only heir was Adrian, since James had died too. Adrian… was a vile monster. Our family legacy was based on a familial type relationship with anyone who worked for us, like Mikey's ancestors," Patrick motioned to Mikey, who nodded his head solemnly. "Adrian brought a great stain to our family name when the slave trade started bringing African Americans over and selling them to plantation owners. Adrian stood at the port eagerly waiting for his share that he had paid for, and when they arrived, he walked them chained together the entire way from the coast to here as he rode in his horse-drawn carriage. Many of them died walking with nothing but a burlap sap as clothes and without shoes."

Candace covered her mouth in shock while Carter looked at the floor, unable to comment on anything.

"What happened to them?" Bobby asked, breaking the silence.

"The ones that didn't escape… died or rather," Patrick stopped and gulped. "Adrian murdered them for either trying to escape or not doing the work or for just pure sport."

"There's a huge well in the cellar," Mikey began. "They weren't able to get water from it. It stayed dried."

"And?" Carl insisted, on edge from the story. "What the fuck did they do with the well?"

"They threw the bodies in there with sulphuric acid to eat away the bodies," Patrick finished. "They grew different, varying flowers on the property and would toss them in by the handfuls along with soda ash to try and cover the smell of rot. But nearly three hundred years later, you can still smell them rotting down there when you go into the cellar. Hell, you can still smell it in the walls upstairs. The bones of this house never forgot what he did and remind you every now and then with a whiff of decay."

"Oh, my fucking God!" Candace hissed in near hyperventilation. "Oh, my fucking God!"

"That wasn't all," Patrick grimly stated. "Adrian hunted the Native American tribe that helped us settle, and one by one, he murdered them and tossed them down the well as well."

"What the fuck," Carl mumbled. "Why?"

"Because his mother had an affair with one of them, and his brother was the result of the affair," Mikey sheepishly replied.

"No wonder this god-forsaken place eats everyone that walks the lands," Carter spat. "There's something fucking wrong with your entire bloodline. Even you."

"Hey, now!" Mikey spat. "Out of every single low-down Ingram my family dealt with after the passing of Benjamin, Patrick is the only one that was not like the rest of them. I am sure he told you about the sanitariums and all, but I bet he didn't tell you how his father beat him nearly every single day for no reason at all. They locked him in his room with a bucket to piss and shit in and slid him food under his door, not allowing him to leave. He is *not* like them."

"This is coming from the alcoholic and drug addict who let a teenager drown so he could party with them!" Carl interjected.

Mikey stood quickly to his feet, enraged. "If you lived here, and you knew what happened here, and you knew you were related to the same people and would be treated the same exact way if you did something wrong, you would've been an alcoholic and drug addict as well. It was the only thing that made everything disappear! And when that happened, I quit cold turkey. I went through months of withdrawals on Patrick's couch to get clean and sober because I *hated* that I was responsible for that kid drowning. I *hated* myself, and if it weren't for the fact I needed to hang around and make sure this fool here didn't get the wild hair to come back to this place and live in it again, I would have ate a bullet by now."

"Everyone, stop arguing!" Candace yelled. "There are more important things to worry about right now than what someone's family did in the past. We need to go to the cellar and find the kids and get the fuck out of this hellhole!"

"Candace is right," Patrick said, agreeing quickly. "We need to get those kids out of here before this place claims them as well."

Patrick moved from Mikey's side and began walking through the sitting room, heading toward the kitchen area.

"The cellar is this way," Patrick said, motioning with his hand for them to follow him. "Be careful walking down the steps. They're old, and they're steep."

Patrick made it to the kitchen and breathed in deeply before opening the door that led to the cellar. He twisted the door handle and gave it a nice yank. The cellar door opened with a loud squeak from its rusty hinges. The steps led down into a dark, dusky nothingness.

"Feel with your feet and hands as you walk down. There isn't any light until we get down into the cellar, so you will be walking blind," Patrick explained.

Patrick led the way as he put both hands out and felt the walls before taking his first step. He cautiously felt with his foot for the step before planting it firmly on the board, testing it with his weight. He took each step the same way, and everyone followed suit, holding the walls and testing the boards as they descended into the dank darkness. The lower they descended, the more a smell that had started off faint began to grow stronger. Soon, they were all coughing and gagging, trying to hold their breath and not breathe in the rank stench that floated in the air.

Out of nowhere, Candace let out an earth-shattering screech and began smacking her arms and running her hands all over her body.

"What's wrong?" Carter demanded.

"It was a spider," she cried in reply. "I'm sorry."

"At least it was just a spider," Carl giggled as he brushed past her and Carter on the steps. "Fucking women."

A hand reached out from between the steps and grabbed Carl's foot. He let out a yelp as he pitched forward, trying to grab onto anything before he hit the steps. His hands only met air, and you could hear his body thud and crunch as he plummeted down the stairs and landed with a thud at the dark bottom. They all carefully but quickly descended the stairs to find him. Patrick felt along the floor with his foot until it came into contact with Carl's body. He grabbed his arms and dragged Carl over under one of the lightbulbs shining lonesome in the dark corridor. He knelt and put his ear to

Carl's chest to see if Carl was still breathing. Patrick quickly put his fingers to his neck to feel for a pulse when he felt a bone protruding from his neck, and warm, oozing blood covered his pointer and middle finger.

"He's dead," Patrick stated.

"No, no, no, no, no," Bobby babbled as he wrapped his head in his hands and sobbed.

"I'm sorry," Patrick mumbled.

Bobby started to panic. "I can't do this. I can't fucking do this." Bobby turned to run back to the cellar steps when Patrick grabbed his arm.

"It's safer for us to stick together," Patrick insisted.

"Ain't no one safe around you," Bobby replied, pursing his lips and shaking his head. "You're a magnet for death, and I ain't dying tonight, too."

"They don't discriminate," Patrick replied. "They don't care if you like me. They don't care you're not a descendant. They don't fucking care. If you leave the group, you will fucking die, too, because that door is held shut by the soul of this house, and it's not going to let you go alone. It's going to fucking eat you. Get your shit together and let's find the fucking kids before it eats them too!"

Patrick turned around to look at Carl one last time, but his body was gone.

"Where the fuck did his body go?" Patrick asked.

"Maybe he wasn't really dead?" Carter offered, looking around in the dark shadows.

"His fucking neck bone was jutting out of his skin," Patrick hissed. "He was fucking dead."

"You know this place don't just eat souls," Mikey answered quietly.

"Fuck this. Fuck all y'all. I'm gone," Bobby spat as he ran toward the cellar steps.

"Bobby, no!" Patrick warned.

They listened to his footsteps running up the stairs, and they heard him run past the squeaky hinged door. Within a few minutes, they heard him scream and a thud. They stood quietly as they listened to his body being dragged across the floor, and then the noise disappeared.

"He's right," Carter began, breaking the silence. "We are all going to die in here tonight."

Chapter Seventeen

CARTER AND CANDACE walked huddled together as Mikey and Patrick led the way slowly through the corridors of the massive cellar under the manor. Candace sobbed quietly, scared not only for herself and her husband but for her kids as well. Carter was right with what he said after they heard Bobby meet his untimely end. They were all going to die tonight. As if her fear had baited some sort of empathy within the house, the entire corridor lit up with every single light bulb that had been dead spring to life. They all stopped and took in their surroundings, checking to make sure there weren't any hidden monsters the shadows had been hiding from them. Up ahead of them was the final passage that led into the heart of the cellar.

Patrick spun quickly on his heels, removed the necklace from his neck, and placed it around Candace's neck. He handed the protection talisman over to Carter. They both looked at him with inquisitive eyes, not understanding what he was doing.

"When you find your kids, you run, and you escape the house," Patrick flatly stated. "Don't worry about me or Mikey. You just run. The amulet and talisman will keep you protected. And when you get out of this house, you keep running until you hit the main road. And even then, you keep running until you have put enough distance between this place and yourselves that you feel you can stop running."

"We can't just leave you two here," Carter argued.

"Yes, you can and yes, you will," Patrick replied.

"What do we tell Amarette then?" Candace asked.

"You don't have to tell her anything. She will know," Patrick replied. "But if she still asks, you tell her that I paid the debt my family owed. And also," he started and stopped.

"Also, what?" Candace asked.

"Tell her I will always love her, even from the other side," Patrick replied.

Candace nodded her head and suppressed the tears that threatened to spill. "I will," she croaked.

"Alright?" Patrick prodded.

"Alright," Candace assured.

"Ok," Patrick said, exhaling loudly, then turned to Mikey. "The same goes for you, old man."

"No," Mikey firmly stated. "I will not let you-"

"Do this one thing I ask of you, please," Patrick begged.

"You are my only family," Mikey replied. "We leave this place together, or we don't leave at all."

Patrick nodded and hugged Mikey tightly. He turned toward the final passage and shakily took a step toward it.

"Did I ever tell you what happened to the sanitarium I was committed to?" Patrick asked.

"Are you seriously trying to make small talk?" Carter asked nervously.

"A week after I was released," Patrick continued, ignoring Carter's remark. "The entire facility went up in a blaze of fire."

They all took it one step at a time, inching their way to the threshold of the heart of the cellar.

"How did that happen?" Candace asked.

"No one knows," Patrick replied. "There was only one survivor, and he was babbling about how his father, the devil, was the one who killed everyone, and he had to burn it down to kill him."

"The devil?" Carter asked.

"Yeah, the devil," Patrick replied. "He was my roommate. He was just an orphan, and there wasn't any room for him at the state home. Most of the orphans were placed in asylums, especially Gaeblers, because they took in any and everybody. I ran into him not too long ago. He couldn't even remember who I was or even remember his time at Gaeblers Sanitarium. He had blocked it all out."

"So he couldn't confirm what happened?" Carter asked as they grew closer to the entrance.

"No, but I could see it in his eyes. Even if he didn't remember it, his eyes remembered," Patrick replied. "*Something* happened that night. I don't know if it was the devil, but something happened that was so terrifying that he blocked the entire memory of being there from his mind."

Patrick popped through the entrance, glanced around the atrium, and gasped. In the center of the room, the well seemed to hum as if it were trying to draw them closer to it. However, that's not what made him gasp. Beside the well stood Nathaniel, waiting as if he knew they were on their way. On top of the brim of the well, Isobel and Joshua stood motionless with blank stares.

"I've been waiting for you all to make it down here," Nathaniel frankly stated.

"Isobel! Joshua!" Candace shouted.

They didn't respond to their names. They just stood there with dead eyes.

"I see you brought my sacrifice with you," Nathaniel said, motioning with his gun toward Mikey. "With his spilled blood, I can bring my kids back."

"You don't have kids, Nathaniel," Patrick replied.

"Sure, I do," Nathaniel laughed as he began to walk behind the well. "They've just been dead for three hundred years."

"What?" Carter asked, confused.

"You still don't get it, do you?" Nathaniel asked, chuckling.

"He's possessed," Patrick stated. "James?"

"Bingo," Nathaniel replied.

As they looked closer at the kids, they saw a rope tied around their necks that had been tethered to the wall. Patrick followed the ropes to measure just how long they were. They were long enough that if the kids fell, it would break their necks.

"You don't have to do this," Patrick protested. "You can let those kids go."

"Now, why would I go and do a thing like that?" Nathaniel asked. "When their spirits leave, the spirits of Lizzy and William can enter their bodies. And with the blood of that one there," he said, pointing at Mikey, "I can bring them back to actual life."

"Why Mikey?" Patrick asked.

"Why, he is my descendant, of course," Nathaniel replied. "Remember how you just didn't know exactly how Mikey's ancestors married into the family? Well, my daughter Jane had kids before she was locked away in that insane asylum. One of those kids had kids, and one of them married into the McGradys, and his bloodline was born."

"Why would you want to kill one of your descendants to bring back your children?" Patrick asked.

"Because they didn't deserve to die!" Nathaniel bellowed. "It was my fault for bringing that Asgina into their lives. She made them sick slowly over time so she could eat their hearts. I just want my babies back."

"So do I!" Candace hissed.

"Your kids were the perfect specimens," Nathaniel chuckled. "It has been a long time since Cherokee blood was spilled on this land, even if it was as watered down as it was. Blood begets blood, and since I was half Cherokee, making my children a quarter Cherokee, your kids' blood matches their blood perfectly. It makes for easier mingling of souls, so to speak."

Candace went to run to her kids when Nathaniel waved his gun around and tutted at her. "At, at."

"Daddy! Stop it!"

Nathaniel turned around to see Lizzy and William standing behind him.

"My darling children," Nathaniel cooed. "It won't be long, and you will be alive again."

"She lies!" Lizzy yelled. "Don't you get it? She wants you to kill them so she can eat their hearts just like ours!"

"What?" Nathaniel asked, shaking his head.

While the ghost children kept Nathaniel busy, Candace and Carter quietly slipped closer to the well from one side, while Patrick and Mikey quietly approached Nathaniel from the other side.

"She's just using you again, Daddy!" Lizzy insisted. "Just like she used our family. Just like she used you to get to your heart, we are the blood of the tribe that abandoned her. If she kills all of those descendants, then they have no rest in the afterlife, and she gains all of their souls to live forever."

"I just want us to be a family again," Nathaniel whimpered. "I just want my babies safe and sound. And I want their mother back. Oh God, how I miss Anne."

Everyone froze in their footsteps as another apparition appeared before Nathaniel.

"Hello, James," she said.

Nathaniel began to heave tears. "Anne, my love."

"What you are doing is wrong, and you know it," Anne responded. "Let those children go."

"I can bring us all back!" James insisted.

"No, my love, you cannot," Anne replied. "We are dead, and we will forever remain dead.

There is no bringing the dead back, no matter how many necromancers try or how many witches tell you in death. We are dead, my love. You have to let it go."

Candace and Carter reached the well and snatched Isobel and Joshua from the brim of it. They quickly removed the rope from around their necks as Nathaniel turned around, and an inhuman bellow escaped his lips. He swung his gun around, and Patrick grabbed hold of it.

"Run!" Patrick screamed. "Run now! Like we talked about!"

Candace and Carter nodded, turned around, and ran as fast as they could, clutching the children to their chests. They weaved through the corridors, and Carter would shake the protection talisman as creatures would pop out of the walls and floors. They hit the cellar stairs and climbed them as quickly as they could, dodging hands that grabbed at their feet. They reached the top and ran through the kitchen, where Candace stopped and gasped, clutching her hand to her mouth. A large trail of blood led from the kitchen through to the main sitting room and disappeared down one of the halls.

"We got to go!" Carter urged, pushing her from behind to keep going forward.

They sprinted through the sitting room and reached the door of the house. To their surprise, the doorknob twisted, and the door opened without a single problem. They raced from the entryway and out onto the porch, taking the few steps leading to the terrace, then tore through the grass, heading for the tree line. They bobbed and weaved and ran as fast as they could without running into trees, as tree branches reached out and grabbed their faces, ripping at their skin. They didn't stop or slow down and came to the clearing on the other side of the woods where the cabin had stood for check-in.

Waiting there in the cold, Amarette stood smoking a cigarette. She quickly threw the smoke aside and ran up to them. She looked behind them, expecting to see Patrick and Mikey not far behind him. Her eyes landed on the amulet and talisman she had given Patrick and met Candace's eyes.

"Where is he?" Amarette demanded.

"He said you would know," Candace replied, clutching Isobel tightly to her chest. "He told me to tell you he will always love you on the other side."

"No," Amarette seethed. "This house will not claim him."

Amarette ripped the amulet from Candace's neck and took the talisman from Carter. "You two keep running like he instructed you."

Candace and Carter nodded as Amarette took off toward the manor.

"Where do we go?" Candace asked.

"He said run until we felt safe," Carter replied, starting to run again. "So that's what we will do."

Candace followed behind Carter as they raced through the main gate and down the driveway that led to the main road. The further they got away from the land, the more the electrostatic feeling they had once they stepped through those woods began to release its grip on them. They continued running until they saw flashing lights and the rest of the campers standing around, giving their statements as to what happened.

"You guys made it!" Evette cheered as they ran up to the group.

"My children need medical attention right now!" Candace demanded, and an EMT took Isobel and Joshua from their arms and immediately placed them in the back of their ambulance to work on. They still sat catatonic, staring blankly ahead.

"What's wrong with them?" the EMT asked.

"I don't know. We found them like that," Carter replied.

"Where are Bobby and Carl?" Evette asked.

Carter and Candace exchanged glances. "They didn't make it."

Evette clasped her hand to her mouth as tears sprang forth. "Oh, my goodness. What happened?" she asked.

"Carl fell and broke his neck," Carter replied.

"And Bobby?" she prodded further.

"Um, we don't know," Candace replied. "All we heard was a scream, a thud, and his body being dragged off by something... just something."

"What happened in that house?" Evette demanded.

"That house," Carter began. "That house is cursed. That land is cursed. We are all lucky to be alive."

"Bobby and Carl were getting married in the spring," Evette whimpered. "Looking at them, you would never guess they were gay, and they kept their relationship really private. They've been together for twenty years or so. I can't believe they're both gone now."

"Where's Patrick?" Joy asked, walking up and interjecting in the conversation.

"When we left the manor, he and Mikey were fighting that Nathaniel guy for his gun," Carter replied. "He told us before we even got in there that when we got the kids to keep running until we were safe."

"So no one knows if they're still alive?" Joy asked, concerned, wrenching her hands together.

"No," Candace replied.

"Mommy?" Isobel called out.

Candace turned her attention from the adults back to the ambulance.

"Lizzy, baby?" she asked, climbing in beside her.

"Where are we?" Isobel asked.

"You're safe," Candace replied.

"And that man?" Joshua piped up.

Candace sobbed in relief and pulled both of them into her chest as they tightly hugged her.

"That man will never try to hurt you again," she croaked through her tears.

"Hey, guys!" Carter said, rushing over and grabbing them both up in his arms. "Are you feeling ok?"

They both nodded.

"I'm hungry," Isobel replied.

"Me too," Joshua seconded. "Can we get some McDonald's?"

"Now you sound more like yourselves," Carter laughed as a tear slipped from his eye. "We will get you food soon."

"Sir, do we need to take them to the hospital to be checked out?" the EMT asked.

"No, I don't think that will be necessary. It seems they were just in shock from getting separated from us."

"Ok, they can sit here until we all clear out."

"Thank you," Carter replied as he kissed the tops of their heads. He looked over at Candace and smiled. "Next time, we stay at Keith's house. Deal?"

Candace let out a small laugh and nodded her head. "Yes, next time, we stay at Keith's house."

"I don't know. I kind of liked it here," Joshua interjected. "Minus all the ghosts and stuff."

"You *would*!" Candace remarked and laughed.

One of the sheriffs approached the two of them. "The ladies over there told me that there were two more dead people in the campground?" he asked.

Carter nodded. "I don't know where their bodies are, though. They were gone when we went back for them. There were some wolves in the area earlier. Maybe they carried them off?"

"There ain't no wolves in this area," the sheriff snorted.

"Oh, believe me. We thought that too until they attacked," Carter replied.

"Probably was just a big ca'yote," the sheriff replied. "Hey, don't I know you?"

Carter glanced at the name tag on the sheriff's uniform. *Tatum.* "Yes, you do," Carter replied. "You pulled us over on the exit ramp at the beginning of the week."

"That's right!" he replied. "Didn't think I would run back into you guys again. Hell of a week?"

"You could say that," Candace replied.

"Do you need me to call anyone for you?" Officer Tatum asked.

"Actually, yes," Carter replied. "Could you call the mayor?"

"The mayor?" Officer Tatum asked. "Why the mayor?"

"He's an old buddy of mine. He invited us down for the Regatta and fishing tournament. He said if we needed, we could stay with him, and well, we need it," Carter replied.

"Hot damn," Officer Tatum replied. "Let me get him on the phone for you."

"Thank you," Carter replied and returned his attention to the kids.

"Y'all want to spend the rest of the week with Uncle Keith?" he asked.

They nodded. "I could go for some Xbox and pizza," Joshua replied.

Carter laughed and tousled his hair. Officer Tatum returned holding his cell phone. "Here you go," he said as he handed the phone over to Carter.

"Keith?" Carter began.

"Carter? What the fuck is going on!"

"You wouldn't believe me if I told you," Carter laughed nervously.

"Try me," Keith replied.

"That room still available for us?" Carter asked.

"Of course it is!" Keith replied.

"Well, we will try and get a ride over there tonight," Carter said. "It's not too late, is it, for us to come over?"

"Not at all!" Keith replied. "Give the phone back to Tatum, and I will tell him to bring y'all over once he is finished up there. Are y'all ok to wait that long?"

"Yeah, we will be fine until then," Carter replied.

"Ok, good. I will see you when you get here," Keith said.

"See ya," Carter replied and handed the phone over to Tatum. "He wants to speak to you."

Tatum took the phone. "Yes, sir?... Yes, sir… sure thing, sir…. As soon as I am finished, sir… bye, sir." Tatum hung up the cellphone and put it back in his pocket. "As soon as I am done with all of this, I will give y'all that ride over to the mayor's house."

"Appreciate it," Carter replied, shaking his hand.

He returned his attention to Candace, and she was staring off into space.

"Whatcha thinking about?" he prodded.

"Hmm?" she asked, blinking her eyes quickly. "Oh, nothing really. Just hoping that Mikey and Patrick make it out ok."

"Yeah, I hope so too," Carter replied quietly. "I really didn't mean all those things I said to him. I hope he knows that."

"I'm sure he knew it was the fear and anxiety talking, babe," Candace replied, rubbing Carter's arm. "Do you think Amarette is ok?"

"God, I hope so," Carter huffed. "Did he really expect her to listen to him?"

"Probably not," Candace giggled. "She didn't look like the type that took orders from men."

"Hell no, she didn't," Carter laughed. "Ugh, I could go for a joint right now."

As if hearing him from across the way, Joy walked over and handed him a joint she had been smoking. "It's the Holy Ghost," she warned.

"I don't even know if I should smoke that," Carter laughed as he took it from her hand. "Last time I smoked, I nearly saw Jesus."

Candace and Joy cackled as Carter toked the joint and blew the smoke off into the air. Through the trees far off in the distance, they heard a loud explosion and saw a pillar of fire rise above the trees. Everyone facing the opposite direction quickly spun around and stared as the fire seemed to reach the heavens, and the billowing smoke crept through the humid air. It looked like an atom bomb had been dropped. All of the emergency teams and cops immediately jumped on their radios to phone in the smoke for fire and rescue to come out.

"Send the trucks, Lifeguard 10, send them all!" Tatum demanded. "Any idea what that's all about?" he asked Candace and Carter.

They shook their heads. "No," Carter replied. "I have no idea what that could be."

"Looks like it came from where the manor is," another officer added.

"Is that where Patrick and Mikey were?" Tatum asked.

Candace and Carter nodded. "Yeah, that's where we left them after we had found the kids wandering around inside," Candace replied. "As well as his girlfriend, too."

"Amarette was here?" Tatum asked.

"Yeah, you know her?" Candace asked.

"Everyone knows Amarette," Tatum replied. "She's the local witch you go to when you need some herbs or to be cured of a hex. She's also one helluva cook."

Tatum hopped back on the radio. "Possible casualties with the fire. Hurry with those trucks before the entire valley catches on fire."

"I guess now all we can do is wait and pray they all made it out safe," Carter whispered to Candace.

"Yeah, I have a feeling that Patrick was the one who blew that house up," Candace replied. "I just don't know why and hope to God it's not what my gut is telling me."

Chapter Eighteen

PATRICK WRESTLED with Nathaniel and his gun while Candace and Carter grabbed their kids.

"Run!" Patrick screamed. "Run now! Like we talked about!"

Patrick watched Candace and Carter swiftly leave the atrium with their kids, and relief washed over him.

"No!" Nathaniel bellowed. "What have you done?!"

Nathaniel violently jerked the gun in his hands, and Patrick's grip slipped. With one final yank, Patrick completely lost the gun out of his grasp, and Nathaniel brought it around hard against his head. Patrick staggered, disoriented. Everything turned into a hazy blur that came and went in and out of focus. His ears rang a bit as he hit the ground on his knees. He struggled to keep awake as his vision threatened to blackout. He lay himself gently down on the dirt floor and let the cool soil comfort him. At this point, he didn't care if he died. He had accomplished what he set out to do tonight and made peace with the fact that this was the night of his rectification.

As Patrick's eyes went in and out of focus, he saw a glint of something blue shining in his eyes. He moved his hand slowly, wrapped his fingers around the shining blue object, and drew it into himself when his hearing was finally restored. Mikey and Nathaniel were struggling over the gun as he sat up and admired the necklace.

"That's Gini's necklace!" Mikey grunted, trying to keep his grip on the gun. "That's what we need to save Ozell and put Gini back into her hole."

A strange energy filled the room, and for a moment, both Mikey and Nathaniel quit struggling with one another as if they had been struck by electricity. Chanting filled the room, and the sound of bones rolling around in a ball.

"I told y'all to forget about me," Patrick murmured, peeling his eyes from the necklace and back to the entrance to the atrium.

Amarette stepped through the entrance, shaking the bone talisman and chanting her Creole spell. Nathaniel dropped his gun and began to twist and contort as her voice grew louder and more demanding. As if a bolt of lightning struck him, Nathaniel lunged forward as James' spirit was pulled from his body. Nathaniel stumbled to the ground and quickly clambered away from the spirit that had possessed him. Fury flashed in James' eyes as he began to walk toward Amarette. However, it was like an invisible force field held him back as she shook her bone talisman and held her amulet up, still chanting.

"I can send you to peace!" she yelled. "I can help you escape this time loop of hell you are stuck in! Don't fight it!" she pleaded with James.

Anne stepped forward. "Release us all!" she demanded.

"I can't," Amarette cried. "I can only send three of you for the time being."

"Send my family," Anne begged. "I can wait."

Amarette nodded as she continued to chant. She took a bottle from her bag and popped the cork with her teeth. She tossed the liquid at the center of the well, and it was like a whirlpool opened within it, leading directly to the afterlife. She continued to chant and mentioned William's name first. William sighed in relief as his ethereal body began to dematerialize into floating particles of light and head to the well. She waited for him to fully enter before she proceeded. She then called out James' name, and just as William did, he began to dematerialize.

"No!" he screamed in rage. "Not without my wife!"

Before she could say Lizzy's name, James grabbed onto Anne, and the energy transference of the spell began to dematerialize her as well.

"No," she pleaded. "Lizzy will be alone with these things!"

"I'm sorry," Amarette cried out. "I can't stop it!"

"Please," Anne begged. "Take care of my baby girl!"

"I will cross her as soon as I can," Amarette promised.

Anne and James burst into dozens of tiny floating light particles and were consumed by the whirlpool. As soon as the last floating light entered the portal, it disappeared. Amarette fell to the floor on her hands and knees as Patrick crawled over to her.

"You're not supposed to be here!" Patrick seethed.

"I couldn't leave you to die," she replied, tears brimming in her eyes.

"We can talk later how about how brave she was and how much y'all love each other because right now, all of the spirits are attracted to her power, and we need to get the fuck out of here," Mikey remarked, helping Patrick to his feet. "Can you walk?" he asked Amarette.

"I am fine," she replied, standing to her feet. "I'm just a bit woozy, is all."

"What do we do about Nathaniel?" Patrick asked, and Mikey stopped and looked down at him.

Nathaniel was slowly starting to come to from his brief unconsciousness after being separated from James's apparition.

"We can't leave him!" Patrick insisted.

"Fuck!" Mikey hissed.

"Give me Patrick," Amarette offered. "I can help him. You get Nathaniel."

Mikey handed Patrick over to Amarette, and Patrick wrapped his arm around her neck and gave her a kiss on the cheek. Mikey bent down and pulled Nathaniel up by the arm, wrapping Nathaniel's arm around his neck and hoisting him to his feet.

"Where the fuck am I?" Nathaniel asked, looking around bewildered.

"Somewhere you don't want to be," Patrick said.

"Let's get the fuck out of here!" Mikey yelled.

Mikey kept a grip on Nathaniel as they hobbled through the atrium's entrance, as blood began to bubble and spill over the top of the well. They ran through the corridors to the cellar steps. Patrick held onto Amarette with one arm and clutched the necklace he had found with his hand.

"Nathaniel must have ripped this from Joshua's neck," Patrick remarked as they took the cellar steps as fast as they could.

"I think so, too," Mikey replied. "I gave that to Joshua when I found it at the lake the day he nearly drowned."

They reached the top of the cellar steps and began their trek through the kitchen to the sitting room as the walls began to seep blood, and soon, it was like a rising flood that they were walking through. The door was still open to the manor as they all made it outside before it could slam shut on them.

"Amarette," Patrick began. "How much juice do you have left?" he asked.

"I am pretty good at the moment," Amarette replied.

"Can you blow this place up?" Patrick asked.

"If I do that, I won't have the power to help you put the raven mocker back into its grave," she replied.

"Fuck," Patrick hissed as they stepped onto the lawn in front of the manor.

"I have a better idea," Mikey offered. "Wait right here. I will be right back." Mikey helped Nathaniel sit down on the ground before he proceeded to run toward the woods.

"Don't get kidnapped again," Patrick yelled.

"Kidnapped?" Nathaniel asked.

"Yeah, you were possessed and took Mikey as a ritual sacrifice, as well as two of the kids that were campers at the resort," Patrick replied.

"Where's my wife?" Nathaniel asked, alarmed. "Is she ok?"

"I don't know where Ozell is, and what Mikey said about her didn't make sense," Patrick replied.

"What did he say about 'er?" Nathaniel asked, standing to his feet.

"That she had been turned into a bird by the raven mocker," Patrick replied.

Nathaniel's face lost all color. "Raven mocker?" he asked, concerned. "There's a raven mocker runnin' loose?"

"Yes," Patrick replied. "And I have the necklace to stop her."

"She's part Cherokee," Nathaniel said, pacing back and forth. "That thing can kill 'er!"

Patrick walked over to his old friend and put his hand on his shoulder to offer him comfort. "We will find her. I promise," he said. "We just have to stick together."

Nathaniel nodded. They heard footsteps running in the woods as Mikey returned carrying a metal box.

"What's in the box?" Nathaniel asked while Mikey popped the lid on it.

"Dynamite," Mikey replied. "I have been saving it for this very occasion when Patrick wanted to finally destroy this hellhole."

"How much you got in 'ere?" Nathaniel asked, peering in.

"Enough to level three city blocks," Mikey replied as he took the bundles out. "Here," he said, handing bundles to Nathaniel. "Tie the fuse to these as I tie the fuse to this set." He slid the box over to Patrick and Amarette. "Y'all tie the rest of them together."

They all hurriedly tied the bundles of dynamite together. When the last ones were tied, and they combined all the fuses together, Mikey walked them around the manor, dropping a bundle every twenty-five feet. When he had made it all the way around the manor, he walked to the porch, popped the door open, and threw the remaining bundles into the sitting room. He then stopped and stamped his foot.

"I could fucking shoot myself in the foot right now. Anybody got a lighter?" Mikey asked, looking between the three of them.

"I do," Nathaniel replied, pulling his lighter from his pocket.

"I didn't know you smoked?" Mikey said as he took it from his hand.

"Not cigarettes, usually," Nathaniel laughed. "That's my joint lighter."

Mikey struck the flint, and the lighter popped to life. "It works!" he exclaimed. "Now, once I light the first fuse, it will be a domino effect from each bundle to the next. So as soon as the fuse is lit, we need to get the fuck out of here if we don't want to be blown to smithereens as well."

Everyone nodded.

"Y'all go on ahead, and I will catch up," Mikey ordered.

"No, remember?" Patrick refuted. "We go in and out together."

"Fine, just stand back then, you idjet," Mikey huffed. "Go over by the trees."

Amarette, Patrick, and Nathaniel ran over to the trees, and when Mikey saw they were far enough away from the house, he lit the fuse and hightailed it to the trees.

"Run!" he screamed, and they all took off into the woods. "It should be about thirty seconds or the first one to blow, and then it's like rapid fire," Mikey said through gasps as he ran with all his might through the thick forest.

The first explosion went off, and he was right. As soon as they made it to the other side of the forest, a loud explosion of them all detonating at the same time erupted through the valley. The force of the exploding dynamite sent them all topping forward onto the ground. They all scrambled to their feet and continued to run as rubble rained down around them. Boards, roofing, glass, and all kinds of carnage fell from the sky as they pivoted and dodged the last assault the manor could muster against them.

When they felt they were far enough to be outside of the reach of falling debris, they all turned around to see the pillar of fire and smoke reaching high in the air. The fire burned heavily, eating its way through the trees that surrounded the manor as Patrick and Mikey stood side by side, watching the legacy of both of their families turn to ashes.

"Do you think that will stop the hauntings?" Mikey asked as his face glowed in the fiery blaze.

"No, but it's a start," Patrick replied. "I believe if we get enough psychics, witches, and priests in here, we can heal the souls of the people who died at the hands of our families."

"I hate to butt into your sentimental whate'er y'all wer' havin', but I need to find Ozell," Nathaniel interrupted. "We still have a mess to finish cleaning up."

"He's right," Amarette added. "We still have to put the Raven Mocker back in her box."

"You still have the necklace?" Mikey asked.

Patrick held it up for him to see. "Yup."

"Let's get to it then," Mikey said and turned toward the resort to start trekking toward Devil's Claw Lake.

Even though a fire blazed, crackled, and popped behind them, the walk to the lake was eerily quiet. There wasn't a single cricket or any other kind of sound other than what their footsteps made in the crunching leaves of the wooded trail. Not even the apparitions of the land seemed to want to interfere with the capture of the raven mocker. Perhaps they believe that if she is destroyed properly, they will be free of the hell they were stuck in.

They all arrived at the sandy beach of the lake as the sound of lapping water against the shore cued them to their arrival in the inky black night. It was almost as if the moon had been swallowed whole while they were inside the manor because it no longer loomed in the night sky. As they walked closer to the sounds of the water, it registered to all of them that something was off with how the water sounded.

"The water sounds closer," Mikey said as he cautiously stepped down on the bank side.

No sooner had he planted his feet where the beach area normally stayed dry. A wave of water crashed over his feet, soaking them with the frigid October water temperatures.

"Why is the lake flooding?" Patrick called out to Mikey as he climbed down the bankside and then helped Amarette down.

"I don't know," Mikey replied, a bit spooked. "It's never done this before."

"Is it safe?" Nathaniel asked as he followed the three of them down onto the beach area. "I know… the stories of this lake. I have seent it with my own eyes."

"That's what I am afraid of," Mikey replied. "This is her lake."

"What's that out there in the middle of the lake?" Amarette asked, pointing across the water.

A silhouette of a building loomed in the middle of the waters.

"That wasn't there before," Nathaniel replied nervously.

"No, it wasn't," Mikey added. "That looks right about the spot that Gini's shack rested below the waters, too."

"Then let's get this over with," Patrick replied. "I don't want to be in this water after nightfall…" His thoughts drifted off to Nelly Roderick and her half-eaten, decayed face.

As they walked down the sides of the bank to get closer to where they saw the building, the feel of the air changed again. It began to grow super cold, like it had been earlier. The warmer water collided with the cooler air, and a mist began to form over the entire lake like a blanket of fog moving in. A gurgling croak that grew in pitch and volume filled the air until it was a tumultuous sound. They clasped their ears as they walked closer to the building and saw a land bridge connecting it to the bank.

"She's here!" Mikey shouted over the sound as they arrived at the bridge.

"What do we do?" Patrick yelled to Amarette as they all still clutched their ears.

"We need to draw her inside the building," Amarette loudly replied.

Hundreds of ravens swarmed in the sky, circling the building below. A loud howl erupted from the bedrock above them, and the wolves they had chased away earlier stood there snarling and snapping, ready to tear into them.

"Dammit, I forgot my damn gun," Nathaniel yelled as he watched them chomping at the bit."

The circling ravens began to nosedive toward them, clawing, pecking, and scratching at their faces and bodies. As if cued by the birds, the wolves began to descend the bedrock, chomping at the bit, growling, and howling. The four of them stood in terror and grabbed each other's hands, waiting for the deadly assault of the wolves' teeth, when a loud ruckus filled the air. Other birds began to emerge from over the trees. Hawks, snowy owls, great horned owls, and even eagles filled the sky with their shrieks as they descended on the ravens and wolves. Cougars emerged from the tops of the cliffs, hissing and roaring at the wolves below, followed by black bears. Leading the birds was a single white dove.

"That's Ozell!" Mikey called out as he pointed to the lone white bird.

Ozell barreled straight down toward the flock of ravens that were attacking the group, and the larger birds followed her. It was a bloodbath in the sky as the ravens were ripped to shreds by the talons and sharp beaks of the birds of prey. The wolves had turned their attention to the descending cougars and bears. They snarled and snapped their jowls as the cougars and bears simultaneously attacked, swiping their claws and chomping down on the necks. The bears picked the wolves up and shook them like ragdolls, sending them flying into the cliffside rocks, crumpled. What few wolves remained ran for safety, as did the ravens in the sky with their enemies in hot pursuit.

Ozell landed on Nathaniel's shoulder and nuzzled the side of his face. Nathaniel stroked her glowing white feathers and kissed her gently on top of her head.

"I promise we will get ya fixed, and then we are going to Hawaii like I promised," he said to her as if he understood what she was telling him.

A thunderous cackle erupted through the valley as the wind began to swirl around them. A water spout popped up to their right and another two to their left, twisting and turning, joining and disjoining. Amarette raised her hands and began to chant, funneling her magick into the twisters. The waters collapsed all around them, soaking them to the bone as the twisters disappeared.

"You think you are more powerful than me, little witch?" Gini's voice echoed through the valley. "I have the energy of the land to feed on for strength. You have nothing. I will feed from you as well. You already can feel your magic wavering and fading, can't you?"

Amarette glanced nervously over at Patrick, then stepped forth.

"I am the daughter of a Creole priestess. My magic runs deeper than yours. Unlike you, my ancestors didn't abandon me," Amarette hissed. "I call you forth, Ava and Camille. I call you forth, Agatha and Mary. I call forth the entire line of the Fontenot family. Stand by my side. Lend me your strength from the other side!"

Swirling, bright lights lit up the lake as if the sun had risen over the horizon. Spirits flew in from every direction, placing their hand on Amarette and granting her the use of their ancestral powers. Her eyes began to glow a buttery color as their powers infused with her own as the raven mocker landed on the land bridge across from her. Gini lifted her hands, and tendrils of black smoke began to creep across the lake toward the group. Fish floated to the tops of the water as the decaying hand of death took their life to feed her. Amarette held up her hands and began to chant. A smoky red mist rose from beneath the water, swallowing and eating the black smoke. It overtook the powers of Gini and crept closer to her. It surrounded her and her shack in one large, inescapable circle.

Mikey took the necklace from Patrick and walked it out across the land bridge as Gini slowly retreated into her shack.

"You have no power over me, you watered-down Cherokee!" Gini hissed.

Mikey grabbed her by her jowls and forced her mouth open as he shoved the necklace down her throat and kicked her into the shack.

"I don't need power," Mikey retorted.

The red mist closed in on the shack as Mikey high-tailed it from the center of the lake back down the land bridge. The boards began to shake and tremble, and he was soon dancing across them, trying to keep his balance as the mist engulfed the shack and dragged it back down to the murky depths it had sprung forth from. A small whirlpool formed in the center that began to suck the boards one by one into the crater now formed in the lake below.

"Mikey, run!" Patrick called out, running as far out as he could.

Mikey balanced himself as best as he could as he scuttled across the land bridge. When he was within arm's length of Patrick, the boards collapsed, and he went under the churning waters.

"Mikey!" Patrick screamed in panic.

Mikey emerged to the top of the roaring waters and paddled as hard as he could to try to get to the shore as the whirlpool's waters tugged and pulled at his body. A hand reached up out of the water and wrapped its arm around his neck, dragging him back under the water. Once again, Mikey emerged to the top, coughing and sputtering up the lake water. Patrick's hand reached out for him, and they could barely touch fingers. Mikey gave one last push of a paddle and grabbed Patrick's hand. Patrick pulled and tugged on him, but couldn't pull him from the swirling, watery current that had hold of him. Hand showed up beside him, and he looked to his left as Nathaniel grabbed onto Mikey's arm, and they both hauled him onto the shoreline, collapsing in exhaustion. They heaved in deep breaths as the waters began to turn to normal and receded to the levels they were supposed to be.

"I thought I lost you, old man," Patrick heaved in between breaths.

"I thought you did, too," Mikey replied, panting, trying to catch a deep breath to calm his lungs.

A glowing light caught their attention from behind them, and the three of them turned to see Ozell perched in Amarette's hand. Light illuminated the small bird, and with a blinding flash, Ozell stood before Amarette stark naked, collapsing into her. Nathaniel jumped up quickly and ran to his wife, removing his jacket and wrapping it around her.

"I'm me again," Ozell cried.

"Yes, ya are," Nathaniel replied as he planted a wet kiss on her lips.

"Did you mean it about Hawaii?" she asked.

"I sure did, honeysuckle," Nathaniel replied.

"You haven't called me that in ages," Ozell remarked, nuzzling into Nathaniel's chest.

"I haven't felt like me in ages," Nathaniel replied.

Patrick walked over to Amarette as the glowing lights that had illuminated her body began to fade. She nearly toppled to the ground as he caught her. She smiled up at him as he gazed down at her face.

"We did it," Amarette whispered to him.

"No, no, ma cherie, you did it," Patrick replied as he kissed her deeply.

"I don't mean to interrupt all y'alls happy parade," Mikey interjected. "But I am wet and cold and would like some dry clothes."

Patrick chuckled as Mikey walked up beside him, and Patrick slapped him on the back. "I can take you home with me to Gretna. You can wear something of mine," Patrick replied.

"That sounds like the best damn idea you have had all night," Mikey teased.

"We are going to scoot on down to our house," Nathaniel quickly interjected as he and Ozell walked toward the other side of the banks.

"Y'all take care," Patrick yelled and waved as they grew closer to the other side of the shore that led to their house.

"I guess we better get on up the hill," Mikey said, walking toward the banks. "Fire and rescue has probably already been called and are up there waitin' on us."

"Yeah, you're right," Patrick replied, following Mikey with his arm wrapped tightly around Amarette. "Hey, did that do the trick?" he asked her as they started up the trail.

"Did what do the trick?" Amarette asked.

"Did we just lock her away, or did we destroy her?" Patrick replied.

"A little of both," Amarette replied. "I drained her of her magic before I entombed her."

"So, how do we set the land free?" Patrick asked.

"One magical feat at a time," Amaette replied, nudging him in his ribs.

"Oh, yes, ma'am," Patrick laughed.

Mikey was right. As soon as they topped the hiking trail, they could see the flashing lights of the fire trucks that worked rapidly to put out the fire they had started.

"Hey! They're down there!" one of the firemen shouted as a few of them ran down to meet them. "Are you guys ok?" one of them asked.

"Never better," Patrick replied.

"Do you mind telling me what in the hell you two were up to setting that house on fire?" Officer Tatum demanded as he strolled up to them.

"Killing ghosts," Patrick replied with a smirk.

"I oughta arrest you two for arson," Tatum hissed. "But from the sounds of the campers, you two saved the day during that terrible weather we had."

"So, are we free to go home then?" Patrick asked. "Because I am tired. I am wet. And I just want my bed."

"Hell Yeahy'all can go home. You really think I am going to arrest the voodoo queen of Franklin County?" Officer Tatum replied. "We still on for tomorrow, Ms. Amarette?"

"Yes, we are, Officer Tatum," Amarette replied as they began to walk toward the gates of the resort.

"What's all that about?" Patrick asked, amusedly.

"Oh, he wants some shine," Amarette replied. "That fire water I make, according to him, is the best in the whole county."

Patrick laughed as Amarette, Mikey, and he walked through the gate and down the long road, looking for his Denali.

"Where's my Jeep?" Mikey asked.

"Probably in a tree somewhere," Patrick replied.

Epilogue

THE SUN SHONE BRIGHTLY over Foxwood Hills as construction crews quickly worked, clearing the debris from the previous week's mayhem. Excavators, bulldozers, skid steers, and various other machinery hummed loudly as they scraped and picked the land free of the burned-down forest and manor. Other crews cleared away the debris left behind from the main lodge and main office. Some of the cabins needed to be remodeled after trees were tossed through the roofs from the tornadoes that had struck.

Those who had rented cabins were finally cleared to return to the property to gather their things from the cabins. A specialty crew worked through the rubble of the damaged cabins to gather the camper's things so they wouldn't get hurt trying to do it themselves. If anything had been damaged, Patrick told them he would compensate them on top of the refund he issued them and then some for their troubles.

Amarette cooked up a feast for everyone to eat before leaving to head to their respective homes, and everyone sat outside at tables under gazebos, enjoying the meal before hitting the road. Patrick sat with Candace and Carter, chatting and laughing while Mikey played with Isobel and Joshua in the field. The kids laughed and romped with him as they tossed and kicked a soccer ball around.

"Everything go back to normal for them?" Patrick asked as he sipped his glass of sweet tea.

"Yeah, no more strange behavior," Carter replied, popping a piece of battered shrimp in his mouth. "As soon as we got far enough from the property, they started talking to us that night. Then it's been hell chasing them around up at my friend Keith's house."

"When do you return to Maryland?" Patrick asked, leaning back in his chair.

"We return this weekend," Carter explained. "I called the hospital I work at and let them know what had happened, and they told me to take another week to destress from it all."

"Well, that's good," Patrick replied.

"Patrick, you have some mail," Amarette called out as she walked over to the table and sat down beside him.

Patrick grabbed the mail from her hand and sifted through the letters. He stumbled across an envelope from Hawaii and tore it open. Inside was a picture of Nathaniel and Ozell drinking mai-tais on the beach, as well as a postcard. They both looked twenty years younger, as if the magic that had worn their age into wear had reversed. Patrick showed Candace and Carter, and they smiled.

"So you all are friends again?" Candace asked, drinking from her soda cup.

"Yes, once the spirits were crossed over by Amarette that had been influencing them, it was like Nathaniel was his old self again that I knew as a kid," Patrick replied with a smile.

"Whoa, look at that ring!" Candace exclaimed, grabbing Amarette's hand. "Someone finally propose?" she asked, eyeing Patrick.

Amarette giggled, and Patrick's face lit up with a smile. "Yes, someone *finally* proposed after what, fifteen years?"

"I admit, it was long overdue," Patrick chuckled.

"So what's the plan going forward?" Carter asked. "You opening again next season?"

"Yes, I am," Patrick replied. "And I am going to be more proactive over here, too. Amarette and I plan to cross over some of the more evil spirits by and by. When it feels like it's safe enough, I am going to build another manor and register it with the state as an orphanage. Give back more to the community."

"Patrick, you know you already give a lot to the community, so don't be modest," Amarette remarked.

"I know. I just can't help but think about my days at Gaebler and all of the kids that were there just because they were orphans," Patrick replied. "Besides, I have all this land and all this money. I want to put my family's name to good and rebrand it from the cursed name it's had through the centuries."

"I think that is a wonderful idea!" Candace exclaimed, holding up her drink. "To a better future."

Everyone tapped their cups together and took a drink.

"What about the raven mocker?" Carter inquired. "How is that situation?"

"For now, she is powerless and entombed in her spot at the lake," Amarette replied. "I have to get some friends and colleagues together to decide what we need to do about her to get rid of her for good before her battery recharges."

"How has Mikey been?" Carter asked as he glanced over to him, running around with the kids.

"He has been…good for the most part. He's staying with me in Gretna and away from here for a while. I didn't realize how much this place wearied him until that night when he lost it," Patrick replied. "So he has been getting some R&R before the new season starts up in April."

"Where has he been living?" Candace asked. "Before staying with you, that is."

"His family's house is through the woods that way," Patrick said as he pointed in the direction of the McGrady's estate.

"Is that place haunted, too?" Carter asked, lifting an eyebrow.

"Patrick chuckled. "Not like my manor was. There's also another estate that I had given back to the Thompson girl over that way," he said, pointing yet again. "I haven't checked in on her for a while, so I don't know how that's been going either, since all of the land is tied together here."

"What happened with her?" Candace asked.

"When she was a teen, social services came and got her. Apparently, her mother had died when she was a child, and she had lived in the house all alone the whole time talking to her mother's corpse," Patrick replied.

"That's awful!" Candace remarked with compassionate eyes. "Is that *the* story, though?"

"No, it's not," Amarette replied. "Some of the local witches said that she had been talking to her mother's ghost the entire time, completely unaware that her mother was dead. She just thought she was sick with her heart."

"Oh shit!" Carter mumbled. "That's some... heavy stuff."

"Yeah, there were some other things that also need to be addressed with the whole thing, but it will have to wait until I can do something about this place here before I attempt to even touch it," Amarette replied.

"What kind of things?" Candace asked.

"A dark coven of witches that have been put back to sleep," Amarette replied. "We need to figure out how to destroy them like the raven mocker. It's heavy magic. It's just a matter of time before they find a way to escape the place they're held prisoner in."

"Were all of the Ingrams crossed over?" Carter asked, changing the subject.

Amarette's smiling face faded. "No, they weren't," she replied. "Lizzy is still here... somewhere. I haven't seen her since that night."

"Why couldn't you cross them all over?" Candace asked, leaning forward over the table.

"I didn't have enough power reserved to try and cross them all over while also going up against the raven mocker. I promised Anne that I would cross her over as soon as I could, but I haven't seen Lizzy to even attempt it."

"Is she hiding?" Carter asked.

"I believe she is," Amarette replied. "She's alone here with all those malevolent spirits, and honestly, I'm not even sure she wants to cross over either."

"How was the fishing tournament?" Patrick asked, turning the conversation away from death and back to normal.

"It was decent. Regatta, too," Carter replied, smiling. "I had never been to one of those before, so it was like a real vacation."

"You coming back next year for it?" Patrick asked. "We should have room here."

Cater laughed. "Actually, I think we are. Just as long as there's no impending doom for us again."

They all laughed, and Isobel and Joshua glanced over at their parents talking to Patrick and Amarette. Mikey kicked the ball, and it went flying past them toward the tree line.

"I got it!" Isobel shouted and giggled as she ran towards the trees.

The wind lightly blew, and the leaves swirled around her feet as she carefully walked through the thorny brush to retrieve the ball. She picked it up and was about to return to Mikey and Joshua when, all of a sudden, she felt cold in the shade.

"Hello," a voice said, and Isobel gasped, dropping the ball.

"Lizzy!" Isobel exclaimed, excited to see her friend again.

"Shhh," Lizzy replied, putting her fingers to her lips. "Don't let them hear you," she said, pointing to the table Isobel's mom and dad sat at.

"Why don't you want them to know you are here?" Isobel asked innocently.

"Because they will try to send me away," Lizzy replied, watching Amarette to make sure she didn't sense her presence. "I don't want to leave. I like it here."

"Don't you miss your family, though?" Isobel asked her, brushing a strand of hair out of her face.

"Yes, I miss William terribly. But he is safe with mommy and daddy now. Daddy is all better and no longer mean," Lizzy replied.

"I think we are coming back again next year," Isobel said with a smile. "We can play again when I come back."

"That would be great!" Lizzy replied as both the girls giggled. "You better get back up there before they realize you are just standing here acting weird again."

"Ok, Lizzy," Isobel replied. "I will miss you while we are gone."

"I will miss you too," Lizzy replied, hugging Isobel. "Now, go before Amarette spots me."

"Bye!" Isobel exclaimed as she ran back up to Mikey and Joshua.

"What took you so long?" Joshua asked.

"I thought I saw a snake, so I was standing real still so it wouldn't bite me," Isobel replied. "It was just a tree branch, though."

"Are you sure that's all it was?" Joshua inquired, giving her a stern look.

"Yup!" she replied with a smile. "I'm hungry. Can we go get some food?"

"Yeah, I am hungry too," Mikey replied with his hands on his hips, breathing hard.

"Are you sure you're not just old?" Isobel asked with a giggle.

"I'm not too old to chase you over there," Mikey threatened, and the kids screamed in fun as he chased them over to the table their parents sat at.

"Mommy, I'm hungry!" Isobel shouted, running up to the table.

"Come with me, and I will make you a plate," Candace replied, standing from her chair.

"Me too! Me too!" Joshua shouted.

"Me too!" Mikey mimicked, and Candace laughed.

"Come on, you two," Candace said and grabbed each of them by the hand.

Mikey laughed as he took a seat next to Carter at the table.

"Tired?" Carter asked.

"You have no idea how much kids wear me out," Mikey replied with a snort.

"Oh yeah?" Carter asked. "Try living with them, especially when the boy keeps hitting growth spurts, so all you hear is *I'm hungry* every five minutes."

Everyone laughed as they watched the kids with Candace getting their food.

"I sure will miss them, though, when y'all go back home," Mikey frankly stated. "Out of all the campers that have come and gone through here, those two were a real treat to have around."

"Is there a Mrs. Mikey?" Carter asked as he popped a fry in his mouth.

"There was a long time ago," Mikey replied.

"Oh… that's right," Carter laughed. "I asked for the attorney."

Mikey laughed really hard. "Yes, you did," he replied.

"What happened?" Carter asked.

"She wanted kids, and I didn't," Mikey replied.

"But you love kids?" Carter asked, confused.

"I do," Mikey replied. "But I wasn't bringing kids into the world on this land or with my lineage."

"I used to think the same way," Patrick replied, sharing the empathetic moment with Mikey.

"Used to?" Carter asked.

"I took a test this morning," Amarette smiled.

Mikey's eyes grew wide, and he jumped up from the table and began to shout, "I'm going to be an uncle!" while dancing around.

"You can be whatever you want to be," Patrick laughed.

"Will he be an uncle?" Carter whispered.

Patrick mouthed no, and they shared a short laugh.

The kids returned, and they all sat around talking and eating until one of the recovery teams arrived at the table with their belongings from the cabin. Carter thanked them and carried the luggage to their rental.

"As soon as you find a replacement for your vehicle, you let me know," Patrick said as he picked up one of the suitcases and loaded it into the hatch. "I will completely pay for it for you."

"There's no need for all of that," Carter replied. "I had full liability on it. It's covered from tornado damage. Hell, I could have run it off the cliff and into the lake four-wheeling it, and they would have covered it."

"Well, the offer stands. If you find a vehicle and the insurance check doesn't cover it all, let me know," Patrick reiterated.

"Ok," Carter replied as he loaded the last suitcase into the rental and shut the hatch.

"OK, kids. It's time to get going," Carver yelled.

"You going back to the mayor's house?" Patrick asked.

"Yeah, he's letting us use his guest house," Carter replied, holding the door open for Joshua and Isobel to climb in. "Buckle up, you two," he demanded, and the two kids strapped themselves in.

"Well, if you're ever in town and need a place to stay, my house is in Gretna," Patrick offered. "Give me a call. We would love to have y'all over."

"I will see how the upcoming summer is planned," Carter replied. "We need to take more family vacations instead of me working all the time, so it would be nice to get away more often."

"I feel like we are leaving family behind," Candace said as she hugged Mikey and Amarette. "Look me up on Facebook so we can stay in touch."

"Will do," Amarette replied.

"What's a Facebook?" Mikey asked, and the two women just giggled.

"It's not for *old* people," Amarette teased. "It's the *internets*."

Candace walked over to the rental and opened her door. She quickly hugged Patrick and hopped into the passenger seat, waving bye to everyone. Carter climbed into the driver's seat and started the vehicle. He gave a quick wave to Patrick, Amarette, and Mikey, put the vehicle in drive, and pulled out of the drive. He passed through the gate and headed down the long drive to the main road.

"I will miss them," Isobel remarked from the backseat.

"Yeah, we will, too," Candace replied, glancing in the backseat with a smile. Her eyes narrowed as she looked closely at what Joshua held in his hands.

"Honey, what is that?" she asked, pointing to the object.

"I found it in the woods when Mikey took us on a hike earlier," Joshua replied, handing the object over to Candace.

"But what is it?" Candace asked, looking it over. "It looks like bones or something."

"It's a raven skull."

Extended Cut Available in Paperback Only

MIKEY DROVE his brand-new Jeep that Patrick had purchased from the car lot in town. Patrick also helped Mikey get his inheritance, which had been put into a trust fund and guarded from him throughout the years. The lawyer Patrick hired served brass tacks whenever he dealt with wills and trust funds. The lawyer who had set up Mikey's trust fund with his parents had been skimming from the investments over the years and wanted to keep it all hush-hush, as it was a lucrative opportunity for him. He had given Mikey excuse after excuse throughout the years as to why he couldn't give him access to the trust.

Mikey paid to have the old plantation house, which his parents had left him, remodeled and brought up to proper code. It had been years since there were any structural changes to the house other than the minor repairs Mikey did to ensure the upkeep of the place. It was time for a modern look at the place. He dropped about $200,000 to have it restored and then zoned as a historical monument. History was always important to him.

Mikey headed over to the Thompson estate to check on the Thompson girl and her family, who had recently moved back into the place. He had only met the girl one time, and that was the day that Patrick had purchased the land from her, so it didn't default to the state. Once she was ready to move back into the place, Patrick gifted her the land back. She was now married with two kids and a third on the way.

After all of the extravagance of that weekend, where all hell broke loose at the resort, Patrick wanted him to check in on her, and he agreed he needed to as well. Unlike Patrick, he knew more about the Thompson estate than just the whispers around town from the covens that Amarette knew. Back in the early 90s, some paranormal shit had gone down in the house that was sold in a parcel of the land prior to Patrick's purchase. This was while he was locked away in the Sanitarium, and he wasn't told about it so that he wouldn't bring the issue of ghosts back up to his parents.

The Calhoun family that had moved out had spoken of ghosts that haunted the area. From Mikey's understanding, it was the Ingram ghosts as well. Patrick had gotten it wrong about the ruins they had found on their property, and it turned out that it was one of the McGrady's houses that they had discovered. James' property that he had been given resided on the Thompson half of the estate. The main reason why James roamed the land over on the Ingram estate was that it had belonged to his father, Benjamin.

Mikey arrived in front of the manor, and it didn't even look like anyone lived there. It was rundown and looked abandoned, with weeds as tall as he was. It had vines just like the ones that covered Ingram Manor. In fact, it looked just like the state Ingram Manor had been before they blew it up. He pulled his phone from his pocket and dialed up Patrick.

"Hey, I'm over here at the Thompson estate. Are you sure she moved back in?" Mikey asked.

"Yes, I spoke to her in person the day she moved in. I signed the paper over to her," Patrick replied. "Have you knocked on the door?"

"You don't understand," Mikey replied, getting out of the Jeep and peering closer at the house. "There is no way anyone lives here."

"Why do you say that?" Patrick asked.

"Because everything is boarded up. It's grown up with weeds, and it looks just like Ingram Manor did," Mikey replied.

"Go knock on the door!" Patrick ordered.

As Mikey walked closer to the building, the wind started to blow, and the clouds began to cover the shining sun. Static hung in the air, and lightning struck the ground right beside the house. Mikey dropped the phone as voices filled the air. These voices were unlike the ones he had heard at Ingram Manor. These were…

"Mikey!" Patrick yelled into the phone.

Mikey picked the phone up and answered. "Yeah, sorry. I dropped the phone."

"What's going on?" Patrick demanded.

"There is absolutely no way anyone lives here," Mikey insisted. "There's…"

"There's what?" Patrick asked.

Mikey didn't answer.

"Mikey?" he said.

No answer.

"Mikey?" he repeated louder.

Still no answer.

"Mikey!" he shouted.

"Mikey is ours now."

Author Biography

Kasey Hill has lived in Franklin County, VA, for most of her adult life and is a versatile writer known for her work in several genres, including urban fantasy, horror, thriller, paranormal romance, and metaphysical/New Age topics. She has authored both fiction and non-fiction, with a particular interest in Wicca, specializing in Trinitarian Wicca as the historical archivist with an upcoming historical account of the shift from polytheism to monotheism in Abrahamic religions, where she has published non-fiction works exploring the subject.

Her fiction often dives into the supernatural and the macabre, blending mythological elements with modern storytelling. She has published multiple novels, poetry collections, and short stories. Notable works include her *Guardians of Light* series in the mythology fantasy genre and her poetry, which has received recognition for its depth and emotional resonance. As she grows in the horror genre, she has a particular penchant for Southern Gothic storytelling, such as her Adult Horror novel *Devil's Claw* and her Young Adult horror series, *The*

Whispering Spirits, featuring *The Haunting at Foxwood Village* and *Dark Coven.* She has several Horror short stories circulating for anthologies and Ezines featuring her unique style of worldbuilding.

In addition to her writing, Kasey Hill has also contributed to the Wiccan and occult community through her non-fiction work, making her a multi-faceted author with a broad range of interests and expertise.

Follow Kasey Hill

- Facebook: https://m.facebook.com/KaseyHillAuthor/
- Twitter: www.twitter.com/kaseyhillauthor
- Website: www.kaseyhillauthor.com
- Blog: www.kaseyhillauthor.tumblr.com
- www.kaseyhillauthor.wordpress.com
- Pinterest: https://www.pinterest.com/kdt21/
- Goodreads: https://www.goodreads.com/author/show/11075849.Kasey_Hill
- Kasey Hill's Fan Group Scream Queens: https://www.facebook.com/groups/1805999022997291/
- Instagram: https://www.instagram.com/kaseyhillauthor/
- Linkedin: https://www.linkedin.com/in/kaseyhill02201988
- Amazon: https://www.amazon.com/Kasey-Hill/e/B00O2WT210

- Newsletter: https://mailchi.mp/4516f70b8165/kaseyhillnewsletter

Companies Owned

- Dark Moon Rising Publications: https://www.facebook.com/Darkmoonrisingpublications
- DMRP Instagram: www.instgram.com/DMRPublications
- DMRP Twitter: www.twitter.com/DMRisingPub

Nonfiction

- Trinitarian Wicca: https://www.facebook.com/TrinityWicca
- Trinity Twitter: https://twitter.com/trinitywicca

Poetry

Tattered Wings

- Facebook: www.facebook.com/tatteredwingspoetry

https://www.facebook.com/pages.of.a.tattered.soul
https://www.facebook.com/CarelessWhispersPoetry
https://www.facebook.com/PerfumePowderAndLead
https://www.facebook.com/tiptoethroughthetulips.poetry
https://www.facebook.com/bittersweetsymphonypoetry

- Instagram: www.instagram.com/tatteredwingspoetry

www.ingramcontent.com/pod-product-compliance
Lightning Source LLC
La Vergne TN
LVHW050918080826
845145LV00001B/120

* 9 7 8 1 9 4 5 9 8 7 8 9 2 *